LOGGED IN

A Laugh Out Loud Romantic Comedy!

Allison McWood

Annelid Press

FIRST EDITION

Cover design and by Graham Kennedy

ISBN: 978-1-7771360-8-6

A WORD FROM ALLISON:

Ask me why I have a deep connection with Algonquin Park. (I'm glad you asked!) As it happens, I have several threads of family history relating to the park which is perhaps why I've always found it to be a profound and alluring setting. My grandparents owned a resort near Algonquin Park, lined with guest bunkies on a quiet bay. I've grown up hearing stories of this idyllic place where my dad spent some of the most memorable years of his childhood, surrounded by the magic of nature. It was a modest resort, animated by vibrant, salt-of-the-earth people. Honestly, can you think of a more compelling setting for a story?

On the creative side of things, I am related to Canadian artist Lawren Harris of the *The Group of Seven,* who often drew his own inspiration from Algonquin Park. He was a cousin from several generations back. I don't know if the sap of the Algonquin pines is running through my veins or whatever, but the park awakens my imagination in a way that is unique and perhaps spiritual. I can't help but wonder if Harris felt the same stirrings of imagination when he hiked the Algonquin trails. I wonder also if his soul has ever somehow hiked alongside me, gazing across the same shimmering lake. He clearly saw the world differently and was intrigued by abstractions. I am most definitely an abstraction so I think we would have gotten along famously.

Logged In features a fictious log cabin resort. Although it is inspired by four different resorts located in and around Algonquin Park, the resort in the book is completely fabricated for comedic effect. The idea of an eco-lodge in the middle of the remote wilderness was inspired by an actual eco-lodge in Algonquin Park - although I have never visited this place and based on the reviews, it is much more upscale, upkept, comfortable and functional than the imaginary resort I concocted. I simply used the model of the eco-lodge as a guideline of how to write logistically about an *off the grid* establishment. Again, the resort in the book does not exist. So please don't try to make reservations. You will be sorely disappointed.

Ironically, I finished writing *Logged In* one week before the entire world shut down and went into isolation due to the Covid 19 pandemic. I freaked myself out a bit with the bizarre timing of this. The story deals with the importance of community and how technology is not a valid substitute for human interaction. This irony stung and haunted me, especially in the first few of weeks of isolation. I really missed my community. My people. My friends. My family. My friends who basically ARE family. (You know who you are) I craved the energy of actual people. I missed hugs. Gatherings. I felt that I no longer had the inherent right to be human. Because let's face it, humans are highly social creatures with an emotional and biophysical need for human contact. As is the case every time I write a book, I wondered if my story would be meaningful or even relevant to anyone. But when the entire world faced not just a health crisis together but also a human tragedy, I knew then that this was a story that I needed to tell. I hope it brings you as much joy as I had writing it. And more importantly, I hope it brings people together.

Have fun reading!

Peace,

Alli

ACKNOWLEDGMENTS

Loving thanks to my dad for teaching me about being a master storyteller and for sharing vivid stories about his childhood up north.

Thanks also to Grandpa Mac from whom I somehow inherited my fondness of fedoras.

To Lawren Harris, thank you for inspiring me to see the world through a unique and vibrant lens.

Many thanks to my awesome editors, Jason Reilly and Daniel Patch who worked tirelessly during a global pandemic to make this book happen.

Thank you to Graham Kennedy for the stunning cover art.

A thousand thank yous to Annelid Press and Dan for literally everything.

Special thanks to Pierre for showing me the importance of community and friendship. Thanks also to the amazing Poilbout family for bringing our community together in a way that is uniquely yours. (and for the free office space by the window) I love you guys.

And finally, thank you to Professor Derek Cohen and Professor Deanne Williams for believing in me, B.W. Powe for your guidance, Peter Karrie for your mentorship, Mrs. Bridle for giving me the little pink notebook, Bono for being Bono, Kimberlee's cocker spaniel for being surprisingly helpful and Darcy the brooding waiter with the ponytail.

THANKS EVERYBODY!

For Grandma and Grandpa McWood

CHAPTER ONE

"What do you mean the software is being used by cats?"

Perplexed heads turned as Bianca Mumford tried to keep up with the brisk, steady current of jetlagged travelers in the Toronto airport. Flustered, Bianca repositioned her Bluetooth. Surely, she had misheard.

"They beat us to it." The voice of product manager Melvin Zudd made Bianca's ear itch with static. "Nobody saw this coming. *Ambrose & Guff* just shipped their product and it's shriekingly similar to ours."

"How similar?" Bianca asked, swallowing a yawn.

"Cats, Bianca. They used our hook. There are trivial differences in their product but..."

"Such as?" Bianca asked bluntly. She assertively clacked her shoes on the sterile, airport tiles. "Can we still launch? Can we brand our product differently? Maybe there's something we can do to salvage the software on a marketing level."

"It's a marketing calamity," Melvin said despondently. "*Ambrose & Guff* have developed software that allows indoor cats to amuse themselves while left alone in the house. Ours, on the other hand, focuses on virtual companionship for cats who have trouble meeting other cats."

"That's a significant difference though," Bianca replied.

"Both enable cats to operate the software autonomously," Melvin argued. "And both target indoor cats who crave stimulation."

"But our product offers something much more meaningful. Every cat deserves the chance to experience a relationship. Even indoor cats who may not even be aware that other cats exist. Our competitor did not consider that cats can amuse themselves. They don't need software for that."

"This has nothing to do with what cats want, Bianca. The cats are not buying the software. Humans are. And the humans are going to buy the product that comes out first."

Bianca pursed her lips.

"Bianca," Melvin said in his most convincing doomsday cult voice, "We are not the first to launch VR software of this nature. Giving cats their autonomy was our brand. Our gimmick. I don't see how we can salvage this. And with our shareholders expecting a product by Friday. Besides, we suspect there may be incriminating similarities in the code."

Bianca felt a headache brewing. The sneaky kind that creeps up behind your eyes and compresses your addled brain. Blinking away the fog of fatigue, Bianca's mind quickly filled with scrambled images of every person involved in this project. Who could have dropped the ball on this one? When? How could she have let this happen? Was it even her fault at all?

God, what if this is my fault?

"Bianca, I think this might explode in our faces."

"Hold on. Can we nail the competition with a patent infringement lawsuit? Is there any chance we thought of this first? Were there any leaks? Moles? Did everyone on the team adhere to the confidentiality agreement?"

"Hell if I know," Melvin exhaled. "Maybe there was a slip up in market research."

"Get Dirk on the phone," Bianca said while consciously trying not to quaver. "If I find out he didn't triple check..."

"What... are we going to do?"

Walking with an even fiercer purpose, Bianca nearly rammed into a family of six who was returning from a trip to Disney. "Mel, I'm still at the damn airport. My connecting flight was delayed seven hours, I lost my spot in business class, my brain, body and luggage are still in Japan... Look, I'll be back at the office in an hour. Sooner if I can figure out what's going on with my luggage..."

"We were supposed to ship in two days."

"I am aware, Mel."

"We can't make this okay in two days."

"How much code do we have to rewrite to make the product suitable for hamsters to use?"

"Are you being serious right now?"

"Guinea Pigs then. Guinea Pigs might make more sense, actually."

"Our engineers do not have godlike speed. This code took them three years to refine."

The color drained from Bianca's already pale face. She slumped onto a bench as a current of people, not unlike focused, goggle-eyed fish walked apathetically past her.

I will not cry. Not here. Not ever.

"Mel, just... just tell everyone not to crap their pants. I'll take care of everything when I'm back in the office. Give me an hour."

"They're calling a meeting. We need you here or the whole thing will..."

"An hour, Mel. I don't have superhuman teleportation skills."

Bianca yanked the Bluetooth from her ear, burying her face in her hands.

***

He must have been the most sluggish taxi driver in Toronto. Driving at a snail's pace, the whiskered cabbie seemed to be taking every sketchy backstreet in the city. Bianca shifted impatiently in the back seat as the driver muttered bitterly under his breath about capitalism and avocado toast.

As the cab turned a sharp corner into the business district, Bianca's stomach flipped. She felt woozy as she gaped out the side window at blips of Bloor Avenue whizzing by. Every shiny building started looking the same to her, melding together into a sterile, urban monotone. People walked briskly, like schools of fish. They looked like automatons, programed to avoid eye contact. Beeping traffic created an almost harmonized soundtrack to Bianca's current mindset. She felt like a trout, flapping around desperately out of water – gasping, struggling, confused, desperate and probably looking like a complete idiot to other trout.

It all came down to this. Seven years in a fickle industry where you are only as impressive as your most recent project. An industry where you can topple from the summit of success after years of proving your aptitude. All because of one, arbitrary blunder. An industry where men outnumber women by an obscene margin.

Bianca had to work like a draft horse to become a senior executive at *Atticus & Blart*. She basically pulled lemurs out of her butt for this company. Even if this whole cat thing was somehow her fault – and she was still holding out hope that the blame would fall on Dirk – surely the CEO would take her years of unwavering commitment into consideration. Right?

Dammit, heart. Stop pounding.

Something deep in Bianca's subconscious was nagging her to hold it together. She was a professional after all. Her team was depending on her. She couldn't just fall apart like a cheap taco. Everyone would peg her as a hysterical woman. Nobody would ever take her seriously again. Her mind jostled with ideas, solutions, delegations, possibilities, compromises, excuses, code that she didn't even know how to write... But everything swirled together in her throbbing brain like a trippy, convoluted mushroom hallucination.

The taxi shrieked to a halt. Bianca was thrust forward, being yanked back into place by a proactive seatbelt. She became aware that she was mouth-breathing and she could feel the pulse throbbing in her neck.

"*Atticus and Blart,*" muttered the weedy driver. "Not that anyone cares."

Bianca stared for a moment at the tall, imposing building outside.

"Are you getting out or what?" the driver asked in a vinegary way.

Bianca blinked. She liberated herself from the vehicular sardine tin and teetered towards the door of her building. The tinted windows were like mirrors and she could barely recognize the zombified corpse looking back at her. She blinked her stinging eyes, took a deep breath and walked into the foyer of doom.

***

Bianca squished her face into a raisin of apprehension before courageously pushing the door open. What she would find in that boardroom, she was certain, would be the stuff nightmares are made of.

A sea of eyes penetrated Bianca, who stood there like a stiff department store mannequin. Some faces were just as stunned as she was while others were saturated in fear and uncertainty. Just as she suspected, there were also looks of accusation and disgust – and those were the stares that impaled her self-confidence. Flannigan from Human Resources was there with a notebook, writing something ambiguously. A few restless legs twitched around the room and yes, there were tears. Mostly from Gordon Smitt. He didn't deal with stress very well.

Worst of all, was the deafening silence.

"Okay." Bianca could only choke out that one word. The tension in the air was as thick as margarine. She was having trouble swallowing.

Her eyes zeroed in on the CEO, Arthur Grosswater, whose deathly intense glare reminded Bianca of a Bengal tiger staring down his prey. He leaned back in his leather chair, heaving a cigar-scented exhale, his eyes still fixated on Bianca and all her insecurities. Could he actually see Bianca's anxiety wafting around her body like a psychedelic cloud of shame?

"I can fix this," Bianca stammered.

"You can't fix this," Arthur growled. "Nobody can fix this. It's over."

"No," Bianca said. Her black bob haircut swooshed back and forth when she shook her head. "Every challenge we face is an opportunity to improve our product. I'm a firm believer in that. It seems like the end of the world now because the news is still fresh. But once we mull this whole thing over and regroup..."

Bianca heard a bitter voice in the group gurgle something about Bianca being an overconfident twat. She swallowed, blinked hard and continued.

"I'm brewing up a solution as we speak," she said as her confidence wobbled. "We are going to pull this off, okay? Who's feeling motivated?"

Crickets.

"Bianca. This is on you," Arthur said, pointing a sausage finger into Bianca's personal space. "Nothing moves forward without a nod from *you*. And if memory serves, this psychotic cat software was your idea in the first place. Can you please just admit your ineptitude so we can..."

"Arthur," Bianca said a little too loudly. "I've got this. Okay? I've... I've got this."

"Are we going to lose our jobs?" asked Gordon. His bespectacled face pinkened with dread. "We're all going to be outsourced, aren't we? All the developers? Oh my god."

"Gordon, it'll be fine," Bianca shout-squeaked. "We're going to figure this out. Nobody is going to..."

"This is outrageous," Arthur exploded with his face reddening like a livid radish. "How could you be so oblivious to what our competition is doing?"

"I've had a lot on my plate," Bianca gasped hoarsely. "I was focused on other elements of..."

"This," chuffed Arthur, "is not a forgivable blip that can be ironed over with a bit of new code. This is a fiasco. Do you realize that your incompetence could lead to the demise of our company?"

"Arthur," Bianca said stoically, trying to hold her posture erect despite her sudden dizzy spell, "I have a plan. I always have a plan. I'm a planning... planner... Anyone want to hear my plan?"

"Bianca," HR Flannigan warned. "Your face is turning fuchsia."

"Last time we missed a deadline we had to downsize the whole company by thirty percent," warbled Gordon. "What about my vulnerable children? Little Eddie and Fern are the real victims in all this."

"Gordon!" Bianca shrieked in a more irrational tone than she had intended. "Stop it! Just... stop!"

"Bianca, you need to calm down," HR Flannigan said with a similar calmness as someone trying to convince a lunatic to hand over the scissors.

"Where were you even when this whole thing went pear shaped?" choked an emotional engineer at the back of the room. "You were supposed to be..."

"I was in Japan for a VR conference!" Bianca snapped sharply. "I literally just landed in Toronto less than two hours ago! Then suddenly I'm swamped by a trillion apocalyptic texts! I've had back-to-back work trips all month! I don't even know what time zone I'm in right now!"

"Please control yourself," HR Flannigan cautioned. "You look unwell."

"Stop talking to me like I'm a porcelain doll, HR Flannigan!" Bianca screamed.

Everyone in the room winced and fell silent.

"I didn't bust my ass for seven years…"

"Language," said HR Flannigan, pointing an accusing pen.

"…without vacation, without sick days, without weekends or any semblance of a social life — I didn't toss my soul into this bottomless abyss just to be labeled as incompetent and singled out and… this was a team project! What about Dirk? I told him to… Seriously, who names their kid Fern?"

"Bianca, this is unseemly," Arthur grunted.

"I am not crying!" Bianca sobbed breathlessly.

"Nobody said you were," said HR Flannigan condescendingly. "We are just concerned for your emotional and mental wellbeing. And liability."

"We're all going to be homeless with no shoes!" wailed Gordon, nervously chewing the side of his cheek. "And if we're going down, then so are you, Mumford!"

Bianca broke down and ugly cried.

Everyone in the room gaped. The sound of her heaving sobs filled the now silent room.

"Christ on a cracker," someone whispered audibly. "She's effing crying."

"Unreal," said another guy. We'll call him Phil.

"Can you all just give me a minute?" Bianca sobbed, her trembling hands forming into fists of ire. With a pinstriped sleeve, she shielded her eyes which now resembled two, brimming infinity pools. "I'm feeling cornered. And being a senior executive, I think the respectful thing for you all to do right now is..."

"Told you she was an overconfident twat."

And that was the very moment that Bianca Mumford lost her mind.

CHAPTER TWO

"Glad to see you managed to compose yourself," said Arthur Grosswater emotionlessly from behind his mahogany desk.

Bianca stared blankly. HR Flannigan had escorted her into the room like an inmate. The whole thing made Bianca feel hollow.

"Are you fit to receive some vital news?" said Arthur menacingly, forming his fingers into a steeple.

"I'm just a little jetlagged. I'm fine."

"You were rocking in the corner, covering your ears and babbling unintelligibly about squirrels."

"Sleep deprivation can sometimes..." Bianca tried.

"Squirrels wearing fedoras."

"I'm fine now."

"You're not fine, Bianca," Arthur grunted.

"You had a nervous breakdown," HR Flannigan observed clinically.

"Don't exaggerate," Bianca winced, trying not to focus on the flickering, fluorescent light above her.

"You locked yourself in the supply closet," HR Flannigan read from his clipboard, "screaming diabolically and telling everyone that you were going on a journey. Then you invited the tech support supervisor to join you."

"I have no recollection of that incident," Bianca half-lied.

"Then you started gnawing compulsively on your left forearm, before trying desperately to escape through a mail slot."

"Seriously, do you have nothing better to do than document literally everything a person does?" Bianca asked resentfully.

"You can't just go around losing your mind every time you are called out on your ineptitude," Arthur said.

"I made one, miniscule mistake in seven years! I'm usually a stickler for details. You both know that. This doesn't usually happen."

"It's been happening quite often of late," objected Arthur. "You're slipping, Mumford. You're losing your verve. Everyone around here is aware of this except you. This little fit you pulled is the final catalyst, I'm afraid."

"I don't have fits," disputed Bianca, wedging a defensive fist in her hip. "Now Gordon, he has fits on a regular basis. Why is he not in here?"

"Also noteworthy," HR Flannigan interjected, "are the reports of you habitually locking yourself in a bathroom stall and crying.

Routinely between the times of 3:00 and 3:05. Every single day, I've been told."

"Who told you that?"

"Do you deny it?"

"Well... no but..."

"Perhaps you are not cut out for..."

"Five minutes of personal time..." Bianca argued.

"Why were you crying?"

"I don't have to tell you..."

"Why?"

"There was no specific reason. I need to stay strong. Alleviate some..."

"Are you succumbing to the stresses of this industry?"

"Hardly!" Bianca fought back. "I just need to schedule a few minutes a day to..."

"You schedule time to cry?" HR Flannigan wrote that down. "Are you unhinged?"

"It's not like I can cry right out there in front of..."

"You are a senior executive. This is worrisome. And your behavior today in the boardroom..."

"Someone called me an overconfident twat!" Bianca's voice cracked. Her vision blurred with warm tears.

"I see," HR Flannigan said, narrowing his left eye.

"Can I just go?" asked Bianca, gesturing towards the door with her thumbs. "I have a lot of work to do."

"No, you don't," Arthur heaved.

"What's that supposed to mean?" Bianca asked tentatively.

"You can't work under this level of duress," HR Flannigan said in his kindergarten teacher voice.

"I'm not under duress. That's nonsensical."

"Squirrels," Arthur stated. "Wearing fedoras."

"You're taking my words out of context," Bianca grasped.

"HR Flannigan will escort you off campus shortly..."

"Wait. Am I fired?"

"Not quite," Arthur said elusively. "I mean we thought about firing you because you basically lost your mind..."

"I've gone seventy-seven hours without sleep. Out of sheer dedication for this company. I'll remind you also that I haven't taken vacation in..."

"... seven years," Arthur finished. "I know, Bianca. That's the problem. You basically live in your office. You literally never go home. You're here on Christmas Day, weekends. You even came to the office after you caught that weird flu in Malaysia."

"Wouldn't you say that's the very picture of commitment?" Bianca interrupted.

"You spread that damn virus around the office like an unpopular opinion on social media," Arthur snarled. "Our entire staff had to take weeks off work, while you remained at your desk, coughing infectious spores into the air. You were literally the only person in the building."

"And this is the thanks I get?" Bianca pushed back. "I sold my soul to this company, Grosswater. You don't realize how lucky..."

"You basically used yourself as a superviral bioweapon."

"You're welcome," Bianca said defiantly, fluffing herself up.

"You need a break," Arthur said firmly.

"By law," HR Flannigan added.

Bianca grappled for a moment. "But... but I don't want to fall behind. I have to prove... it's a competitive industry..."

"We can't have you dropping dead from sheer exhaustion," added HR Flannigan. "We don't have insurance for that."

"We care..." Arthur yawned.

"While it's true labor laws don't apply in our industry..." said HR Flannigan.

"... about productivity," Arthur finished.

"... there's the whole liability thing and that's not in our budget this quarter," HR Flannigan finished.

"I don't understand what's going on," Bianca said. Her mouth quivered with perplexity.

"We are sending you away."

"In what sense?"

"The company is paying for you to take a leave of absence."

"For… how long?"

"The summer."

"Nope."

"It's already arranged."

"My team can't function without me."

"We are sending you to an idyllic eco-lodge in Algonquin Park."

"You're banishing me to the remote wilderness to fend for myself?" Bianca's reviled lip curled. "You can't do that. It's immoral. I've only ever lived in the city. I won't survive out there. What if I die?"

"It's not like that," Arthur said. "HR Flannigan, tell her it's not like that."

"It's not like that," explained HR Flannigan. "You will be happy there, Bianca. Free from the brutal stress of the I.T. industry."

"But I enjoy the brutal stress of the I.T. industry," Bianca said, blinking back tears. "It gives me a sense of purpose."

"Imagine," HR Flannigan said dreamily, gesturing to an imaginary, floating scene of utopian beauty. "Tucked away in a rustic, log cabin. Lake twinkling in the moonlight. A loon. Do you like loons? Orange fire crackling, warming you. The aroma of wholesome meals wafting from the main lodge. Air that's fresh enough to inhale. Wildlife beckoning you. Maybe you'll see an otter."

"What exactly is an eco-lodge?" Bianca grimaced. "Is that some hippie way of saying there's no toilet?"

"You will have all the modern conveniences of home," HR Flannigan pitched. "Just in a more relaxing, naturalistic setting."

"Why do I get the sense that you're lying through your face?" Bianca said nasally.

"Bianca, try to understand," Arthur interrupted like a rude thunderbolt. "You do not have a choice. This trip is mandatory."

"Think of it as an all-inclusive, prepaid vacation," smiled HR Flannigan. "Paid for by the company. A token of appreciation for all your hard work here."

"What if I say no?"

"Then you're fired," said Arthur, ham-fisting his desk.

"Will there be a job waiting for me when I get back?" Bianca swallowed.

Arthur Grosswater and HR Flannigan exchanged an elusive look.

Sweat beads formed on Bianca's forehead.

"If you return with your sanity," Arthur smirked, "then yes."

CHAPTER THREE

Strange as it may seem, Bianca had no recollection of ever seeing her condominium building during daylight hours. Coming home in the middle of the day felt like a volt of shock, seeing the sun streaming down the hallway when she stepped out of the elevator. She actually had to squint.

As she ambled down the hall, she got a whiff of some conflicting aromas, wafting from under doors. Strangers were making lunch. Sniffing the air, Bianca found this concept to be weirdly wonderful. Cheesy scrambled eggs with bacon. Rice with exotic spices. Boiling hotdogs. Normally the air was odorless each morning when Bianca ventured to work at Ridiculous O'Clock. This intriguing assault on her senses was something entirely new.

Bianca's bacon-induced daydream abruptly stopped when she heard the elevator doors open. Brisk footsteps were happening behind her. With her unreasonable work schedule, Bianca had never really encountered anyone else in the hall before. She discreetly got a glimpse of a twenty-seven-ish guy with a hipster beard walking deliberately behind her. She quickened her pace and avoided direct eye contact. As she approached the door to her condo, the hipster continued to follow.

Graphic artist, Bianca guessed. Possibly a psychopath.

Fumbling for her key, Bianca's heart fluttered like a panicked moth in a jar. The graphic hipster psycho stopped directly next to her. Bianca squeezed her eyes shut and waited for the inevitable.

"Hey," the guy said with a casual grin.

Bianca forgot to breathe for a moment as grinning guy (possibly not a psychopath) opened the neighboring door. His vintage, flannel shirt was unbuttoned, revealing a faded *Pink Floyd* T-shirt underneath. He smelled vaguely of corn chips.

"Did you just move in?" he asked. "I've never seen you before."

Bianca gaped. She had lived in this condo for five and a half years. Was this guy on glue? How could he have no idea she lived next door? Wait though. Bianca had no idea who he was either. She squinted at his face, struggling to retrieve it from her long-term memory archive. Surely, she would have remembered that crooked grin. And that hair that probably took hours to look so meticulously unruly. A twinge of embarrassment tickled her innards as Bianca realized how antisocial she must seem. She had not meant to let five and a half years go by without ever once having asked to borrow a cup of flour.

Bianca's eyeballs scoured all the doors around her in the paisley-carpeted hallway. She mused for a moment. Had she formally met anyone in her building at all? Her community was at work. She felt a sense of belonging, purpose and identity at

Atticus & Blart. She shared many things in common with her coworkers, who all had the same University degrees and worked towards a common goal. What reason would she have to wonder aimlessly around her condominium complex, making friends? That would be counterproductive. It would, however, have prevented this incredibly awkward situation with this guy who was apparently her neighbor.

Was she slipping into a state of utter reclusiveness and social irrelevance? Was she only functional within the context of *Atticus & Blart?*

"Brenden," the guy said, extending his hand.

Bianca's eyeballs lolled towards her neighbor's hand. In all her befuddlement, she forgot to reply. Bianca reddened.

"I'll just..." Brenden said, gesturing awkwardly towards his door.

"I'm not weird or anything," Bianca blurted.

Wow, Bianca. That was smooth.

"Good to know," Brenden smirked.

"Senior executive," Bianca said curtly. "Bianca. Bianca the... senior executive. Just as a frame of reference so you know I'm normally eloquent and interactive. Social. You know. In my environment. I just don't have time to meet people. In this building, I mean. I actually know a lot of people."

Brenden nodded slowly.

"I have friends," Bianca nodded. "Lots. They're exclusively at work though. I miss work."

Brenden awkwardly pointed at his door. "I have a cat so I should probably..."

"Cat?" Bianca suddenly looked ill.

Brenden scrambled into his condo, leaving Bianca standing pathetically in the hall.

**

Questioning suddenly her decision not to install blinds on her wall-to-wall windows, Bianca squinted in a headachy manner as she walked through the door. Her condo looked different in the daytime. The walls were a slate color. Who knew? Everything seemed smaller and more compact than she remembered. But then, she had grown accustomed to fumbling around in the dark at 4:00 am, groping around the kitchen for a quick espresso... Wait. She had a potted bonsai tree? Bianca hoped it was artificial because to her knowledge it had never been watered.

Bianca smacked her briefcase on the granite breakfast bar and nestled her butt onto a postmodern barstool. Today, her stainless steel kitchen seemed more institutional than usual. Decorating her apartment with sterile modernism seemed like a trendy idea at the time but was not proving to be very comforting at present. The stark, generic painting on the wall was not offering any sympathy.

Bianca instinctively powered on her laptop and attempted to log into her work account. Her fingers tapped out a familiar rhythm as Bianca's eyes became glassy windows of weariness. She audibly gasped when the face of Arthur Grosswater appeared on her screen, grimacing at Bianca disapprovingly.

"For the luvva!" Bianca startled, nearly teetering backwards on her barstool.

"Nice try, Bianca," said Arthur Grosswater's face.

"Jeez!" Bianca huffed. "What are you doing in my computer, Grosswater?"

"I had a feeling you would try to log in."

"I was just logging in to see if there were any loose ends before I…"

"We have blocked you from your account," said the face.

"You are taking this too far."

"You are cut off, Mumford. When I said you were being sent on a mandatory leave of absence, I meant it."

"Starting tomorrow."

"Today. I trust you've packed."

"I only found out about my banishment this morning. When would I have time to pack? What do you even bring to a backwoods shack? Flipflops and a hatchet?"

"Be ready. A driver will be collecting you at the west entrance of your building tomorrow morning at 6:00. And leave your devices at home. You are to use this opportunity to completely disconnect."

"And this is supposed to alleviate my stress levels *how?*"

"It's nature, Mumford. People like nature."

"The notion of sleeping in a primitive, log structure and voluntarily being where the mosquitos are…"

"Nature."

"Wearing nude pantyhose is about as natural as I can manage."

"Try to think of it as being rebooted."

"Can I at least bring my special pillow? The last thing I need is to have neck spasms. In the forest."

"About four hours by car," Arthur said randomly.

"What?"

"Trudy."

"Who's Trudy?"

"And the water taxi."

"Grosswater, you're not making any sense right now."

"I'm not actually Arthur Grosswater. I'm an algorithm. Whether or not I am directly or accurately responding to your comments is dependent on probability."

"You are a sociopath."

"Algorithm."

"You've always had the personality of an algorithm."

"Be mindful of how you speak to me."

"But it's not you."

"Good point."

"If I were to point out that the only clothing I own is pantsuits and insensible shoes..."

"Possums."

Bianca rolled her eyes. Talking to Algorithm Arthur was about as productive as talking to Real Arthur.

"Mumford? Are you there? Mumf..."

Powering off Arthur Grosswater was the most satisfying thing Bianca had done all day.

CHAPTER FOUR

No stranger to the surreal ambience of 6:00 am, Bianca waited outside the west entrance of her building with three large designer suitcases and a high-end carry-on satchel. The sky was a weird struggle between night and day as only a handful of poor wretches peppered the empty sidewalks, barely self-aware. Assuming they were mindlessly jaunting to places of business, Bianca secretly envied the handful of poor wretches.

Bianca inhaled deeply, memorizing the familiar stench of cigarettes, toxic emissions and the strange vapor that was wafting from a sewage grate. It was an urban aroma. Comforting. It smelled like civilization. A peopled city. Creature comforts. The grind. Purpose. Bianca loved this stinky city which had become her cocoon. She integrated comfortably into the system and could not imagine being disconnected from the familiar rhythm of Toronto.

She was swallowed by a sense of dread when she saw the headlights of a white limo approach her challengingly like the eyes of a glowing-eyed jungle cat. The limo, much like her thumping heart, slowed to a halt in front of Bianca's building. Bianca swallowed hard.

Snapping out of her morbid trance, Bianca suddenly realized that her luggage was being grabbed by a white-gloved hand. A grizzled driver opened the car door, waiting attentively for Bianca to climb into the backseat. They looked at each other for a moment as Bianca's eyes widened with apprehension. The driver cocked his head.

"Bianca Mumford?" the driver asked with a smoky rasp.

Bianca nodded slowly. She craned her neck to get a better view of the limo's interior.

The driver dimpled into an ironic smirk. "Hop in."

Bianca reddened. "Thank you," she murmured, tentatively finding a seat in the back. Her rear end sunk dreamily into the plush, leather seat. Possibly the last luxury she would experience for the next couple of months. She startled when the driver shut the front door loudly.

"I'm Randy," the driver said eagerly, extending his gloved hand over the front seat and into Bianca's circle of personal space.

Breathing out a long breath, Bianca shook Randy's hand limply, as though reluctantly handling a dead fish.

"Not a morning person, I guess," Randy jested as he put the limo into drive.

"I am actually," Bianca finally managed. "A morning person."

"Really?" Randy smirked as he pulled out into the sparse, early morning traffic. "You seem a little caffeine deprived."

"I am adequately caffeinated," Bianca said primly. "But thank you for your concern."

"Algonquin Park," Randy said, reviewing his marching orders. "Lucky you."

Bianca rolled her eyes and grunted.

"You're a little overdressed for Algonquin Park, don't you think?"

"All of my clothes look like this," Bianca huffed. "I wasn't given adequate notice to go shopping."

"What brings you to Algonquin?"

Bianca squeezed her eyes shut tightly, like a toddler who doesn't want anyone to see her with a forbidden cookie. "Personal time," she said, barely audible.

"I could use me some of that," Randy nodded. "Judging by your pantsuit and designer luggage, I take it you're a hard-working career lady."

"Senior executive," Bianca said, wearily resting her temple against her fingertips.

"*Atticus & Blart,*" Randy nodded at a memo. "You must be a valuable member of their team for them to send you on this dream vacation."

But this was not a vacation. This was a deliberate slap in the face from an ungrateful corporation that has no semblance of conscience, empathy, gratitude or common sense. It was a public flogging. Sending her to a musky wilderness, miles from civilization was a sadistic form of unmentionable torture. And Lyme Disease.

"Maybe you'll see a moose!" Randy bubbled.

"I don't believe in moose," Bianca said dryly.

Randy involuntarily sprayed some sparkling water from an inaptly timed sip. "You don't believe in moose?"

Bianca discreetly shook her head.

"What do you mean you don't believe in moose?"

"They don't exist."

"They do though."

"Don't be daft."

"Algonquin has lots of them," Randy insisted. "Sometimes at around dusk, you can see them come right up near the road."

"I've never seen one."

"Have you ever left the city?"

"What reason would I have to leave the city?"

"To see a moose."

"Not real."

Randy suddenly burst into a fit of laughter.

A sinking feeling consumed Bianca as she watched Randy wipe away a tear of amusement with his finger. She had always assumed that moose were mythological things, somewhat like mermaids or Narnia. The notion of a lanky beast with an oddly shaped head, sporting a rack of impossible antlers, ambling awkwardly through the forest on disproportionately long legs burgeoned on the absurd. The elusive and secretive nature of such beasts was even more difficult to believe. She heard tales of people portaging for days in hopes of spotting moose, only to mope back to their suburban bungalofts in disappointment – much like all the disillusioned tourists who flock to Loch Ness.

Double-checking his blind spot, Randy quipped, "Can't imagine a girl like you roughing it in Algonquin. In a pantsuit."

"They're putting me in a log cabin."

"You say that like it's a bad thing."

"I'll probably die in there."

"Or not."

"They could have at least sent me to Oahu."

"Meh."

"What's wrong with Oahu?"

"They don't have moose," Randy smirked.

Bianca pursed her lips indignantly.

"You've got this, Bianca Mumford."

"You seem pretty sure of yourself."

"Look at you. A strong, grown-up woman. Competent. Independent. Nobody becomes a senior executive without a can-do attitude."

"This is entirely different."

"Maybe not."

"None of this was my idea. I want to be in my comfy condo with hot flowing water and ambient road noise."

"You need a break."

"Why do people keep saying that?"

"You are wound tighter than a ball of..."

"Anxiety?"

"Yarn. Wow. You really do need a break."

"I don't know you so..."

"If this isn't a vacation..."

"Stop."

"And none of it was your idea..."

"Can you *not?*"

"What is the purpose of this trip?"

"Ugh..."

"Are you running from the law?"

"No! I..."

"Are you in some kind of trouble?"

"Randy..."

"Mental health leave?"

Bianca bit her lower lip.

"Oh," Randy rasped softly.

"I'm not crazy or anything."

"Never said you were."

"I just got a little emotional at work yesterday."

"Happens."

"It was no big deal."

"I'm sure it wasn't."

"Everyone has a breaking point."

"Truth."

"I mean, lots of people gnaw on their arms."

"...what?"

"And I wasn't really frothing. Tommy Fung will say anything for attention."

Randy blinked.

A wave of nausea welled up inside Bianca. She could not unsay the frothing thing. Why did she even say that? Now the driver was thoroughly traumatized. She could see it in his bewildered eyeballs and the maze of worried creases forming in his forehead. Bianca felt agitated, as she was rapidly losing ownership of this dialogue. If she was at work, she never would have spluttered out personal details of her life. She would never let her guard down or make herself vulnerable. She would command the room. Control every conversation. Maintain composure. Exude strength. Why were things so different in the backs of limos?

"Do you have anyone?" Randy asked. His smoky voice tenderized like a compassionate veal scallopini.

Bianca shrugged, careful not to appear fragile.

"Family, I mean. Or a man?"

Bianca's nose crinkled into an indignant pout.

"I can see by your *spaghetti western squint* that you don't have a man and that it's none of my business."

Perceptive.

"Do you have any family you can talk to? About your troubles at work?"

Bianca slowly closed her eyes and breathed in.

"You don't?"

"They're busy," Bianca said. "My family. But I can handle..."

"They're busy?"

"I come from a hard-working family," Bianca said sharply. "I was raised to take care of myself. Besides, you're making this out to be a bigger deal than it is. I had a misunderstanding with my employer."

"Over whether or not gnawing on your arm is cause for a mental health leave?"

Humiliated, Bianca covered some faint teeth marks on her arm. She could not stomach the look of empathy plastered all over Randy's face.

Why can't limo drivers just mind their own business?

"Fine," Bianca said, pulling a cell phone from her satchel. "I'll put your mind at ease. I'll call my dad right now."

Bianca dialed and waited. She perked up but deflated when a recorded message informed her that her father would be out of the country until the end of July. She noticed Randy's eyes narrowing through the rearview mirror. Taking a deep breath, she faked a conversation with her dad.

"Dad?" Bianca said bluntly into the phone. "Yes, it's me. Just thought I'd call to pass some time in the car... Yup, Algonquin... Bear spray? Okay, I'll keep that in mind. Say, did you end up getting that schnauzer you wanted?... Aww, that's adorable. What did you call him?... Mr. Flooferson? Oh my god, dad. My heart just exploded. Text some pictures, okay?... Yes, I'm fine now, thanks for asking... Yup, it's all good. I was a little overwhelmed. Grosswater overreacted. You know the drill... I know, yes. I'll try to unwind and make the most of it... Yes, Dad, I know I can talk to you about anything... I'll call when I get there, okay?... Love you too, Daddy... Ciao."

Bianca put the phone away and looked smugly at Randy.

"See?" she said hoarsely.

CHAPTER FIVE
(DAY 1 IN ALGONQUIN PARK)

Gravel crackled under the tires. Bianca woke with a kink in her neck from a boredom-induced catnap. She blinked the sleep from her eyes and looked out the tinted window. Towering pines encrusted the perimeter of a pristine lake. The lake water looked like glass, reflecting the pillowy clouds above. The sky looked like it had been masterfully colored with a blue crayon. All of this would have eased Bianca's nerves, had it not been for the black nimbus of mosquitos, waiting eagerly for her to come outside.

"Isn't it grand?" Randy said with a toothy smile. "Ready to head out?"

"Perhaps you didn't see the plague of pestilence waiting for me to open the door?"

"Mosquitos?" Randy laughed. "They're not a plague. They were here first. If anything, we are the pestilence."

"I'm not opening this door."

"Surely, a strong, powerful executive like you can handle a few bugs?" Randy winked.

Bianca blew the black bangs from her forehead in frustration before bravely opening the door. Once outside, she compulsively started swatting every member of her body.

"Where's the lodge?" Bianca said, crinkling her nose and looking around. There were no cabins in sight. Only a solitary, rickety canoe, wedged into a sandy shore.

"Over here!"

Bianca spun around to find a ghoulishly lanky fellow approaching with an enthusiastic wave.

"Who's that?" Bianca stage-whispered to Randy.

Randy shrugged.

"Bianca Mumford?" the lanky fellow asked in an endearingly nasal voice. He brushed some dirt from his hand and offered it to Bianca.

"I thought there was a lodge," Bianca said, looking cautiously at the lanky fellow's hand and flaring her nostrils.

"It's not accessible by land," he explained. "We take this water taxi."

Bianca looked nauseated at the sight of the rickety canoe. "You mean *that?*"

The lanky fellow bashfully smiled, revealing a mouthful of uneven teeth, yellowed from coffee. "We try to reduce our carbon footprint. No motorboats allowed. Are you ready to go?"

Bianca looked pleadingly at Randy and mouthed *don't leave me here.*

Randy plunked Bianca's luggage on the ground next to her. "Get in that canoe," Randy instructed, "and do this thing like a boss."

Bianca watched in horror as Randy's crunchy footsteps made their way back to the limo.

The lanky fellow gaped at the luggage. "Um…"

Bianca spun around, her black hair shimmering in the sunshine. "Is there a problem?"

Flummoxed, the lanky fellow pointed at Bianca's luggage which was now sitting pretentiously on the gravel. "I…" he stammered. "I mean… this."

"My luggage?"

"I don't think it'll fit in the canoe."

"Make it fit. I need my stuff."

"Wow," the lanky fellow said, scratching his head and running his fingers nervously through his mousy locks. His eyeballs quivered. "Well, maybe if you wedged the satchel between your knees…"

"Fine," Bianca grunted while dragging one of the impossibly heavy suitcases. "I'll do it myself. But don't expect a tip."

***

"I'm Tucker, by the way," winced the lanky fellow as he dipped his paddle into the water. The suitcases weighted the canoe down, making the bow drag through the sandy lake bottom.

"Tucker," Bianca nodded cordially. She sat primly in the ridiculously lopsided canoe as though nothing out of the ordinary was happening.

"First time here?" Tucker grunted in mid-stroke. His gangly muscles tightened visibly with each labored paddle.

"Why do you ask?" Bianca said, suddenly self-conscious of her pinstripes. She discreetly fastened the top button of her business-casual blouse.

"I ask everyone that," Tucker said. His voice had a tendency to randomly squeak like a rusty gate. "And also the pantsuit."

"This is a very versatile pantsuit."

"Also the luggage."

"What's wrong with my luggage?"

"Did you not know about the water taxi?"

"This was an impromptu trip, planned by my employer. I was not alerted about the dress code or the luggage restrictions."

"Gotcha," Tucker nodded submissively.

Bianca observed that the dark circles around Tucker's eyes made him look like a timid racoon. "Are you unwell?" she asked, confidentially. "You look a little rakish."

Tucker reddened. "I eat a lot of kale. Maybe a little too much kale."

"I sort of feel like I'm being escorted across the River Styx."

"I just look like this," Tucker shrugged. "Genes. Metabolism. Not everyone can be beautiful like..."

Bianca raised an eyebrow.

"...Gwen Stephani," Tucker blushed.

"So Tucker," Bianca said, feeling like a conspicuously displaced octopus in a tree, "what is this place? This eco-lodge? What does that even mean?"

"Oh!" Tucker perked up. "Here at *The Whispering Beaver*..."

"Wait, the what?"

"*The Whispering Beaver*," Tucker repeated.

"What in the actual f..."

"The eco-lodge. That's what it's called."

"I'm not staying anywhere involving whispering beavers."

"You don't like our name?" Tucker looked genuinely hurt.

"Why would anyone name their business *The Whispering Beaver?*"

"Isn't it obvious?" Tucker asked with his lower lip protruding in earnest defense.

"Not even a little bit."

"Whispering," whispered Tucker. "Because it's so tranquil and placid. See, whispering makes you think of quiet things. And the word itself sounds like a gentle breeze. Lake water licking the rocks. Leaves rustling. Or you know. Someone whispering."

"You don't have to literally whisper. I know what whispering is."

Tucker pursed his lips, disappointed that his poetic explanation was not more effective. "So that's why we're called that. And also beavers are cute and industrious."

"And being an eco-lodge means what?" Bianca asked.

Tucker beamed. "We are completely off the grid."

"Off the grid?" Bianca repeated nervously. "Are you saying there's no toilets or electricity? Because if that's the case, you can turn this canoe around right now."

"Didn't you read the brochure?" Tucker chuckled. "We generate our own electricity from a little waterfall in a cove by the lakeshore."

"Well," Bianca said with a stiff smile. "That's... primitive."

"It's actually pretty cool," Tucker smiled eagerly. "We have a little shed with a generator. I can show you if you want."

"So we're talking *real* electricity?"

"Is there another kind?"

"Is there light?"

"Sure."

"And hot water?"

"Most of the time."

"And flushable toilets?"

"There's... toilets," Tucker nodded elusively.

Bianca felt a tension headache brewing.

CHAPTER SIX

While Tucker agonizingly dragged the oversized luggage into an ambiguous grove of trees, Bianca trudged up a hill to a little log cabin with an *office* sign squeaking as it swung back and forth in the breeze. Tufts of wispy smoke wafted from a chimney, alerting Bianca that someone was currently manning the office. A plethora of multicolored impatiens smiled from their window boxes, while a droopy oak tree moped above the cedar-shingled roof. The windows sported gingham curtains. The cuteness was palpable. Bianca would have been charmed, had someone not been churning butter in her gut.

Bianca's feet wobbled a little as she ventured up the stone steps. Of course, they adorned the footpath with river rocks. Why wouldn't they? The screen door shrieked open as Bianca poked her head inside, in search of someone. Anyone.

"Oh my gosh!" a matronly woman gushed.

Bianca was caught off guard when she was suddenly being hugged by said matronly woman who was aproned and wearing an obsolete shade of lipstick. The woman wiped her hands on her apron and smiled warmly. She was wearing a floral housedress.

She must have been someone's mother. Someone's pioneer mother.

"You must be Bianca!" the woman said, clasping her hands together with glee. "We've all been eagerly awaiting your arrival! How was the drive? You come to us from Toronto, no?"

Aghast, Bianca nodded.

"Sit, sit," the woman coaxed, patting a chair next to a desk that was wedged into the front room. The chairs did not match each other or the desk. "You can call me Trudy."

Trudy. Way to be elusive, Algorithm Arthur.

"*The Whispering Beaver* is delighted to have you in it."

"Please never say that again."

Trudy sprayed a raspberry laugh and jestingly pushed Bianca in her arm. "I think I'm going to like you."

"Same," said Bianca stiffly.

"Now then," Trudy said, rubbing her hands together in anticipation. "We're putting you in the Fox Hole."

"What does that mean?" Bianca asked, tentatively edging farther away from Trudy.

"Your cabin," Trudy blinked. "We name our cabins after woodsy things. Wildlife found right here in Algonquin Park."

Bianca stiffened.

"Not to worry though," Trudy said confidentially, cupping her mouth with her hand for effect, "the foxes are harmless. Mostly."

Bianca paled.

"I'm sure Tucker already told you about our little waterfall," Trudy squeaked. "We are completely off the grid, but you will enjoy all the creature comforts of home. Mostly."

"Awesome sauce," Bianca said sarcastically.

"Your luggage should be waiting for you when you arrive at your cabin. Your key," Trudy added, handing Bianca a hand-carved keychain with a fox on it. "You'll find your cabin all the way down the path, next to the Wolf Den."

Bianca gaped with her lips parted.

"Oh!" Trudy laughed breathlessly at herself. "You thought... oh dear! It's not really a wolf den! That's the name of the cabin next door! Don't worry though. Your neighbor won't disturb you. He's a quiet fella. Mostly keeps to himself. Now then, about your meals..."

"I avoid carbohydrates."

"Aww, that's cute," Trudy twinkled dotingly. "Meals are served here at the main lodge in our cozy dining room. You've been assigned table number nine. I like the number nine."

Bianca blinked.

"Tucker will be out and about tending to things," Trudy counted on her fingers. "If you need anything at all, just ask him or me or any other member of *The Whispering Beaver* family."

"Aaaaand you said it again."

"We can arrange picnics. Outings. Guided canoe tours. Or you can just unwind in the Fox Hole and feel all those urban insanities just melt away."

Bianca wriggled uncomfortably in her mismatched chair as Trudy nodded just a little too sincerely.

"What are you getting at, Trudy?" Bianca asked with a sideways glance.

"Your boss told us about your um…" Trudy circled her finger in a cog-like motion next to her temple, insinuating the loss of Bianca's sanity.

"I am perfectly fine," Bianca insisted.

"Yes, you are," Trudy said, pinching Bianca's cheek. "Of course, you are. Or were, I suppose. But not to worry because your boss filled me in on everything and we are here to help you recover."

"I can take care of myself," Bianca said confidently. Sort of.

"Mmm-hmm," Trudy said, goggling at Bianca's poor choice in clothes. "We're here to help, Love. Anything you need, just ask a member of our team. Until 9:00 p.m. Then we're all off duty."

Bianca furrowed her brow as a strangely timed glop of bird plop splashed on the windowpane beside her.

CHAPTER SEVEN

The rustic log cabin challenged Bianca to a staring contest. Bianca stood hopelessly, gawking at the cloudy windows which gaped challenging back at her. She could almost hear the theme song from *The Good, the Bad and the Ugly* whistling in her mind. The logs were crafted and notched masterfully. Between each log was a layer of white chinking which looked like buttercream icing smushing out between layers of cake. Rickety steps led up to a droopy, covered porch. A screen door with a defiant tear dared Bianca to enter.

Pine needles crunched beneath her feet as Bianca took her first reluctant steps towards the aptly named Fox Hole cabin. It was a bit of a hole. Outdated. Not that she knew the difference between a modern cabin and an outdated one. It looked dilapidated and pathetic from the outside. Like protective arms, the needled boughs of towering pines seemed to hover protectively around the cabin. Even the pines could see that the cabin could not defend itself against the elements.

Might as well get this over with.

A rusty nail gave up hope, protruding through a splintery, wooden step as Bianca put her foot down. The wood buckled and Bianca lost her footing. Shaking her head in disapproval, she cautiously climbed up to the porch, each step creaking as though Bianca's feet were causing the wooden slats physical pain.

Bianca peered through the foggy window. Everything looked blurry through the weathered glass. It was like looking through a portal into her own, worst nightmare. It looked cramped in there. And rural. She opened the torn screen door which quickly slammed shut behind her. The slam echoed over the lake, probably disturbing everyone and making them peer out of their stupid cabin windows.

Squinting, Bianca inspected the room. It was small. But had a homey warmth. Unlike her cold, metallic condo which looked like something out of a science fiction catalogue. The tartan couch and knotty pine coffee table were not her style at all but the cozy vibe in the room made Bianca's constricted chest loosen slightly. Although she would never admit that.

She switched on a lamp. Electricity. (Sigh of relief) A dull, yellowish light struggled through the lampshade, creating a lulling, ambient fug. Bianca gasped a little when she saw an acrylic painting of a bull moose, penetrating her with his creepily realistic eyes. Suddenly queasy, Bianca felt like she was being chosen as a potential mate during rutting season.

Not real, not real, not real.

Bianca ran her hand over the hotel-white comforter on the bed. Mmm. Cushy. However, when she sat on the bed, the boing of springs alerted her that the comforter was just an affront to cover up the fact that they hadn't changed the damn mattresses since the place opened seventy-one years ago.

A cramped bathroom was tucked away at the back of the cabin. Through the open door, Bianca spotted a toilet. (Yay) She peered through the door and found a narrow shower (also yay) which was relatively clean, save for some stubborn scum that had accumulated from years of use. Some silly little spa shampoos and mini soaps were lovingly displayed in a wicker basket by the sink. Bianca smirked. Rip-off brand. Nice try though.

The cabin was stuffy, and Bianca crumpled her nose at the vague musk in the air. With some grunting effort, Bianca cranked open a few windows to vent out some of the mugginess. As she did so she got a glimpse of the neighboring cabin through a grove of overprotective pines. The Wolf Den. It seemed to be the identical twin of Bianca's cabin except for the roof that sagged lazily on the left side.

There was movement inside the Wolf Den. Bianca was unexpectedly intrigued, wondering if she could catch a glimpse of the elusive neighbor who Trudy described. She craned her neck as a lumbering figure inside the neighboring cabin skulked past a window. She squinted, struggling to focus. His windows were just as murky as her own. He was an imposing figure. Not huge by any means, but intense. Hair. Lots of dark hair. His movements were anything but graceful. Could he be a medium-sized sasquatch?

The figure stopped abruptly at the window, as though feeling Bianca's curiosity boring through his body. He swung his head around and looked directly at Bianca through the window. Bianca gasped audibly and quickly pulled the gingham curtain shut.

CHAPTER EIGHT

It felt like summer camp. Or at least it would have felt like summer camp if Bianca had ever been to summer camp. A copper bell clanged from the main lodge, causing all the *Whispering Beaver* guests to emerge from their cabins, in search of food. As usual, Bianca was prepared. She showered and changed from her icky car clothes. She conditioned and combed her hair into a flawless, bodied bob. After inspecting her reflection from every geometrical angle, she approved herself as acceptable for a dinner out.

While ambling towards the lodge, she slipped a few times in her maroon, patent shoes. However, she collected herself each time, pretending that she meant to slip. Even among backwoods people, she was determined to maintain a professional air of poise and elegance. Because reasons.

The shrieky, screen door alerted Trudy of Bianca's arrival at the main lodge dining room. Trudy smiled warmly, albeit stiffly when she eyeballed Bianca's demure, black cocktail dress, adorned with burst crystal.

"Sweetheart," Trudy said maternally, "you look..."

Bianca inspected her attire self-consciously, hoping her dress wasn't accidentally tucked into her sheer pantyhose.

"What?" Bianca asked. "Is this too casual for dinner?"

"You look precious," Trudy assured her, waving her hands in a *never mind* kind of way. "Table nine is waiting for you, Dear. It's right over there in the corner. Lizbeth will take care of you shortly."

Bianca walked awkwardly towards her table, her shoes slipping a few times on the knotty pine floor. She could feel the eyes of people all around, staring at her from their tables. A gaggle of flannelled fisherman who still reeked from their recent catch. A family with twin toddlers who sat in their highchairs, gnawing on fistfuls of crusty bread. An impossibly old couple looking wizened, milky-eyed and holding weathered hands. A sickeningly cute honeymooning couple, cozying up on the same side of the table. A morbid teenager who resented Bianca for existing.

Why is everyone looking at me?

Bianca wedged herself into her seat in the corner. Eating alone was degrading but there was no reason anyone else in the room had to know how awkward she felt. She sat with perfectly erect posture, clearing her throat importantly and looking superiorly at the single piece of paper that served as a menu.

"Hey, darlin'," a perky waitress said, filling Bianca's glass from a jug of icy water. "The name's Lizbeth. I'll be taking care of you."

Bianca looked up, wincing at the smacking noise Lizbeth was making with her gum. Lizbeth was, Bianca supposed, the cover girl for *Backwoods Magazine.* Her dirty blond hair was tossed into a hasty ponytail with strands of un-consenting, stray curls escaping a lazy scrunchie. She wore bulky layers of conflicting flannels, which made Bianca's eyes ache. Her lips were painted Barbie doll pink and she wore clunky Birkenstocks with wool socks underneath.

"Bianca, right?" Lizbeth asked, licking pink lipstick from her teeth.

Bianca merely gaped.

"I heard all about you," Lizbeth said confidentially. "No judgement though. It could have happened to anyone."

"What?" Bianca asked. But she knew. Apparently, everyone here was warned about her brief bout of insanity.

"Do you want me to go over the menu with you?" Lizbeth quickly segued.

"I'll order the…"

"Jedd," Lizbeth nodded cheerily. "He's our chef. A wizard in the kitchen, really. Although sometimes I have to help him out since he lost his sense of taste in a freak accident." Lizbeth continued nodding and smiling, remembering something fondly.

"Right," Bianca said dryly. "So with the rump roast…"

"Jedd's a good guy," Lizbeth said, still nodding.

Bianca blinked, waiting to see if Lizbeth was going to continue in her nostalgic stream of consciousness.

After a beat…

"Medium rare," Bianca tried.

"Have you met Jedd?" Lizbeth asked, smacking her gum good-naturedly.

"I have not."

"Oh, Jedd's great. He's been here since the place opened. *The Whispering Beaver* was his daddy's idea. Built all these cabins himself when Jedd was just little. So much love went into these cabins. This is a great, little place, eh?"

"It's outstanding," Bianca muttered. "Listen, it's been a long drive and I'm peckish. Do you mind if I order?"

"Handlebar mustache," Lizbeth gleamed. "A white and wiry one. Oh Jedd. He reminds me of a grandpa. Hey, do you want to hear about my grandpa?"

Bianca's stomach grumbled angrily.

Suddenly, the screen door slammed at an even louder volume than usual. Every head in the dining room turned. A lumbering shadow appeared on the wall.

"Oh gosh," Lizbeth stage whispered. "He's here."

Bianca rubbernecked to get a better look at the mysterious creature who just entered the dining room. She recognized the imposing figure as being the shadowy rebus who glared at her from the cabin next door. She was eager to put a face to the shadow.

"Who is that?" Bianca whispered.

"Kraven Kane," Lizbeth shuddered.

"Who's Kraven Kane?" Bianca asked.

"He comes here every summer," Lizbeth said, doe-eyed with intrigue and possibly fear. "Just shuts himself in. Keeps to himself. Only meanders out for meals and then lumbers back into his cabin like the mysterious riddle he is. We've been given our orders to give him his space."

Bianca studied Kraven, who sat in the opposite corner of the dining room, obscured in the shadows. He reminded Bianca of a lumberjack with his buffalo plaid flannel shirt rolled up to his elbows. Despite Kraven giving off the antisocial nuance of a Kodiak bear, he was smaller than his energy suggested. His shoulders were hardened with rock-solid muscle. Bianca imagined him swinging an axe. She wasn't sure how she felt about that.

Kraven's unkept tangle of black hair was tied in a messy ponytail with a rubber band that looked like it had not been pulled out in weeks. His unruly, black mane framed a severe, square jaw, etched with prickly, black stubble. Most ambiguous were his searing eyes, which surveyed the room from their concave sockets. The color and cryptic intensity of his eyes reminded Bianca of an Egyptian mau.

A shiver ran up Bianca's spine. She looked around to see if anyone else felt a sudden chill in the room.

"Excuse me," Lizbeth said like a deer in the headlights. "I need to promptly bring Kraven his basket of warm, cheddar biscuits. He likes his warm, cheddar biscuits."

Bianca's lips parted as she unintentionally gawked at Kraven. It was impossible not to look. She had never seen anything like him. Did he have the spirit of a bear? Timber wolf maybe? She noticed Lizbeth tremble a little bit as she brought him a basket of biscuits, covered with a checkered tea towel. Kraven dipped a biscuit into a bowl of carrot soup, then mashed the biscuit into his mouth whole. Bianca was agog. He chewed with the finesse of a cud-chewing cow, swallowed wolfishly, then stifled a belch in his flannel sleeve.

Is this guy a man or an animal?

Kraven's razor-sharp eyes sliced through the room and zeroed in on Bianca. She jolted, suddenly realizing that she was staring like a warped voyeur. She gasped audibly, abruptly looking down at her glass of water, memorizing the ice cubes clinking inside. She could feel Kraven's piercing stare penetrating her. Those eyes. They could bore through steel. Bianca pursed her lips, hoping he would lose interest in her. Even from across the room, Bianca could hear Kraven's exasperated exhale. Everyone in the room could hear. It was guttural and throaty.

Did he just growl?

Bianca had a foreboding feeling that Lizbeth was right about leaving this one alone.

CHAPTER NINE

Dusk was settling in, offering Bianca just enough twilight to guide her path as she sashayed back to the Fox Hole. As she approached the cabin, she noticed a bizarre contraption set up beside it. A large metal box with a door propped open was strategically placed between the cabin and the mysterious pines. Bianca squinted at a graphic on the side that looked somewhat like a bear. Curious, Bianca climbed inside the contraption to investigate.

"What are you doing inside the bear trap?" Tucker's voice sliced sharply though the dense silence.

Bianca let out a shrill noise, not unlike the unassuming victim in a horror movie. The hatch suddenly slammed shut, trapping Bianca inside.

"Aw Jeez," Tucker quavered. He knocked on the bear trap, making a tinny noise. "I'll get you out of there! No worries!"

Tucker pried open the bear trap and offered his hand for Bianca to climb out. Bianca grudgingly accepted the chivalrous gesture.

"Why?" Bianca barked.

"Huh?" Tucker asked stupidly.

"Why is there a bear trap outside my cabin?" she demanded.

"Shhh," Tucker said, putting a cartoonish finger to his lips. "We don't want to alarm the other guests. It's a secret."

"What are you talking about. Tucker?"

"See," Tucker explained, "the ranger came by and said there have been reports of a bear..."

"WHAT!"

"Shhh. I told you. It's a secret."

"There's bears here?"

"Of course there's bears here. It's a giant forest. So the ranger said that the bear was last seen sniffing around your cabin. And since your cabin is right at the end of the property here, hidden in the trees, sort of, we figured this would be a good place to set up the trap. But you can't tell anybody, okay?"

"This is unacceptable."

"It's a humane trap."

"Nobody told me there were bears!"

"Isn't that kind of implied?"

"Great," Bianca said, thrusting her hands in the air. "My first night here and I'm going to be eaten by a bear."

"It's only a black bear so probably not," Tucker offered.

"*Probably* not?"

"Black bears usually don't attack."

Bianca exhaled.

"Unless there's cubs."

Bianca stiffened.

"Or if it's like a rogue bear or something and it has mental problems," Tucker shrugged.

Bianca felt her rump roast objecting.

"But don't worry," Tucker assured her. "In Ontario, there's more reports of people being killed by racoons than black bears."

"I'm going to be killed by a racoon?" Bianca shrieked. "I can't be killed by a racoon! That would be embarrassing."

Tucker shrugged.

"Tucker, I'm not sleeping in a cabin with bears right outside!" Bianca wailed.

"You're not very good at this *secret* thing, are you."

"Did you see that tear in my screen door?" Bianca asked, "Was that the work of a rogue bear?"

"You're making me nervous a little."

Bianca grabbed a flashlight from Tucker's pocket. "Go in there," she demanded.

"Wha?"

"I'm not going in that cabin until you make sure there are no bears."

"They don't really know how to use doors."

"Tucker!"

"Right, okay. I'll uh… I'll check it out for you. No worries."

Tucker skulked dramatically up to the front door of Bianca's cabin, flattening himself against the wall and peering inside. Bianca looked on in suspense.

"Bear?" Tucker called feebly. "Hey, bear?"

"Are you scared?" Bianca stage whispered.

"I don't know."

"I thought you were confident that bears can't use doors."

"I hadn't ever thought about it before, to be honest," Tucker admitted. "Now you've got me wondering."

"Go in!" Bianca hissed.

Gulping, Tucker stealthily slunk into the cabin, taking deliberate steps and beamed the flashlight around the room. The flashlight briefly illuminated a hand-carved bear, standing on its wooden hinds in the corner.

A squeaky scream emitted from deep inside Tucker.

Bianca reactively screamed.

Tucker impulsively hugged Bianca.

They screamed in stereo.

Tucker suddenly stopped.

"Oh wait," Tucker said in his usual, nasal voice.

Bianca peered through the door and spotted the wood carving.

"Tucker!" Bianca scolded him.

"The good news is, there's no bears in there. That'll make it easier to sleep."

"I have a feeling sleep won't be happening anytime soon," Bianca moaned.

***

Afraid to move, Bianca was folded securely in a stiff envelope of bedsheets, her cushy comforter protectively hiding her from razor-clawed predators. An insolent spring insisted on jabbing her kidney but she did not dare reposition herself. She was feeling about as safe as she could from the imminent bear who was certainly lurking about outside.

A wooden chair was propped up against the double-locked door and the windows were closed and curtained so she would not look delicious if a bear tried to peep inside. Her mind whirred. Her eyeballs lolled around the dark room. Every sound outside made her jolt.

Did the hatch just close?

Did they catch the bear?

A dangling branch was not helping matters as it scratched against the cedar roof. Bianca wondered, in all her exhausted delusions, if that was the sound of a giant bear claw trying to gauge a hole through the roof. Images of bears falling from the ceiling haunted Bianca. She could think of no worse way to die. Alone, on a sandwich, a hungry bear sprinkling some pepper on her head.

Just as she was finally starting to drift off to sleep, Bianca heard a different noise. Actual footsteps were thumping, making noticeable vibrations in the ground. Bianca stifled whimpers as the footsteps became louder and closer. The familiar creak of the porch steps made Bianca tremble. She nearly stopped breathing when the porch began to squeak under the weight of a terrifying beast outside. Peeking from behind her hiding place under the comforter, Bianca saw an umbral creature looming behind the curtain.

God, no. It's the bear.

Holding in her tremoring breaths, Bianca fumbled for her cell phone.

No signal.

She silently slipped out of bed in her red and black, satin lingerie and padded across the room.

Still no signal.

Bianca wrestled with the notion of peering out the window at the beast. What if he saw her? Could a bear shatter a window?

Claw through the screen? Those flimsy chairs wedged under the doorknob seemed pretty wimpy in retrospect. Surely her makeshift blockade could not stop a famished bear from shouldering his way into the cabin. But she had to see what she was up against.

Bianca skulked up to the window, flattened herself against the wall and edged the curtain just enough that she could sneak a glance outside. Looking back at her were a pair of intense, green eyes, shrouded by a shock of matted, black hair.

Bears have green eyes?

Bianca forgot to breathe for a full eleven seconds. She heard the creature grunting unintelligibly from outside, with strange inflections. Did the bear see her? Were those feeding grunts? The kind a bear makes right before he sinks his teeth into a scrumptious Bianca? Audibly whimpering, Bianca scanned the room for something – anything she could use to defend herself.

Bianca suddenly spotted the pile of guest information booklets, deliberately positioned on the coffee table. She had not bothered to read them. One of the booklets boasted a picture of a black bear with bold print across the top.

Be Bear Aware?

Inchworming ridiculously across the room to avoid casting unnecessary shadows, Bianca grabbed the bear booklet and read with adrenalized speed.

Be loud.

Make yourself big.

Okay, Bianca. You've got this.

You've... got this.

... Okay.

Bianca took a painfully deep, trembling breath, mentally apologizing to anyone she was currently on bad terms with. After saying a half-assed prayer about shepherds, Bianca psyched herself up and charged at the window.

"GO!" Bianca screamed, pounding on the window. "GET OUT OF HERE!"

The creature startled, then grunted.

Before she could change her mind, Bianca burst out of the cabin with a weaponized canoe paddle. She did her most convincing impersonation of a charging gladiator. She waved her arms around ridiculously, making faces that were more embarrassing than scary.

"SCRAM, YOU STUPID BEAR!"

Sheer horror slowly oozed out of her body like a thick syrup and was replaced by dumbfounded humiliation. A familiar figure lumbered back into the darkness, towards the neighboring cabin.

"Kraven?" Bianca said hoarsely to herself.

Standing stupidly on the porch for a few lingering moments, Bianca suddenly realized she was conspicuously showcasing her lingerie. She made a futile attempt to cover herself.

From deep in the piney shadows, Bianca was pretty sure she heard a throaty growl.

CHAPTER TEN
(DAY 2 IN ALGONQUIN PARK)

Well, that night was a bust.

Early mornings were surprisingly chilly in Algonquin Park. Nearly suffocating from humidity all night in a cabin that lacked climate control, Bianca was perplexed by the crispy bite in the air when she emerged from her burrito of bedsheets. She threw an itchy, wool blanket around her shoulders before plunking herself on the tartan couch.

As she set up her laptop, she swallowed a yawn. Bianca had slept a whopping thirty-five minutes. Between the impending threat of rogue bears and the mortification of a strange, hairy man seeing her in her skimpies, sleep was not in the cards. Not to mention, Bianca fretted until sunrise about what her lumberjackish neighbor would think of her after mistaking him for a wild animal and screaming at him to be elsewhere. Scantily clad.

Why does it even matter what he thinks of me?

Shaking the image of Kraven's ominous cat eyes out of her mind, Bianca squinted in a deep focus at her computer screen. Yes, Arthur Grosswater blocked Bianca from her work account.

But unbeknownst to Grosswater, Bianca had three alternate accounts in case she was hacked. She tapped her password, which was embossed on her brain thanks to muscle memory. Her heart twittered at the thought of immersing herself in work – anything to distract her from the drone of solitude and the taunting, early-morning birdsong outside.

No connection.

Uttering mild obscenities under her breath, Bianca shut her laptop and attempted to use her phone.

No signal.

Bianca twitched.

***

"What's your Wifi password?" Bianca asked when she arrived at the main lodge.

Trudy blinked.

Bianca blinked.

Suddenly, Trudy sprayed out an explosive laugh and nursed a cramp of hilarity in her side.

"What's funny?" Bianca asked, nonplussed.

"Oh Hun," Trudy said, gasping for breath and holding Bianca's shoulder to steady herself. "You are so cute."

Bianca cocked her head.

"Wifi is a dirty word around here," Trudy bubbled.

All the animation drained from Bianca's face.

"We don't encourage *devices* around here," Trudy said, using air quotes. "All those little screens. People talking with their thumbs. Technology is the enemy of nature."

"Technology equals progress."

"It sucks your soul out through a bendy straw, Dear. But nature revitalizes you. Regenerates all the brain cells that were nuked by your little screens."

Bianca shook her head in disbelief.

"When we say we are off the grid," Trudy said, raising a proverbial finger, "we mean WAY off the grid."

"What about your little waterfall?"

"Our little waterfall can't conjure the internet. It generates just enough electricity to make our guests comfortable."

"The internet gives me comfort."

"What reason would you have to access the internet," Trudy said while practically glowing, "when the Lord Jesus painted you a beautiful landscape outside?"

"I just need a signal to…"

"You're not trying to log into work," Trudy said, furrowing her brow and playfully wagging her finger.

"I don't know."

"Mr. Grosswater made it quite clear that you are to disconnect entirely from your work and recover from your episode."

"It wasn't an episode."

"Your undoing then."

"I fail to see how briefly checking in at work to make sure my team isn't completely unravelling..."

"Mr. Grosswater gave me orders to report back to him if there was any sign of you misbehaving," Trudy said as she innocently eyeballed the ceiling.

"I'm in hell."

"Heaven, Dear."

"What about my phone?"

"Sorry, Hun. No signal."

"That is just blatantly irresponsible."

"The point of you being here..."

"What if there's an emergency?"

"Provide an example."

"An *emergency*," Bianca repeated. "What if someone needs to contact me?"

"Like from work?" Trudy asked. "That isn't allowed, Dear."

"What if I am in distress and need to contact someone for assistance?"

"Every cabin is equipped with a crisis whistle," Trudy explained. "Blow that."

"A crisis whistle?"

"It's very loud, Dear. And shrill. The crisis whistle can be easily heard by every member of our helpful staff. Just blow on that thing and one of us will come-a-running."

"So if I'm being eaten alive by a wild animal, I'll just go ahead and blow the crisis whistle."

"That's what it's for, Dear."

"So Tucker the human twig can stave off a wild animal if need be."

"He is quite agile, Tucker is. I once saw that boy pull a live squirrel off his own face. That little sucker was really holding on tight with those claws. Tucker put up quite a tussle."

Bianca gaped.

"Table nine is waiting for you, Love," Trudy sang. "We put a nice daisy in the vase, just for you."

Bianca felt suddenly seasick. She quickly scoured the dining room. The obscure table in the far corner lacked Kraven. Bianca exhaled slowly like a relieved balloon. She would not have to endure that radioactive stare, at least for one breakfast.

Taking her seat at table nine, Bianca discovered that there was indeed a daisy flirting at her from its little vase. She peeked under the checkered tea towel and found some cold toast hiding there with an assortment of jams. Bianca crinkled her nose and allowed the toast to continue hiding.

"Hey girl," Lizbeth said cheerily, filling Bianca's coffee cup. Her frenzied hair was piled atop her head like a sloppy bird's nest. "Want some eggs?"

"Poached," Bianca replied drowsily. "With a singular sausage. Please blot the grease off first."

Lizbeth noticed Bianca staring blankly at Kraven's empty table.

"He's not here this morning," Lizbeth said mysteriously.

Bianca shifted in her seat.

"Is everything okay?" Lizbeth asked, taking an uninvited seat beside Bianca.

"Tired," Bianca yawned.

"Didn't sleep well?" Lizbeth asked, rubbing Bianca's arm.

Bianca heaved.

"Awww," Lizbeth continued. "First night in a new bed is always hard."

Bianca's head involuntarily swerved back towards Kraven's table.

"He sure is an unusual sort," Lizbeth said.

"Wha?" Bianca caught herself staring and looked again at the flirty daisy.

"Kraven," Lizbeth answered. "I wonder why he didn't show up this morning?" Lizbeth scratched her head and got her fingers tangled in the frizzy kerfuffle. "It's egg day. Kraven loves his eggs."

Bianca fidgeted nervously with the daisy.

"You seem upset," Lizbeth observed. "Did something happen? Last night maybe? Is that why you didn't rest easy?"

Bianca inhaled tightly, squeezing her eyes shut.

"Is it... Kraven?" Lizbeth said.

Bianca's stomach dipped.

Should I say something?

I have to tell someone.

But why HER?

I don't know anyone else.

Yes, but why HER?

"Okay," Bianca blurted before she could change her mind. "Something happened. Last night. It was quite terrifying actually."

"Oh gosh," Lizbeth said with wide eyes. "Didn't you blow the crisis whistle?"

"It was Kraven," Bianca stage whispered. "But you can't tell anybody, okay? Because it was awkward and just plain shameful."

"Cross my heart," Lizbeth promised.

"I thought there was a bear," Bianca said ominously. "You know. Because of the trap. I heard something outside. So I... now keep in mind, I thought this was a bear... I charged outside with a canoe paddle. But... it was Kraven."

Lizbeth nodded slowly.

"Are you hearing this?" Bianca hissed. "Kraven was lurking around outside my cabin. Looking through my window like a sociopath."

"Yep," Lizbeth nodded. "That sounds about right."

"What?" Bianca squeaked. "Are you saying he does this often?"

"He's a little creepy," Lizbeth shrugged. "None of us can figure that one out."

"Why aren't you taking this more seriously?"

"I'm sure it was a misunderstanding. More or less."

"I'm traumatized."

"Awww."

"Lizbeth, I don't think you understand. I was wearing slinky lingerie at the time. Red and black, to be more specific. The colors of unquenchable desire and other unmentionable things. I bolted out of that cabin like a crazy little skank."

Lizbeth nodded and smiled, remembering something affectionately. "There was this time a couple summers ago when

Kraven disappeared for a solid six days. Never once showed up at the lodge during that whole time."

"Lizbeth…"

"We… Jedd, Tucker and me… we were all placing bets on what he was eating if he wasn't showing up for any meals. My guess was squirrels…"

"Lizbeth, can you try to understand how awkward this is for me?" Bianca pleaded. "The guy is staying right next door. What if he is a sex offender or something?"

"I figured he'd cook the squirrel outside on a spit," Lizbeth said beaming with intrigue. "That would be so *Kraven* of him. But Jedd, he figured Kraven was catching himself some fish. That makes more sense, actually. But it's fun to imagine Kraven eating squirrels."

Bianca hid her face in her hands.

This is going to be a LONG summer.

CHAPTER ELEVEN

The sun beat down on Bianca's face without mercy. She skipped the eggs. Poached or not, Bianca could not stomach eggs today. She could not bear the agony of steeping in the funk of her own awkwardness. Alone in a dining room full of probing eyes. And a daisy.

The word was out. Lizbeth would probably tell everyone in this godforsaken place about what happened. Bianca was hunted like an unassuming gazelle by the world's weirdest jackal. But the story that was bound to circulate would not be about the jackal's weirdness. It would focus on the partially naked gazelle who was only trying to defend herself.

As she was returning to her cabin after breakfast, she heard a faint growl. A tranquil growl, like the sound a grizzly might make while sipping margaritas on the beach. She spotted Kraven by the lake, sitting cross-legged on a sagging dock. His fingers were pinched together in a meditative way. His eyes were closed.

What in the world...

A particularly large conifer trunk offered an ample hiding place for Bianca, who was strangely enticed. She peered from behind the tree and watched, mesmerized as Kraven drifted into a Zen state. His black lashes sealed his eyes shut as he droned a monotonic hum from deep in his throat.

Determined to get a closer look, Bianca spotted a canoe by her little dock with a single paddle lying diagonally across it. She padded softly towards the canoe, pushing it discreetly into the lake. The canoe wobbled treacherously as she attempted to put a foot in. She steadied herself by gripping both sides of the boat, white knuckled. Using her tiny butt, she struggled to balance the boat which teetered back and forth. Once she found her center of gravity – sort of – she reluctantly dipped her paddle into the water, shushing the ripples ridiculously.

The monkish drone emitting from Kraven echoed soothingly across the lake. Goosebumps formed instantly on Bianca's forearms. The sound was primal, and it was freaking her out. Or seducing her. She felt woozy. From the awkward wake of the canoe. Or other things.

I can't see him. Stupid tree.

An insolent willow was hedging Kraven's dock. Bianca would have to find a creative way to edge the canoe around the willow without being discovered. Lilly-dipping amateurishly, Bianca paddled in stupid circles while craning her neck to get a better view of her mysterious neighbor. Squinting and angling her neck just so, she managed to catch a glimpse of Kraven who was still mentally lost in another dimension.

Frustrated by the willow bough that rudely swayed in the breeze, Bianca stood unsteadily in the canoe and leaned out as far as she could arch. She noticed that Kraven's buffalo plaid shirt was unbuttoned to relieve him of the sweltering, morning sun that flickered off the water. Sprouts of black hair adorned his chest like a lush garden of... well, chest hair. His face was tilted upward towards the sun. Sweat trickled in rivulets down his ruggedly square jaw and his lips parted blissfully. He glowed in the sun like a heavenly body.

Holy....

"FRIG!" Bianca shrieked as she lost her balance and toppled from the capsized canoe. She flailed gracelessly through the air and landed with a smack in the lake. Spluttering and gasping, Bianca splashed around like a buffoon. "Help!" she shrieked. "Somebody!"

Kraven suddenly jolted as though he just woke from a long, deep coma. Hearing the hysterical howls and seeing waterlogged Bianca flailing like an idiot with her black hair stuck wetly to her head, Kraven sprang to his feet, poised for rescue. Then he relaxed a little when he saw that Bianca was drowning in water that was only about two feet deep.

Realization sunk in as Bianca sat upright in the water which was just shallow enough for a toddler to wade in. Bianca huffed breathlessly and perhaps indignantly. She caught her breath and made a futile attempt to fix her hair. Her pantsuit was soaked through. Slimy, green lake things clung to the sopping material. Gasping, she looked up at Kraven who was leering down at her with those otherworldly eyes.

"Weirdo," Kraven growled throatily.

CHAPTER TWELVE

Weirdo?

Nope. Bianca was not going to tolerate this. After dredging herself out of the lake, wringing the moisture from her pantsuit and using her fingers as a comb, Bianca trudged stoically up the hillock towards Kraven's cabin. She lost her shoes somewhere in the lake but whatever.

In a huff, Bianca rapped on Kraven's cabin door with a purposeful fist. There was a dramatic pause which made Bianca's heart palpitate like an angry pigeon flapping around in a rafter. Just as she lifted her white-knuckled fist to knock again, the door opened suddenly. A man-sized buffalo plaid shirt flew out the door and percussed Bianca in her face.

The door slammed shut.

What the...

Bianca knocked with more verve, scraping her knuckles on the splintery door.

The door creaked open again.

In the doorway stood Kraven, looming over Bianca like an alpha rottweiler.

"Weirdo?" Bianca shrieked.

Kraven eyeballed Bianca up and down, leering at her sopping, nyloned feet and waterlogged pantsuit.

"WEIRDO?" Bianca shrieked at a higher volume and with clearer pronunciation. "Are you really in a position to call me that when... when... I mean look at you!"

Kraven blinked.

Bianca continued, pointing an accusing finger. "You, Sir, are freaking me out. Lurking around here like a deranged lumberjack. Impersonating rogue bears in the middle of the night."

Kraven raised an elusive eyebrow.

"Don't think I didn't know it was you," Bianca hissed. "Who else around here has gooseberry eyes? The kind that can cut glass? What you did was a criminal offense. And don't assume that just because I am of the female variety..."

"Not from around here?" Kraven said with a low rumble. His eyes were lingering just a moment too long at the special place right below Bianca's collar bone.

"That," Bianca said indignantly, holding her suit jacket closed after suddenly realizing how see-through her blouse was when wet, "is impertinent. But just so you don't ask again, I'm from Toronto."

Kraven rolled his eyes.

"Which means I've got street smarts," Bianca hissed. "And these skills are easily transferrable to a forest. I've taken self-defense classes. Hence, I know how to murder a man with a stiletto shoe. Let that sink in for a minute. I've also taken harassment seminars at work which basically makes me unbreakable. So don't mess with me, Lumberjack. Do you understand? If you take me on, you will lose. And I would really prefer not to hurt you."

The corner of Kraven's mouth twitched, implying a smirk.

Bianca turned to leave but swerved back around.

Kraven exhaled loudly.

"And another thing," Bianca barked. "You are the weirdo. Not me."

Kraven glared at Bianca for a moment, making her feel like she was looking into the headlights of an alien spacecraft.

"Take the shirt," Kraven droned before slamming the door in Bianca's face.

Confounded, Bianca looked down at the buffalo plaid shirt, draped over her arms.

CHAPTER THIRTEEN

I can't believe I just did that.

With trembling hands, Bianca peeled off her wet clothes like an underripe banana. Her tenacious pantsuit clung like an unforgiving barnacle and she grunted audibly from the effort. Trillions of goosebumps formed up her arms and legs as her damp skin objected to the crisp air. She shivered. Partly from being waterlogged and dripping with lake water, partly from the harrowing encounter she just had with Kraven.

Why did I confront him?

Now everything's weird.

Weirder.

Why did I have to be so impulsive?

Standing naked, sopping and shivering in a cabin is apparently not an effective way to make a person feel less vulnerable. The clacking sound of Bianca's chattering teeth snapped her out of her stunned, internal musings. She foraged around the room for something to wear. A row of respectable pantsuits hung pretentiously in a stiff, hangered row in the closet. But the crumpled pile of plaid flannel which had been mindlessly strewn on the bed seemed to beckon Bianca. Kraven's shirt looked so soft and fuzzy. It had been well-worn, giving it a vintage quality. Comforting. Warm. Woodsy. Bianca had never worn flannel in her entire life, but the shirt was just sitting there. Wanting her to put it on.

I wonder what it would feel like.

Bianca hastily adorned herself with Kraven's shirt. The garment was much too large for Bianca, but she made do by rolling up the sleeves and letting the shirt drape flatteringly over her delicate frame. The shirt's length fell just below Bianca's knees, looking much like a nightshirt or an ultra-casual dress. She squirmed around in the shirt's looseness, enjoying the fuzzy tickle on her skin.

Modelling her new makeshift outfit in the mirror, Bianca smirked with satisfaction. She may or may not have admired her own butt for a few too many lingering moments. She looked cute. From every angle. Even stylish in a rural sort of way. Black and red were her most flattering colors, making her black hair and Mediterranean blue eyes pop. And the comfort level of this strange, new fabric was alluring.

Flannel. Who knew?

The creaky porch alerted Bianca that someone was about to knock on her door.

"Bianca?" Tucker's voice squeaked.

Bianca opened the door, revealing Tucker sheepishly standing on the porch with a tray of food.

"You left this morning without eating your eggs," Tucker said. "I... I mean *we* thought you might be hungry. Do you like clams? I brought clams."

"Tucker..."

"Sorry. It's all I could find in the kitchen." Tucker's eyes wandered down towards Bianca's goose-pimpled knees. "You're not wearing any pants."

"This," Bianca said, tugging the fabric downwards to imply extra length, "is a dress. Rural chic. It's a thing."

"Oh," Tucker said, nodding uncertainly. He was still staring at Bianca's knees.

"Tucker..."

Tucker jolted. "Right. Okay. You probably want to eat your clams in private so..."

"Tucker, I need to ask you something."

"Anything you want, it's yours," Tucker said a little too quickly.

"What have you got on Kraven Kane?"

"I don't get it."

"Why is he *like that?*"

"You're saying things that I don't understand."

"Does he... I don't know... Does he scare you a little?"

"You're scaring me a little right now, to be honest."

"Is there any way I can move to a different cabin?"

"Why?"

"So I don't have to sleep next door to the human muskox."

"You mean Kraven?"

"Tucker..."

"Why are you so obsessed with Kraven?"

"I'm not..."

"Wait, are you wearing his shirt?"

"Dress," Bianca lied defensively. "Rural chic."

"Sorry, there's no vacancies."

"I can't change cabins?"

"Sorry."

"Can't someone trade?" Bianca begged. "Maybe that teenager with the macabre quality? I'm sure he wouldn't mind. He seemed pretty apathetic."

"Enjoy your clams."

"I don't eat shellfish."

Tucker turned and was just about to mope away when he got an exuberant second wind. "Do you like canoes?"

"No."

"I was not expecting that answer."

"Canoes are unnatural."

"Unnatural?"

"Like imitation beef. Or dating your sister."

"So I guess that means you're not interested in the guided canoe tour. There's one tomorrow."

"Wobbling around on the water?" Bianca exhaled. "When there is perfectly good ground to walk on? Yeah, no."

"I'm the guide."

"I'm a terrestrial creature."

"Please?"

"Still no."

"It's fun though," Tucker said, jumping excitedly. He looked like he was about to pee his pants.

"Canoes are not fun for some people," Bianca said, feeling cornered. "Try to understand that, Tucker."

"But last time we saw a beaver."

"No beavers."

"Trudy said that we should encourage you to embrace the Algonquin spirit. She said it would be healing or whatever."

"Tucker," Bianca inhaled deeply. "Look. It's not that I don't appreciate the effort and concern of your staff. It's nice. Really. Annoying but also sort of nice."

"Thank you."

"But you really need to just let me process this whole... well, nightmare on my own terms."

"We're just trying to make you comfortable."

"I get that. But the only thing that would make me comfortable would be sitting at my desk, performing impossible tasks with ridiculous time constraints. I live for that stuff. It's empowering."

Tucker scratched his head.

"I need to work," Bianca insisted. "All this relaxation is giving me withdrawal symptoms. I've developed a twitch. Did you notice my twitch?"

"I have a twitch too!" Tucker perked up. "We're twins!"

"No."

"Oh," Tucker said, lowering his head in shame. "I'm sorry to bother you. I guess the clams were a bad idea."

"It's not that I don't appreciate the clams," Bianca said, feeling a twinge of remorse. "It's just that I'd rather not contract food-borne norovirus. In a cabin. With questionable plumbing."

"I'll just leave now," Tucker sniffled.

"Tucker, come on. Don't look so defeated. You're making me feel bad. I didn't mean to..."

"You look real nice in Kraven's shirt."

"For the last time it's rural..."

The screen door slammed shut as Tucker slogged away.

"...chic."

CHAPTER FOURTEEN

Embers of glowing red and orange crackled in the stone fireplace, the only source of light in the dim room. A fire poker provoked the embers, causing sparks to crackle and reignite the ashen logs. A blue Maine coon cat walked past, tail in the air, casting an eerie silhouette on the wall. Letting out a raspy meow, the coon cat smushed his head into the dangling palm of Kraven Kane, who was lying on the couch in deep thought. He kneaded the cat's head affectionately with his knuckles.

Pensively, and squinting as though trying to decipher something floating invisibly in the air, Kraven wallowed in the beautiful silence of his cabin. The motoring purr of the coon cat was the only sound in the room, save for a few popping sparks. Whatever was happening inside Kraven's head would remain a mystery to everyone except himself – and possibly the cat who seemed to look at Kraven with an intuitive glare.

Kraven's eyelids fluttered. The dim firelight was stinging his eyes with drowsiness. He perused a few sheets of lined paper upon which was indecipherable handwriting. His own. He blinked a few times before giving up entirely. With a loud, primal exhale, he scrunched the paper into a ball and tossed it into the fire. The paper disintegrated instantly in the flames and featherlight ashes flitted through the air, extinguishing before they floated to the pine floor.

Kraven uttered a noise. A moan maybe? The cat seemed to empathize, his serious, dark face squinting analytically into Kraven's soul. Kraven stared back into the cat's eyes ominously but could not keep a straight face for long. Kraven's face softened into an almost-smile.

"Good boy," Kraven rumbled.

As he drifted halfway into a hazy sleep, Kraven was startled by the faraway sound of a shrill whistle. His eyes popped open, he bolted from the couch, causing the coon cat to spring three feet in the air. Dashing to the window, Kraven looked outside into the darkness. The lights were on in the Fox Hole. A small figure was flailing around inside.

The shrill whistle was relentless.

Kraven looked at the clock. 9:20. The *Whispering Beaver* staff was off duty for the night, probably venturing towards their respective homes.

Kraven mused for a moment.

Should I go over there?

But she's weird.

What if she needs help?

She doesn't want my help.

But the crisis whistle...

She knows how to murder a man with a stiletto shoe.

Good point.

But...

City girls can take care of themselves.

(Sardonic laughter)

The coon cat joined Kraven at the window, nuzzling him, craving attention. Kraven stroked the cat with a purpose as he continued glaring intently out the window. What would the city girl do next? What could be happening inside that little cabin that would warrant a frantic blow of the crisis whistle? Perhaps she broke an acrylic nail or needed someone to squish a spider.

Kraven suddenly spotted Bianca charging out of her cabin in a frenzy, followed by a very confused possum. Bianca shrieked like a banshee with her signature canoe paddle, threatening the poor creature, whose eyes bugged open in befuddlement.

Kraven covered his mouth to stifle a gravelly laugh. His eyes actually danced with amusement as Bianca hysterically shooed the possum, who lumbered into the darkness in a WTF kind of way.

Not lost on Kraven was the fact that Bianca was wearing his shirt. He could see the red and black buffalo plaid in the gleam of the porch light.

The corner of Kraven's mouth curled up into a smirk.

Not bad.

CHAPTER FIFTEEN
(DAY 3 IN ALGONQUIN PARK)

"I'd like to report a possum," Bianca said matter-of-factly the following morning at the lodge.

Trudy blinked.

Bianca blinked.

"A possum, Dear?" Trudy repeated.

"I had to pee," Bianca explained. "I went into the bathroom like any normal person would. And right there, sitting on the toilet, was a possum. Staring at me with its sinister little raisin eyes."

"Love, are you sure..."

"I know what a possum looks like."

"It's just..."

"I looked it up in the wildlife leaflet you left on my coffee table. It was definitely a possum. When I looked directly into its eyes, it pulled me into its abyss."

"You can't report a possum, Dear."

"Are there supposed to be possums sitting on my toilet?"

"Well, no…"

"Do you endorse the presence of possums on toilets?"

"Sweetheart…"

"I blew the crisis whistle," Bianca quaked. "Because I was in crisis. The possum could have given me a disease. Or taken over my mind with its demonic glare. But nobody offered me assistance because it happened after 9:00 pm. What good is a crisis whistle if it is only heard during daylight hours?"

"What would you like me to do?" Trudy asked with her best customer service smile.

"Get rid of it."

"The possum?"

"It's evil."

"Possums eat ticks," Trudy assured Bianca. "They are our friends."

"I want it gone."

"It's wildlife, Dear. This is his home."

"What am I supposed to do if another possum appears on my toilet?"

Trudy pondered. "Give him some privacy?"

"How did it even get into my cabin?"

"They are stealthy little critters when they set their mind to something," Trudy said, smiling and shaking her head as though she was affectionately recalling a specific possum.

"I want to lodge a formal complaint."

"Against the possum?"

"Against your establishment," Bianca said, reddening with impatience. "And your flimsy emergency response protocol."

Trudy sprayed Bianca with a lip fart of laughter. "Oh honey! A possum isn't an emergency! You are too cute!"

After pinching Bianca's cheek for good measure, she noticed Bianca fidgeting with the oversized, buffalo plaid, flannel shirt she was wearing.

"Honey," Trudy said confidentially, "you're not wearing any pants."

"It's the style," Bianca said defiantly. She was minding less and less about the fashion blunder she was committing and caring more about the soothing sensation of fuzz enveloping her body. It was comforting and God knows, Bianca needed comfort.

"Darling girl," Trudy said, guiding Bianca to a discreet corner and covering her knees with a placemat, "if you need clothes, we have some for sale in the tuck shop."

Bianca could not believe she was getting fashion criticism from a woman who was basically wearing a repurposed, floral curtain from the 1960's.

"I'll be taking my breakfast to go," Bianca said, quickly changing the subject.

"I don't think so, Dear."

"Why not?" Bianca sighed.

"I received a message from Mr. Grosswater."

"How? There's no internet or phone lines."

"We have one phone for reservations and such," Trudy explained. "Remember that little hut by the water taxi when you first arrived? We have a nice rotary phone plugged in there. Tucker paddles me over twice a day to pick up messages."

"That's convenient," Bianca said, rolling her eyes.

"Mr. Grosswater has been staying in close contact with me so we can monitor your progress."

"Oh my god."

"Anyhoo, Mr. Grosswater made it very clear that you must integrate into our little community here."

"You mean commune?"

"Tucking yourself into your cabin and avoiding people and experiences is not going to help you heal."

"Can't I just bide my time in my cabin until September rolls around?"

"Not if you want a job to come back to," Trudy said, doing her signature finger wag. "You need to return to work refreshed and inspired... or not at all. Those were Mr. Grosswater's very words, I'm afraid."

Bianca gaped.

CHAPTER SIXTEEN

Resentfully chewing her average mushroom frittata, Bianca was becoming increasingly aware that she was being talked about. The centenarians at table seven thought they were whispering, but since both were a little hard of hearing, they spoke at a conspicuous volume. Bianca pretended not to notice.

"Wonder why she's all alone."

"Nice teeth. Nice hair."

"With teeth like that, she should have a man."

"Maybe she's one of those girls that doesn't like boys."

"Heh?"

"You know. Those girls who prefer girls."

Annoyed, Bianca dropped her fork loudly.

"See that? She dropped her fork."

"Heh?"

"I said she *dropped her fork.*"

"Is she not wearing pants?"

Bianca was rescued by Lizbeth who swooped in like a much-too-helpful albatross.

"How is your mushroom frittata?" Lizabeth asked, smacking her gum. It was grape flavored today, the evidence wafting from her fruity breath.

"Good," Bianca exaggerated blandly.

"Really?" Lizbeth said, her hazel eyes gleaming with rapture. "Wait here!"

Bianca nearly got whiplash from watching Lizbeth dash clumsily into the kitchen.

Suddenly, Bianca heard a chair screech across the floor. She jerked her head around and gasped when she discovered that Kraven had taken a seat across the table from her.

"What's your problem, Toronto?" Kraven said throatily.

Bianca's lips parted for a moment. "Did you just call me..."

"Seriously, is there something wrong with you?" Kraven asked.

"*Me?*" Bianca choked in shock. "You were the one out on the dock, summoning the devil."

"I was meditating."

"Whatever floats your boat."

"Speaking of canoes..."

"Don't."

"Were you stalking me?"

"What?" Bianca squeaked indignantly. "I can't believe you would even... well yes..."

"Wow."

"But don't act like you weren't stalking *me.*"

"You don't know what you're talking about."

By this time, Bianca and Kraven were both leaning in across the table, having an epic grimacing contest. Sadly, they were interrupted by Lizbeth and a very mustached Jedd.

"Excuse me," Lizbeth bubbled. "I hope we're not interrupting anything."

"Lizbeth," Bianca said, not taking her eyes off Kraven, "this is not a good time."

"It'll only take a sec," Lizbeth promised. "I brought Jedd. Say hi, Jedd."

"Greetings!" Jedd said rhapsodically. Jedd's voice had a naturally scratchy texture, like a canoe paddle scraping against a rock. He sounded like he needed a lozenge.

Bianca gaped at Jedd and Lizbeth with utter disbelief.

"I told Jedd that you like the mushroom frittata," Lizbeth gushed.

"Is it true?" Jedd asked, smiling with his quirky overbite. His large teeth gleamed beneath his white, wiry mustache.

Bianca nodded slowly.

"I am honored," Jedd said, modestly bowing.

"I'm so proud of Jedd," Lizbeth praised. "Mushroom frittatas are hard."

"This is the happiest day of my life," Jedd said, unable to contain his childlike enthusiasm.

"We're kind of in the middle of som…" Bianca tried.

"Did Lizbeth tell you about the accident?" Jedd asked eagerly. "When I lost my sense of taste?"

Bianca blinked.

"I told her," Lizbeth offered. "We're all here for you, Jedd."

"I've never made a frittata before," Jedd added. "Nor have I ever tasted one. In fact, before this morning, I didn't even know what a frittata was. I heard there was a city girl staying with us and I thought to myself, *'Jedd, that city girl would order something called a frittata cuz gosh darn it, that's one fancy word.'* It is kind of fun to say, ain't it? *Frittata. Frittata, frittata, frittata.*"

Bianca and Kraven looked at each other blankly.

"The fact that you liked your mushroom frittata." Jedd said, wiping away an emotional tear, "it just means the world to me, girlie. It makes my heart sing. Sorry for being so sentimental. It just does."

"Oh Jedd," Lizbeth said, squeezing Jedd's hand.

Kraven cleared the phlegmy annoyance from his throat. The sheer volume and texture of the sound caused Jedd and Lizbeth to spirit away like a couple of startled housecats.

Kraven continued as though nothing had happened.

"I was not stalking you," Kraven grumbled.

"So you always lurk around in the dark, peering in the windows of unassuming women like a circus freak?"

"Do you always assault people with a canoe paddle?" Kraven said snidely. "In your *fun-jammies?*"

Bianca's face instantly turned into a stewed beetroot.

"You shouldn't have been looking," Bianca pouted.

"You ambushed me with a canoe paddle. Where else was I supposed to look?"

"Why were you even there in the first place?"

"I just thought..."

"Oh I know what you thought," Bianca hissed. "I could see it in your gooseberry eyes."

"You are incorrigible, Toronto," Kraven snarled.

Bianca bit her lip indignantly.

"Excuse us," Lizbeth interrupted sheepishly. "Sorry to interrupt again. Jedd here was wondering if he could get a picture with you."

"With me?" Bianca asked, defeated.

"Because of the mushroom frittata," Jedd explained. "Your feedback made me so happy. I want to remember this moment we had today. Forever."

"It's just a…" Bianca began.

Kraven kicked her under the table.

"Sure," Bianca sighed. "Go for it."

Jedd scooched over next to Bianca and put a weathered arm around her.

"Smile!" Lizbeth said, poising the camera.

Jedd's mouth brimmed with happiness and oversized teeth. His eyes turned into crescents of joy.

A cringe was the best smile Bianca could manage. The flash made Bianca see triangles. She blinked away the triangles.

"Thanks so much!" Lizbeth squealed. "I'll send you copies."

"Don't trouble yourse…" Bianca tried.

"Pretend like we were never here," Jedd said earnestly as he stood to his feet. "And if you need any more mushroom frittatas, you just holler. Understand?" He finished with a wink.

Bianca gaped as Jedd and Lizbeth disappeared into the kitchen.

"Nice shirt, by the way," Kraven sighed. "Remind me where we left off?"

"We were talking about how you are a perv," Bianca said, rolling her eyes.

"Don't start with me, Toronto."

"What was I supposed to think," Bianca spat, "when you were looking in my window during the witching hour?"

Kraven let out a loud snort, somewhat like a bear sniffing around a tent. "You don't belong here."

What's that supposed to mean?

I mean, he's not wrong but..

Seriously, what's that supposed to mean?

"What's that supposed to mean?" Bianca said out loud.

"Possum," Kraven exhaled.

"You little weasel," Bianca seethed. "You were spying on me last night? Again?"

"You blew the crisis whistle," Kraven groaned. "Why would you do that for any other reason than to draw attention to yourself?"

"If you heard the crisis whistle, why didn't you..."

"Didn't want to be clubbed with a canoe paddle."

Bianca huffed.

"Listen, Toronto. I don't want things to get weird."

"Too late."

"Apparently we are going to be neighbors for the next couple of months."

"Excuse me while I ralph in this basket of cornbread."

"You've made it clear you don't want any help from me or anyone else."

"Because I don't need any."

"So just stay out of my way, Toronto."

"Wait, what?"

"Stay away from me," Kraven said a little louder. "You're freaky."

Bianca gaped stupidly as Kraven brisk-lurched out of the dining room, causing ominous vibrations in the floorboards.

CHAPTER SEVENTEEN

That was the worst breakfast of my entire life.

With her face smushed shamefully into a pillow, Bianca wished she could avoid the rest of the season in a trance-like brumation somewhat like a humiliated bearded dragon.

How did this Kraven thing escalate so quickly?

Third day here and I already have a mortal enemy.

A sheepish knock sounded muffled as Bianca's head took shelter in her pillowy refuge.

"Come in, Tucker," Bianca moaned. She had learned to recognize Tucker's tentative knock.

"I brought stuff," Tucker squeaked, awkwardly dragging a laundry bag behind him.

"I don't need stuff, Tucker," Bianca said, rolling over. "Thanks though."

"Pants," Tucker said, displaying a pair of spandex shorts.

"No," Bianca said after examining Tucker's offering.

"But it's free of charge."

"I'm not wearing pants with *Whispering Beaver* written across the butt."

"All our souvenir pants have that."

"Fire your merchandizing people," Bianca said, tossing the spandex shorts back to Tucker.

"But it's free."

Bianca cocked her head.

"Well," Tucker stammered. "Not free exactly. More like on me."

"Then you wear them."

"I just thought you could use these shorts to accessorize with Kraven's shirt. Since you seem so eager to wallow around in it."

"It's a dress."

"Shirt."

"Why would you assume it's Kraven's?" Bianca said, triangulating an eyebrow. "It's just a generic buffalo plaid shirt... dress."

"It smells like Kraven."

Bianca choked.

Damn.

It does smell like Kraven.

Bug spray and campfire smoke.

And something else.

Jasmine blossoms?

Weird.

"Thanks," Bianca said grudgingly, "for the clothes. Just leave the bag here. I'll rummage through it later."

"Groovy," Tucker said with a bashful smile. "Oh, by the way," Tucker added on his way out the door, "I guess I'll see you at 3:30 this aft."

"Why would that be happening?"

"The guided canoe tour."

"Tucker, I said no."

"But your name is on the sign-up list."

"How did it get there?"

Tucker shrugged.

"Take it off."

"Take what off?"

"My name."

"From the list?"

"Yes."

"Can't."

"Why on earth not?"

"It's written in pen."

"I said before that I don't want to go."

"You're pretty much committed at this point."

"But I'm not consenting."

"We need a minimum of five people to go, otherwise we have to cancel the whole thing," Tucker whimpered. "You don't want to let the other four people down, do you?"

Bianca's eyes narrowed.

***

Bianca tore the sign-up sheet off the lodge wall and slapped it on Trudy's desk.

"No," Bianca said firmly.

"Hun..." Trudy tried.

"You can't go around signing people up for things against their will," Bianca argued. "Especially activities involving tippy things like canoes."

"We needed a fifth person," Trudy shrugged.

"What about that enthusiastic Asian man in the Shimmering Otter cabin?" Bianca begged. "He seems like he'd be game for anything."

"He checked out yesterday," Trudy said sympathetically. "Besides, I was speaking with Mr. Grosswater…"

Bianca gaped.

"He told me that he requires a check list of every activity you've participated in here at the *Whispering Beaver.*"

"You love saying that, don't you?"

"Mr. Grosswater said," Trudy continued, "that he needs evidence that you have done everything humanly possible to recover your sanity."

"Just tell him I'm vegging in my cabin," Bianca said on the brink of tears, "achieving a state of absolute tranquility."

"He wants everything documented," Trudy winced. "He wants tangible evidence that you have been communing with nature."

"That's psychotic."

"Dear," Trudy said, cupping Bianca's little, white hands in hers, "We really do want you to be well."

"I…"

Trudy raised a finger and continued. "We are on your team, Bianca. We may seem like oddballs to a city girl like you, but if you open your mind a little, you'll see we're real genuine folks."

Bianca softened and closed her eyes.

"Listen," Trudy said, leaning in. "I wasn't supposed to tell you this, but this whole retreat of yours… See, Mr. Grosswater… How do I put this?"

"What are you trying to say, Trudy?" Bianca asked, wriggling.

"This is a kind of test," Trudy said flatly.

"What?"

"Mr. Grosswater is... oh my. He would just flog me if he knew I was telling you this..."

"Trudy..."

"He has somebody else in mind," Trudy swallowed. "For your job."

"No," Bianca said with her eyes reddening.

"You being here..."

"Is Grosswater's devious plan to get me out of the way while he does his dirty business."

"He's trying to make his final decision," Trudy said, putting a reassuring hand on Bianca. "If you can pull yourself together by the end of the summer..."

"My head is swimming..."

"And you can prove that you're up for any challenge, no matter how seemingly impossible..."

"Oh god..."

"We've got you, Bianca."

"I don't even know you," Bianca's voice cracked.

"I just want to set you up for success," Trudy said earnestly. "I don't mean to be intense. It's just that you're such a sweet girl under all those pinstripes. I can just tell. I can read auras."

"I should have known Grosswater was up to something," Bianca quavered. "Shipping me off like a random UPS parcel."

"We're going to put that crotchety hector in his place," Trudy said, putting her hands on her hips defiantly."

"We?"

"We are going to preen you to be a veritable Algonquin girl by the end of this summer," Trudy added, glowing with determination.

"Trudy," Bianca said, blinking the sting from her eyeballs, "I am completely out of my element. Surely you can see that."

"You listen to me, young lady..."

"Who is it?" Bianca said, wiping dribbling snot of emotion from her nose.

"Sorry?"

"Grosswater," Bianca sniffled. "Who is he considering replacing me with? You know, if I screw all this up."

"Once he launched into that monotonic rant of his, I stopped paying attention," Trudy apologized. "But if memory serves, I think I remember him grunting the word *dork.*"

"Dirk?" Bianca's spine instantly straightened with a starchy wrath.

"That makes more sense, actually," Trudy nodded.

"Dirk Thumperson?" Bianca screeched like a cat in heat.

Trudy nodded stupidly in a circular way. She was not good at deciphering one Dirk from another.

"I don't believe this," Bianca said.

"Dear, if you can't believe this, then neither can I," Trudy said, shaking her head in empathetic disbelief. "Neither can I."

"Dirk," Bianca barked. "He was supposed to triple check the final... Ugh! Dirk."

"I like you better than Dirk," Trudy said maternally.

"Dirk didn't even show up for my public flogging when I arrived home from Japan," Bianca spat. "Coward."

"Shhh," Trudy shushed. "You are safe now. *The Whispering Beaver* will let no harm come to you."

"Please stop."

CHAPTER EIGHTEEN

Dang. I'm twenty minutes late.

Ah well. Maybe they'll leave without me.

But they did not leave without Bianca. Three ominous canoes wobbled on little swells of water in the lake. Tucker waved earnestly from the first canoe. Behind him was the notoriously scowling teenager who had clearly been coerced into participating.

I feel ya, kid.

The second canoe contained the soppy, honeymooning couple. They were giggling ridiculously at something that was not funny – possibly a bird.

If I ever fall in love, I'll slap myself.

In the third canoe...

Jesus H. Murphy.

Seated at the back of the final vessel was...

No.

Just no.

Why him?

Dammit, Kraven.

"Hey, Toronto," Kraven grunted, ogling his flannel shirt draping over Bianca's little body.

Bianca's stomach curdled.

"Hop in!" Tucker called to Bianca. "We've been waiting for you."

"Can I trade spots with Wednesday Addams?" Bianca asked, gesturing towards the teenager who seemed numb to the fact that he was just referred to as a girl.

"No time," Tucker said, already paddling into the shimmering lake. "We're already behind schedule. I need to get you guys back before dusk."

Less than a moment later, the second canoe followed the first towards a maze of finger lakes. Bianca watched defeatedly as the canoes became silhouettes under the afternoon sun.

"Are you going to get in or are you going to continue staring at me like a bewildered lemur?" Kraven grumbled.

"I'm not being in a canoe with you," Bianca said, fervently shaking her head. Her spandex *Whispering Beaver* shorts were riding up her butt. This was not a good omen.

"Sit in the front," Kraven said, jerking his head. "I'll steer."

"Are you going to paddle me to the remote outskirts of nowhere, offer my body to the malevolent lake gods and leave me for dead?"

"We'll see how it goes," Kraven said emotionlessly.

***

"You're lily-dipping," Kraven droned monotonically.

"I don't even want to know what that means," Bianca replied.

"You're not even trying," Kraven said while effortlessly paddling.

"I'm trying really hard, actually."

"Then why is our canoe so far behind the rest of the group?"

"We aren't that far behind."

"We've been paddling next to that same spruce tree for the past ten minutes."

"Can you just *not*?"

"Do you even know how to paddle?"

"I am a senior executive…"

"So no."

"I am highly competent and can do anything I set my mind to."

"When are you going to set your mind to paddling then?"

Bianca bit her lower lip hard.

"I don't suppose you'd like some advice," Kraven offered sardonically.

"About canoeing or life in general?"

"Either."

"No."

"Hold the paddle with one hand," Kraven sighed, "and cup your other hand over the top. See? Like how I'm doing it."

"I have my own technique."

"Which is why we are floundering around like idiots."

"You are a ruffian," Bianca said. "You realize that, right?"

"Dip the paddle into the water," Kraven continued, blatantly ignoring Bianca. "Pretend like you're slicing a cake. Or you know. Murdering a man with a stiletto shoe."

"Don't tempt me," Bianca grunted, trying harder to pull back the water with her paddle.

Muscles ached in Bianca's body that she was not even aware she had. Huffing for breath, she focused on the rows of conical trees that reflected off the water. Anything to deflect her attention from Kraven.

"I can't see them," Kraven said, shielding his eyes with his hand and looking around the empty lake.

"Tucker wouldn't leave us behind."

"Don't be so sure about that. He's a bit of a tool."

"He's a nice kid. Back off."

Kraven triangulated an eyebrow. "Never pegged you as someone who'd defend a crunchy tree hugger."

"Grow some tact."

"Not a big fan of irony, I see."

"My point being," Bianca was getting flustered, "nobody is going to leave us behind. Tucker's done this hundreds of times. He probably knows this lake better than anyone. I'm sure people get separated from his canoe all the... time."

Bianca looked around the expansive lake that now seemed to dwarf their pathetic, little canoe. They looked so insignificant. Proverbially swallowed by the vastness around them. Water licked the sides of the canoe. Bianca decided the water was doing this on purpose to antagonize her. Why else would her innards be flip-flopping along with the tippy canoe?

"Where.... Did they go?" Bianca quavered.

"One of these finger lakes," Kraven said, pointing to a series of narrow streams, fracturing out of the main lake. "Not sure which one they would take though," he said, barely audible.

Bianca swallowed hard.

Alone.

In a canoe.

With this intimidating bonobo.

So this is how it ends.

"I'm going to guess they took this route," Kraven said, nodding towards the second finger lake. "It has a wider mouth." Aptly timed, he turned his head around and squinted at Bianca.

Bianca squinted back. Harder.

"Maybe we should just head back to the lodge," Bianca suggested. "If we make a wrong turn, we could be stuck out her all night."

Kraven paddled with more intensity.

"Kraven?"

Kraven silently paddled towards the finger lake.

"Did you hear me?" Bianca said, raising her voice. She was startled by the echo it generated off the water.

No answer.

Just a low growl.

"Kraven?"

CHAPTER NINETEEN

Tucker and his entourage were nowhere in sight. Bianca's esophagus constricted with panic. Dusk was threatening to creep in like a meticulous spider. Not a word was uttered in the canoe of awkwardness. Kraven's body was resembling more of a shadow than a tangible person. Bianca felt like she was being paddled to her demise by a spectral entity.

An aptly timed pike thrashed dramatically out of the water.

Startled, and uttering the vocalization of a velociraptor, Bianca lunged towards Kraven, pushing him down with full force.

"IT HAS TEETH!" she shrieked. "GET DOWN!"

Kraven was knocked to the floor of the canoe by a flailing Bianca, thwacking his head against the solid wood rim. The stern quickly sunk with the weight of both bodies. The canoe jostled, jerked, tottered, wobbled and plunged. There was a disturbing, wooden *'FWWWUMP'* sound. And seemingly in slow motion, the canoe capsized.

"FOR THE LUVVA!..." Bianca screamed in mid-air. Her body splayed ridiculously while airborne. She groped desperately for

Kraven. Mainly to use him as a human raft when she smacked down on the water. Spluttering, Bianca grabbed Kraven's shoulders to avoid drowning. Kraven, on the other hand, was floating calmly and without incident. He was surprisingly buoyant for a sociopath.

"Have you taken leave of your senses?" Kraven asked, nonplussed.

"Did you..." Bianca gasped. "Did you see that? It was evil!"

"That," Kraven said, shaking Bianca off of him like an annoying burr, "was a fish."

"Are you legally blind?" Bianca said, scrambling to grab hold of Kraven's shoulders again. "That thing could have eaten us."

"I had one of those for lunch yesterday," Kraven smirked.

"You eat mythological sea serpents?"

"I told you," Kraven repeated. "It's a fish. Don't you have fish in Toronto? I mean other than sushi? Also, can't you swim?"

"Of course I can..." Bianca said, letting go of Kraven defiantly. Then she preposterously flapped her arms in a mad attempt to stay alive. "swim."

"Don't drown just to make a point," Kraven said, rolling his eyes. "Just wrap your arms around my neck and I'll swim us to shore."

"You mean ride on your back?" Bianca gasped, thrashing. "That's obscene."

"Do what you want then," Kraven said blandly.

"I want," Bianca gagged with a strangulating grip on Kraven's neck, "a piggy-back-ride."

"You're asphyxiating me."

"Swim."

"Bossy."

"Assertive."

"I can't believe you can't swim."

"What reason would I have to swim in the city?"

"Pampered."

"Excuse me?"

"City girls," Kraven complained. "You lack basic survival skills."

Bianca's mouth manipulated into a number of strange shapes before she found the words. "Have you ever spoken convincingly in front of thousands of people?"

Kraven smirked.

"Who only speak Japanese?"

Kraven smirked.

"Marshalled an international staff of more than five hundred?"

Kraven smirked.

"Persistently thrived in a cutthroat industry with primarily members of the opposite sex?"

Kraven smirked.

"Avoided sleep for nine consecutive days?"

Kraven smirked.

"Defended your decisions to emotionless executives? On the first day of your cycle?"

And still, Kraven smirked.

"Well?" Bianca squeaked.

"No," Kraven said dryly. "But I can swim."

"You don't think very highly of me," Bianca observed.

"What makes you say that?" Kraven said elusively.

"You think I'm a nefarious twat."

"I wouldn't say nefarious twat. Precisely."

"Then..."

Bianca gasped when a loon suddenly popped up next to her and yodeled maniacally.

"What *he said*," Kraven grunted, gesturing towards the loon.

Bianca pursed her lips.

***

A firm hand, dappled in black hairs reached down to Bianca, who was clinging to a driftwood log. Mouth-breathing, Bianca pondered the hand for a solid six seconds.

Kraven sighed. "Do you want out of the lake or are you hoping to morph into a water nymph?"

Taking a deep breath, Bianca reached up. She felt her elegant little hand throb inside Kraven's crushing grip. Bianca was pulled out of the lake like a slippery, dripping eel. She panted a little more dramatically than she needed to as she found her footing on the shore. Shivering, she wrung the moisture from her shirt.

"You wrecked my shirt," Kraven observed.

Bianca looked down at the sopping shirt that was now clinging a little too provocatively to her body. She grasped for a reply. "...Where's the canoe?"

Kraven shrugged.

"You just let it drift away?" Bianca asked, curling into a ball on a sunny rock to keep warm.

"If you have a suggestion as to how I could have towed a canoe ashore while simultaneously rescuing a helpless waif..."

"I'm not helpless."

"The canoe can float," Kraven said, peeling off his wet shirt. "You? Not so much."

"What are you doing?"

"Sculpting the likeness of Bono out of cheese," Kraven replied sarcastically.

"That's indecent," Bianca shivered.

"Leave Bono alone. He's a decent man with iconic vocals."

"The shirt, I mean." Bianca's eyeballs had no idea where to look, so she chose to focus on a peculiar fungus. "You're making me... uncomfortable."

Kraven defiantly slapped his chest. "What are you, Amish?"

Bianca swallowed hard.

Kraven stared at Bianca for a moment, as she hunched on the rock, tightly groping her arms and shivering.

"Take it off," Kraven said gravelly.

"Excuse me?" Bianca said, smoothing down her wet hair for no reason.

"Shirt."

Appalled, Bianca's mouth dropped open for a minimum of thirty seconds. "I am a lady," she primly insisted while holding her shirt tightly shut. "I don't disrobe in front of random men I barely know." Then she muttered under her breath, "And wish I had never met."

"You're shivering." There was ethereal concern in Kraven's voice which was lost on Bianca.

"I am a tough cookie," Bianca said with chattering teeth.

"Sure, but…"

"I was right about you."

"What?"

"Ogling me through my window…"

"Seriously?"

"In the middle of the night."

"Are we doing this again?"

"So you could think all kinds of unchristian things about my *lady business.*"

"Gawd."

"Anything to get my shirt off. Typical."

"Give it a rest, Toronto."

The authoritative snarl in Kraven's voice gave Bianca an additional shiver up her spine – one that was not lake water-induced. She watched sheepishly as Kraven crouched by a blackened circle on the ground where abandoned ashes conjured the memory of fire. He built a nest of tinder in the circle.

"What are you doing?" Bianca asked, craning her neck to get a better view.

"I thought we could hang our clothes by a campfire…"

"Campfire?" Bianca sniggered. "What are you going to do? Rub two sticks togeth…"

Slowly cocking her head, Bianca watched Kraven, intrigued. He was, in fact, making a fire with two, dry sticks. His short breaths were rhythmic as he created vigorous friction. Pearls of sweat formed on his forehead as little tufts of smoke started to crimp out of the wood.

"Do... do people actually do that?" Bianca asked in a faint voice. "Make fire out of sticks? I thought that was an elaborate rumor."

Kraven ignited the tinder nest, stood back and admired his fire with a glow of pride. Bianca may have gawked a little too long at the flames which were reflecting in Kraven's gooseberry green irises. She found him slightly less nauseating in this moment.

"Are you going to warm by the fire?" Kraven asked, huddling next to the campfire. His torso pinkened with warmth from the flames and rivulets of water slowly evaporated from his rocky shoulders. "Or are you going to sit over there with all your principles and remain soggy?"

Bianca gaped at Kraven. Her heart thumped like an overzealous basketball on the pavement.

"Well?" Kraven asked, the corner of his mouth curling up into an ambiguous dimple.

Bianca reddened and instantly looked down at her soppy self. She focused on a tenacious snail, laboring across the rock, leaving behind a glistening trail of snail goo.

"Fine," Kraven exhaled conspicuously. "Freeze. It'll be a while before they come for us."

"Our canoe will float back," Bianca nodded, trying to convince herself.

"The current is flowing the other way," Kraven said, nodding towards the lake. "The canoe will likely wash up by the lodge. When they realize we're missing, they'll send someone out to find us."

"Tucker?" Bianca raised an eyebrow.

"Likely," Kraven answered.

"We're screwed," Bianca said evenly.

A beat.

Kraven sprayed laughter into the flames, making them flicker orangely.

"Sit," Kraven ordered, nodding towards the empty space next to him. "Dusk is sneaking up on us. It'll get crisp out here soon."

Bianca awkwardly obeyed, nestling her moist behind in the dirt. "I hope they find us before dark."

"Doubt it," Kraven shrugged. "No motorboats allowed on this lake. Tucker will have to paddle around every finger lake until he finds us."

"Well look at you," Bianca said sarcastically, unintentionally wriggling closer to Kraven's heat-generating body. "The Gerbil of Optimism."

"Gerbil?"

"That's not a thing?"

"No," Kraven snorted with quasi-laughter. He punched her teasingly in the shoulder. "You're weird, Toronto."

Dammit.

Why did I think the Gerbil of Optimism was a thing?

Did I see it in a satirical cartoon or something?

Ugh! Never mind.

Must recover.

Salvage my last scrap of dignity.

Say something, Bianca. Anything.

"Gerbils are very metaphorical in Toronto," Bianca lied. "We reference them all the... time." Her voice trailed.

"Really." Kraven was unconvinced. But intrigued.

"It's a very literary city," Bianca grasped.

"I've heard."

"You have?" Bianca's head swerved around in shock.

They locked eyes for a moment.

"Very educated population," Kraven said, softening his tone. His voice didn't sound so much like a jagged growl this time. It was more like a sandpapery croon.

Bianca quickly looked away. She wondered where the tenacious snail was. She missed the tenacious snail.

"You would rather be stuck here with literally anyone but me, eh?" Kraven heaved.

"You assume a lot of things."

"Am I wrong?"

"Well, no," Bianca smirked. "But you still assume a lot of things and I find that off-putting."

"The shirt doesn't look repugnant on you," Kraven breathed nervously.

"Repugnant?"

"It's a word."

"I know it's a word."

"Then?"

"I'm just struggling to understand why such a knuckle dragging Neanderthal is so eloquent."

Jaysus, mouth! Why do things like that fly out of you when I'm trying to maintain composure?

Frig. His eyebrows are turning into the letter V.

"Did you just call me…"

"No."

"Yes."

"You misheard."

"You think I'm a knuckle dragging savage?"

"Neanderthal. I mean what?"

"Wow, Toronto. You are so demure. I'm sure your mother would be proud."

Bianca pursed her lips.

"She..." Bianca stammered. "She... is. Why wouldn't she be?" Her voice trailed sadly.

Kraven swerved his head towards Bianca, who had become uncharacteristically quiet. When he saw her fidget nervously with her thumbs with a dejected look on her face, his Adam's apple undulated with remorse. Chewing the side his cheek, Kraven focused on a single spark that popped playfully from the flames and twizzled into the quickly darkening sky.

Silence.

Awkward silence.

"Sorry," Kraven swallowed.

"For what?" Bianca played dumb.

Kraven shrugged.

The air that Bianca stressfully blew out of her mouth was a visible vapor. Kraven watched her sitting vulnerably next to him with her teeth chattering and her nervous eyes roaming around like a watchdog on high alert. He slowly melted like a stick of butter in the microwave. His arm twitched. He lifted his arm and crooked his elbow into what may have been a hug-shape. He quickly put his arm down the moment Bianca changed position. He pondered. He gingerly raised his arm again, putting it tentatively around Bianca's shivering body.

Bianca flinched.

Kraven quickly pulled his arm away.

"What in the hell..." Bianca shrieked, rising to her feet.

"Sorry..." Kraven stuttered. "I'm... I'm so sorry."

"Did I say you could touch me?"

"I just..."

"Pig!" Bianca said, backing away from Kraven and using her two index fingers to form a crucifix."

"I thought you needed..."

"You know what I need, Kraven?" Bianca hissed. "Space!"

Kraven's face liquified into a puddle of regret. He watched Bianca cautiously as she stumbled away.

CHAPTER TWENTY
(DAY 4 IN ALGONQUIN PARK)

When Bianca's eyelids fluttered open the following morning, she felt something heavy draped over top of her. Confused, she sat up and looked around. A familiar crispness in the air nibbled her skin. Bianca found herself covered in the shirt Kraven was wearing the day before. Incidentally, it was identical to the shirt he gave Bianca. Buffalo plaid must have been his favorite color. The shirt was still warm, and it smelled like campfire smoke. Bianca inhaled the scent. She watched for a moment as the morning mist swirled atop the lake.

I love this moment.

Wait, what?

"Morning, Toronto," Kraven grunted while lugging firewood from a grove of triangular conifers.

Bianca scrambled. When she stood to her feet, she suddenly noticed she was only wearing her bra and underwear. Screeching like a howler monkey, Bianca covered herself with her makeshift blanket, aka, Kraven's shirt. Which, by the way, Kraven was not currently wearing.

"Where are my clothes?" Bianca demanded.

"Drying by the fire," Kraven shrugged.

"Why are they not currently on my body?"

"They were wet," Kraven enunciated. "If you slept in them, you would have turned into a banana popsicle."

"Why banana?"

"That's the best kind of popsicle," Kraven said, strategically positioning a new log into the campfire. "Everyone knows that."

Bianca had no valid argument against this statement.

"You had no right to strip me naked!" Bianca barked. "Especially out here where nobody can hear me scream!"

"You're wearing undergarments," Kraven defended himself with a sly grin.

Bianca huffed indignantly. "You.. you saw me... you saw me without..."

"Get over yourself, Toronto. It's not like I've never seen you in your underthings." Kraven pursed his lips to stifle a giggle. "Red and black, lacy underthings."

Reddening with both fury and humiliation, Bianca protruded her lower lip.

"This is indecent," Bianca argued feebly.

"I disagree," Kraven rationally replied. "My mother raised me to be a gentleman."

"The kind of gentlemen that disrobes women while they sleep?"

"You are so ungrateful."

"You want me to thank you for exploiting me?"

"In what way did I exploit you?"

"How should I know? I was asleep!"

No response.

"Kraven?"

"Shhh!" Kraven hissed, focusing intensely on something in the distance.

"Is it a boat?" Bianca asked eagerly. "Is it Tucker?"

"Better," Kraven said, walking with a purpose towards the misty lake.

Bianca giraffed her neck to see what Kraven had spotted. He was lurking gingerly without making a sound. Whatever Kraven was pursuing was obscured in the mist. Wrapping Kraven's shirt tightly around her body like a cape, Bianca padded closer to Kraven. Alas, she tripped over a root and fell on her face. The cape of decorum flew off her shoulders and landed outside of her reach. Bianca scrambled nakedly.

"What an impressive rack!" Kraven said in awe, paying Bianca no mind at all.

"*Excuse me?*" Bianca squeaked indignantly, frantically covering her upper body.

"It's the most magnificent thing I've ever seen!"

Bianca dimpled proudly for a moment before remembering that she was outraged.

Kraven did a double take as Bianca stood conspicuously in her underthings, grasping for the buffalo plaid shirt.

"Good God, Woman," Kraven hissed. "Would you cover yourself with something and get over here? You're going to miss the moose!"

"Very funny," Bianca said, sliding her arms into the sleeves.

"Don't you want to see it?"

"Don't mess with me, Kraven."

Kraven blinked.

"Whatever you're trying to lure me into…"

"Why do you question my motives?" Kraven asked.

"Because they're not real."

"My motives?"

"Moose."

"Moose?"

"Moose."

"Like the one wading in the cattails over there?"

"Nice try."

"Why would I lie about a moose?"

"Because you are pathological. Also, because moose do not exist."

"On what planet?"

"I don't believe in moose."

Kraven blinked.

"So you don't believe in that glorious creature… right there."

As if on cue, the moose turned its iconic head and looked directly at Bianca.

"Toronto!" Kraven excitedly stage whispered. "Look now! He's looking right at you!"

"I'm not falling for it."

"If this is some kind of urban humor, it doesn't translate well."

"If I look, you will catch me off guard and do something vulgar."

"Really. That's what I'm going to do right now. Something vulgar."

"Most likely."

"Such as?"

"Perhaps you will grab my bum."

Kraven blinked.

Kraven suddenly exploded with laughter.

Bianca gaped.

He knows how to laugh?

Huh.

Sadly, the booming laughter echoed off the lake and spooked the moose, who darted into the conical, Algonquin trees.

"Dammit!" Kraven cussed. "You scared away the moose!"

"Okay, first of all, moose are pretend things and can therefore not be scared away. Secondly, you are the one with the thundering guffaw."

"You are the one who said the nonsensical thing that inspired said thundering guffaw."

"Nothing I said was amusing."

"You think I want to *grab your bum?*"

"Or jugs. I can't read your mind."

"That's a little presumptuous, don't you think?"

"In what sense?"

"Don't you think that if I wanted to grab a member of your body, I would have done so when I had the chance?"

"What did you to do me while I was sleeping?" Bianca asked, pointlessly covering all her special places.

"Nothing."

Bianca suddenly looked a tad hurt.

Is this his passive aggressive way of telling me I'm unattractive?

Jerk.

Suddenly, a nasally phantom voice echoed eerily through the mist. *"Helllllloooo?"*

"Good grief!" Bianca startled. "What in the heck was that?"

"The best thing that's happened all summer," Kraven said, looking more lumberjackish than ever. He stood majestically atop a rock with one hand on his hip and the other shielding his eyes as he gazed into the distance.

A glowing beam from a flashlight carved through the mist. The tip of a canoe appeared, followed by the gaunt face of Tucker. Behind Tucker was Jedd. Both faces gleamed with relief when they spotted Bianca and Kraven.

"I see them!" Tucker squeaked. "Look Jedd! It's them!"

"Mercy me!" Jedd exhaled jubilantly. "I am so happy I could just spit!"

"We're coming!" Tucker hollered towards the shore. "We're coming to save you! Stay put, okay?"

Bianca ran to the shore, waving her arms like a spaz. "Over here! We're over here!"

Kraven raised his finger, about to say something. Then smirking, he decided to refrain.

The faces of Tucker and Jedd suddenly paled when they saw Bianca waving her arms around.

"Whoa!" Tucker said, stunned.

"Well, I'll be a monkey's uncle," said wide-eyed Jedd.

Kraven covered his mouth and subtly snorted with laughter.

Bianca looked down.

She had not yet buttoned her shirt.

Jedd slapped his hand over Tucker's eyes.

CHAPTER TWENTY-ONE

"Oh my gosh!" Trudy gasped, clasping her hand to her mouth. Her excited teeter caused the floating dock beneath her to create an unsteady wake. "I think I see them!"

"Where?" Lizbeth panted eagerly, steadying herself next to Trudy on the wobbling dock.

"Over there, Dear!" Trudy said, using one hand to point and the other to place on her chest to calm her heart.

"Oh thank the Lord!" Lizbeth sighed.

"We got 'em!" Tucker squeaked from the approaching canoe.

Trudy wiped a tear of joy from her left eye. "Bring them on in!" Trudy projected. "I need to hug them both!"

Lizbeth crouched onto the oscillating dock and reached for the side of the canoe while Jedd got some rope and secured the canoe to the dock. Trudy offered a hand to assist Bianca and Kraven onto dry land.

"We were so worried, Dear!" Trudy whimpered maternally while squeezing Bianca much too tightly. "Are you okay? Are you intact? Traumatized? Oh my, the thoughts that swirled through my head all night. I couldn't sleep a wink thinking about you two!"

While turning purple from asphyxiation, Bianca felt a strange warmth emitting from Trudy. She could not identify the warmth or the emotion it inspired within her.

I can't breathe.

But I don't hate this.

But I also can't breathe.

"We found your canoe upturned on the shore," Lizbeth said breathlessly. "Last night. Right over there by the Woodpecker cabin."

"We thought you went home to be with Jesus," Trudy said emotionally, using her flapping hands to fan away the garish memories of the previous night.

"Oh Trudy," Lizbeth said, squeezing Trudy's hand.

"This is all my fault," Tucker moaned as he climbed out of the canoe. "I should have paid attention. I didn't realize their canoe was so far behind. Otherwise I would have waited."

"Don't you dare blame yourself, Son," Jedd croaked scratchily.

"You two are related?" Bianca asked.

"Well," Jedd said, putting his arm around the rakish young man, "Not officially. But we're all family here, aren't we?"

"Where did the two of you end up?" Lizbeth asked, concerned.

"Just some…" Bianca stammered. "I don't know. Some place. A clearing just off one of those finger lakes."

"What did you do all night?" Lizbeth asked earnestly.

Bianca and Kraven looked at each other for a moment.

With his hands in his pockets, Kraven chose not to speak.

Bianca blushed.

"There was this one time," Lizbeth went off on one of her tangents, "when a guest took a canoe out and never returned. I mean, he returned a few hours later but we had no way of knowing that at the time. All kinds of ideas came to me, you know? Like what could he be doing out there?"

"Do you need anything?" Jedd asked, putting a fatherly hand of Bianca's shoulder. "Do you want a mushroom frittata?"

"I really don't," Bianca answered politely.

"Did he fall in a hole?" Lizbeth said, still lost in the realm of her story. "Did he encounter a portager with questionable motives? Did a moose charge him? Where he went, I did not know. He kept me wondering for a solid five hours."

"Wait," Tucker said, pointing his finger between Kraven and Bianca. "What *were* the two of you up to? All night? Alone? In a forest?"

"Son," Jedd interjected diplomatically. "there are some things that should remain private between a man and a woman."

Tucker squinted challengingly at Kraven.

"Tucker," Bianca said. "Nothing happened."

"But I saw…" Tucker squeaked like a rusty gate again.

"Lad," Jedd said, lifting a warning finger. "You saw nothing. You hear? You saw a fully clothed woman. A demure woman. Nothing else."

Bianca hid her reddening face with her hand as Kraven's gleaming eyes implied that he was chuckling in his mind.

"Did a tree fall on him?" Lizbeth continued in her stream of consciousness. "Maybe he met a nice girl and they settled down in Opeongo. See, I did not know what happened to him. Until he came paddling back with a bucket of large-mouth bass and a smile. His name was Gary."

"I think I need to rest for a bit," Bianca said.

"Or was it Larry?" Lizbeth said, scratching her head.

"You do what you need to do," Trudy said, kissing Bianca's head. "We are here for you, Dear."

"You sure you don't want a mushroom frittata?" asked Jedd.

"I have never been surer of anything in my life," Bianca replied.

Bianca felt the eyes of Kraven – the eyes of everyone, for that matter – watch her as she ambled up the hillock to her cabin.

CHAPTER TWENTY-TWO
(DAY 5 IN ALGONQUIN PARK)

A foreboding sky was cloaked with onyx clouds, sagging with rain. Storms had set in for the day and Bianca was somewhat relieved that for one day she would be exempt from more disturbing encounters with nature. She took advantage of the fact that the entire *Whispering Beaver* staff were taking her canoe trauma far too seriously. They were not pressuring her to participate in the special rainy day crokinole tournament in the lodge's common room. They discreetly left comfort food on her porch, along with soothing aromatherapy oils and a cozy blanket, lovingly crocheted by Trudy. Tucker even attempted to make tranquil nature sounds outside Bianca's window, which was weird.

They sure are taking my emotional wellbeing seriously.

Really going above and beyond.

It's burgeoning onto the absurd how hard they're trying.

But it is kind of sweet.

And psychotic.

But also, kind of sweet.

I literally don't have to leave my cabin.

I should milk this for as long as I can.

As the rain pelted outside, Bianca was left alone with her thoughts. The unavoidable blotch of woe embedded in Bianca's mind was the fact that Kraven saw her practically naked. This deeply troubled Bianca. Upon reflection, she realized that nobody had ever seen her naked since she was four when her nanny supervised her bath. Even that was weird. But this was weirder by far.

Kraven was much too bold when he… well…

But I was cold. He didn't want me to be cold.

Even so, a woman has her reputation to think of. Her dignity.

But banana popsicles.

Okay. The man has decent taste when it comes to popsicle flavors.

Did he really care… about me?

It was rather chivalrous of him to use his own shirt.

Bra. Underpants.

When has anyone looked out for me before?

I can take care of myself.

Yes, I can. But why should I HAVE to?

He's weird.

I am so humiliated.

Only mildly.

What?

I do have a nervous habit of staging outrage.

Staging?

Maintaining airs.

Airs are exhausting.

It's part of my image.

Images are exhausting too.

But I'm a professional.

Stay on topic.

But the topic is getting too real.

Shouldn't I be more mortified than this?

I AM mortified.

Am I though?

I didn't actually want him to undress me.

Did I?

I don't like where my mind is wandering right now.

Think about something else. Now.

Bianca's was a mind with no off switch. Being alone with her thoughts was like being trapped in a blender with way too many musings and ponderings, spinning around in a whirring frenzy.

What about my job though?

Is Dirk sitting in my swivel chair right now?

Dirk smells.

Is my swivel chair going to smell like Dirk from now on?

Will it matter?

Do I even have a job anymore?

I wonder what Dad and Chad are doing.

Wait, when have I ever wondered about that before?

They don't wonder about me.

No time.

Then I don't have time to wonder about them.

But here I am wondering about them.

Because I have too much time.

Maybe rain isn't such a great thing.

It gives me time to think.

About. You know.

Things.

People smile a lot around here.

And hug.

People who smile or hug in Toronto get arrested.

Frig. Now I need a hug.

This place is effing with my head.

Then there's the whole mess with Kraven.

Shhh. No Kraven.

Yes, but Kraven...

Stop it.

You can't escape him now. He's permanently embossed on your brain. In a bad way.

Or not.

But mostly in a bad way.

Am I permanently embossed on HIS brain?

"Bianca?" Tucker's voice warbled from outside. "Good news! I brought the *Basket of Love!*"

Raising an eyebrow, Bianca opened the door, finding Tucker dripping outside in a translucent rain poncho. He was carrying a huge basket filled with various items.

"What in the actual f..."

"Surprise!" Tucker squeaked. "Are you surprised?"

"I have no idea what's going on right now," Bianca said, dazed with both shock and maybe some humility.

"You should know," Tucker gleamed, "Trudy doesn't do up a *Basket of Love* for just anyone."

"Really," Bianca said, eyeing the basket carefully.

"She must feel a real special bond with you," Tucker offered. "Otherwise she wouldn't have included her famous coconut brownies and a pair of chenille socks."

"Jam?" Bianca asked, holding a small mason jar between her thumb and index finger.

"That's not just any jam," Tucker said in a deathly serious tone. "That's the *Fam Jam.*"

Bianca squinted, squinched her nose and shook her head interrogatively.

"It's Trudy's special blend," Tucker explained. "I can't tell you what's in it or I could be eternally silenced. But I can tell you, she only gives is to people she regards as kin."

"Like family?" Bianca asked hoarsely.

Tucker nodded vigorously. "See," he continued. "we all put something in the *Basket of Love*. That's what makes this so special. Lizbeth put in some gum. She loves her gum. Jedd put in a bottle of his secret sauce. And I um… I put in a picture of…"

"You?"

"Sort of," Tucker said, looking down and scuffing the floor with the toe of his sneaker. "Do you like it or is it stupid?"

"What..." Bianca cracked, "what am I supposed to do with..." she wiped a small tear from her eye.

"You don't like it," Tucker deflated.

Bianca bit her lower lip.

What is up with these people?

What did I do to deserve...

"Thanks, Tucker."

Tucker's face curled up into a smile.

*** *

The Basket of Love?

Kraven squinted out the window at drippy Tucker in his ridiculous poncho who was waving awkwardly at Bianca before fumbling down the rickety porch steps. Kraven fervently kneaded the head of his nuzzling coon cat who joined him once again at the window. The cat was just as brooding and annoyed as Kraven.

How come SHE gets the Basket of Love?

She has no interest in love or anything the word implies.

Am I envious right now?

Nah.

I didn't come here to be inducted into an honorary family.

Or obsess over some weird...

Not obsessed.

Intrigued. Baffled. Agog.

Big difference.

I wonder if Trudy's famous coconut brownies are in that basket.

Gawd, Kraven.

With his eyeballs twitching with ideas, Kraven sat at a splintery desk in the corner, biting the cap off a pen. Frantically, he scribbled unintelligibly in a notebook at a staggering speed, occasionally stealing a glance out the window at the elusive Fox Hole cabin. He stopped a few times to shake a cramp from his wrist, only to delve back into his literary spasm once again.

The coon cat meowed a rusty meow as he competitively walked across Kraven's page.

"Not today, Beckett," Kraven grumbled as he brushed the cat off the desk with his arm.

The cat imitated Kraven's grumble, then curled up resentfully by the fireplace.

CHAPTER TWENTY-THREE
(DAY 6 IN ALGONQUIN PARK)

Bianca awoke the next morning to nature sounds.

"No thank you, Tucker," Bianca sleep-moaned, squirming in protest in her bed. "No more nature sounds please."

The nature sounds persisted.

Bianca blinked and looked around the room. Tucker was not standing outside her window making soothing nature sounds. Not today. Bianca slipped on a shirt and some souvenir shorts. Yawning a yawn seemingly wider than her head, she padded towards the window and looked outside. She blinked the dreamy delirium from her eyes as she scoped out the pine needled area around her cabin. There was no evidence of wildlife anywhere, save for some wildflowers bending in the breeze. And a few too many zippy mosquitos zapping around. Probably craving Bianca's delicious city blood.

The sunrise was doing something funky on the lake. Bianca figured she had nothing else to do at this early hour so decided she might as well walk down to the dock. The morning sun, after all, was showing off with its orange theatrics. It would be rude to ignore such a display. Bianca pulled her flannel shirt more snugly around her as she started her amble down the hillock towards the lake.

A sudden and conspicuous kerfuffle in the tree above her made the rubbery trunk wobble unexpectedly. Bianca gasped. Pine needles started rustling and a morose groan emitted from a slick, black creature perched on a branch like a ginormous bat.

"Holy Hell!" Bianca screamed shrilly as she jounced abruptly, crouching with fear under the tree. Her breaths tremored. Her legs were flexed in preparation to flee as she squinted at the bat-like thing with curious revulsion.

Whatever that thing was, it was not mentioned in the wildlife leaflet. Bianca was paralyzed with panic. She squeaked like an anxious puppy toy, lost her footing and tumbled ridiculously down the hillock. The thing in the tree shrieked like a prehistoric pterodactyl. Gasping for breath, Bianca pulled herself across the ground, using fistfuls of grass for traction. All the while, she looked up in horror at the *tree thing.*

Bianca swerved her head towards Kraven's cabin, quickly pondering the benefits and consequences of calling for help. She did not have time to decide, as the bat-like creature repositioned itself in the branches, glaring at Bianca judgmentally.

Bianca's eyes narrowed with recognition. "What," she panted, "in the hell are you doing in that tree?"

"Don't judge me," the morbid teenager said, blinking apathetically.

"I thought you were *Wrath*," Bianca said, catching her breath. "Or *Avarice* or some such nonsense."

"Thank you," the teenager said monotonically.

"Would it be unreasonable of me to ask why you've gone incog up in a Douglas fir?"

No response from the Douglas fir.

Bianca exhaled as she watched the *child of the corn* scrunch into a vulnerable ball on his branch. He snuffed audibly, wiping his nose with a sleek, ebony sleeve. Did she hear a faint whimper? Slowly, every tense tendon in Bianca's body ebbed. She had a hunch she knew what was going on with this kid.

"I'm coming up there," Bianca said, trying to shimmy up the trunk.

"You're making an arse of yourself," the teenager said dryly.

"Says the guy in a tree... Wait, are you wearing a cape?"

"Shut up."

"Can you give me a hand at least?" Bianca asked, wedging her heel into a knot in the trunk. "I'm a little new at this."

Rolling his eyes, the teenager reached down and helped Bianca scale the tree. She tentatively found a spot on the branch next to the teenager, hugging the trunk for support.

"Bianca," Bianca huffed from tree-climbing exertion.

The teenager scowled.

"Mind if I ask…"

"I mind very much."

"I offered my name," Bianca said, matching the dryness in the teenager's tone. "The protocol is to return the favor with your name."

The teenager shrugged.

"You don't have a name?" Bianca asked.

"Names limit people."

"What do people call you then?"

"They don't."

"Oh…" Bianca scoured the scenery around her in search of inspiration for her next comment. "You don't want to be here, do you."

"Why are you in my Douglas fir?"

"I feel like we're vibing."

"I don't vibe."

"I don't want to be here either. At this… what do you call it… *place*."

"You don't?" the teenager swerved his head to face Bianca for the first time. His eyes were aquamarine. Who knew?

"Is it not clear that I don't belong here?" Bianca chortled.

The teenager clenched his jaw. Twice for effect.

"So what are you in for?" Bianca asked ironically. "School detention? Co-op placement? Cultural exchange?"

"Parents made me," the teenager sulked. "You?"

"Nervous breakdown."

"Cool," the teenager perked up.

"Why did you climb up here?" Bianca asked. "Scaring the pee right out of me?"

The teenager shrugged.

"I think I get it," Bianca nodded, looking straight ahead at a nesting swallow.

"Nobody gets it," the teenager said, stiffening.

"It's hard being taken out of your element," Bianca explained. "They made me get out of my office. They made you get out of your... coffin..."

A smirk snuck out of its hiding place and formed on the side of the teenager's stone-cold lips.

"So your parents sent you off to a remote cabin by yourself?" Bianca tried. "That's harsh."

The teenager shrugged.

"What city are you from?" Bianca tried again.

"Suburbs."

"That's lovely."

"It's like living in a realm where I'm persistently being splashed in the face with acid."

"Toronto," Bianca nodded. What else could she do?

"I'd do anything to live in the city," the teenager said, gazing straight ahead into another dimension. "The hordes of people. Ignoring each other. I could really disappear in a place like that. Get swallowed into a nice, dark abyss."

Bianca nodded and gaped for a lingering moment, hoping this was some kind of sardonic, youthful humor. "That's... pretty much how it is."

A long, painful silence ensued. The teenager enjoyed this silence. It reminded him of the *eternal sleep.* Bianca, on the other hand, was feeling the back of her neck heat up like steamy kettle.

This kid has issues.

And yet, I identify with him on many levels.

Oh my god.

I'm more screwed up than I thought.

The authoritative scream of a shrieky screen door alarmed both Bianca and the young antichrist. Kraven lumbered out of his cabin, doing a double take when he spotted the awkward duo in the fir.

The macabre youth's eyes widened with horror.

Bianca's eyes widened with seasickness.

"It's him," the youth said with the timbre of a movie trailer narrator.

"But…" Bianca started. She did not wish to be suddenly stranded in a tree.

"I am the darkness," the youth said quickly as he leaped acrobatically from the tree, disappearing into the forest.

"Oh for the love of…" Bianca whined.

"What are you doing in a Douglas fir?" Kraven asked evenly. He was now standing under the tree, looking disapprovingly at Bianca.

"I have my reasons," Bianca said in a pathetic attempt to be prim.

"I don't even want to know," Kraven said shaking his head and lumbering in the direction of his cabin.

"Wait!"

Kraven stopped abruptly but did not look up at Bianca.

"I… I don't know how to get down."

"You're serious."

"Please don't leave me up here," Bianca begged with attempted dignity. "I don't know how to be in a tree."

"How did you get up there in the first place?"

"I was counselling a troubled youth."

"Fine. Don't tell me."

"Can you please just..."

Kraven grunted.

"I thought you said your mother raised you to be a gentleman," Bianca said challengingly.

Kraven protruded his lower lip.

"Put your foot in that notch," Kraven droned, "and give me your hand."

"My shoes have no traction..."

"Do you want my help?"

Bianca pursed her lips tightly and wedged her heel into a barky notch. The bark crumpled and Bianca panicked.

"Your hand, Toronto. Give me your hand."

"I'm slipping," Bianca fretted, grasping firmly to a branch.

"Why won't you just..."

Whimpering, Bianca found herself clinging to a branch with both fists, dangling stupidly like a pair of out-of-style pants on a clothesline.

"Toronto..."

"I don't want to die this way!" Bianca cried.

"Gawd, Toronto. You're not going to die," Kraven said, spreading his arms. "Jump."

"Are you daft?"

"I'll catch you."

"No you won't. It's a trick."

"I've assumed the position. Just jump."

"It was so much easier climbing up..."

"I won't let you plummet to your death."

"Promise?"

"Jaysus Thunder."

"This feels like one of those asinine trust exercises."

"I won't let you fall on your head. I have enough problems. I don't need that on my conscience."

Bianca squeezed her eyes shut and pinched her lips together until they whitened. With extreme reluctance, she let go of the branch. She fell, screaming and sprawling freefall in what seemed like slow motion. Within seconds, she felt her body percuss against Kraven's chest. She felt the rocky muscles of his arms flex around her.

"Did I hit the ground?" Bianca quavered with her eyes still squeezed shut. "I hit something hard."

"That was me," Kraven said matter-of-factly.

Bianca opened her eyes. Looking down at her were a pair of laser green eyes, which seemed surprisingly less animalistic up close. They had a soft glow that Bianca could not decipher. Despite the fact that she was safely on the ground, Kraven's rocky arms still tensed around her body. She wriggled to free herself but without any great effort. After all, Kraven did not seem to be in any hurry to let go. It would be rude to thrash around like an Alcatraz escapee.

"Are you okay?" Kraven asked in that gentle, sandpapery way he sometimes had.

Bianca could feel his breath on her face when he said this.

Minty.

Wait, why would a guy in a forest bother sucking on mints?

"You can let go of me now," Bianca announced.

Or not.

Actually, no. Please don't.

Dammit. He let go.

I mean... thank god. I felt like I was being smushed by a reticulated python.

In a good way.

Wait, no. I mean...

"Thanks," Bianca said, reddening. She covered her face and traipsed briskly towards her cabin without uttering another word.

"That's it?" Kraven called over to her. "I basically saved your life and all I get is a monosyllabic grunt of thanks?"

Oh my god, what if he saw me blushing?

Bianca's screen door shrieked closed behind her.

"Whatever, Toronto," Kraven throatily grumbled.

CHAPTER TWENTY-FOUR
(DAY 7 IN ALGONQUIN PARK)

A swift hand grabbed the last bag of peanuts from the tuck shop shelf. Bianca's face melted into a grimace. Did she even need to turn around and see who beat her to the bag of nuts she so obviously wanted? Bianca slowly turned her head and growled when she saw Kraven looking back at her challengingly.

"Are you trying to make some kind of a point?" Bianca exhaled.

"I want peanuts."

"I don't believe you."

"Believe what you want," Kraven said smugly. "I've got the peanuts."

"I was clearly about to take them."

"That was not clear."

"The gentlemanly thing to do..."

"I tried the gentlemanly angle," Kraven said. "It had a negative effect on you."

"When have you ever…"

"Oh, I don't know," Kraven said sarcastically. "Maybe that time I caught you when you fell out of a tree…"

"I didn't fall. I jumped intentionally."

"I helped you stave off pneumonia when you were marinating in that soggy shirt…"

"I wasn't that wet."

"When I heard you crying and shrieking fearfully in your cabin. I came over to see if you were okay…"

"When did you ever…"

… *Oh.*

The bear.

I am such an idiot.

Kraven squeezed the bag of peanuts in his fist defiantly. "My peanuts."

"I said thanks," Bianca said pathetically. "That one time."

"You are oblivious," Kraven snarled.

"Maybe…" Bianca stammered. "Maybe we could share…"

Kraven triangulated an eyebrow.

"… the peanuts." Bianca finished.

"I'm not going to eat them," Kraven grunted.

Bianca frustratedly blew the bangs off her forehead. "So you admit," she said, pointing an accusing finger in Kraven's face. "you took the peanuts to be a jerk."

"I wanted to feed the chipmunks."

"You are such a bad liar."

"Because I lack experience as a liar."

"Somehow you don't seem the type to feed chipmunks."

"Really," Kraven said, taking a step back to behold Bianca's palpable nerve. "And what is my *type* exactly? Please. Educate me."

Bianca gulped, following the contour of Kraven's head as it cocked. According to her bulging eyeballs, she was not prepared to have her impulsive accusations challenged. "Uh..."

"You don't have a clue, Toronto."

"I just want peanuts," Bianca said smally.

"This has nothing to do with peanuts."

"It does a little bit," Bianca said sheepishly. "I'm hungry."

"*What,*" Kraven enunciated much too clearly, "*type.* Do you think I am?"

"You're... the creepy type."

"Creepy."

"Dammit," Bianca grasped. "Can I have a do-over?"

"Take your time," Kraven exhaled, crossing his arms.

"Enigmatic... Is that better?"

Kraven looked at Bianca enigmatically.

"What is that look?" Bianca asked nervously.

"It's my enigmatic look."

"See, it's things like that..."

"Is enigmatic necessarily a bad thing?"

"I can't figure you out."

"Some things are too profound to be figured out."

"I need to understand things."

"Control freak?"

"No! I just like... being in control. Of..."

"I'm not that hard to figure out."

"You're a human sudoku."

"What is it about me that you find perplexing? Or creepy, if you prefer."

"For instance, I've never seen anyone who looks like you."

Kraven swallowed.

A beat.

"Same," Kraven said, looking ambiguously at Bianca.

Bianca gaped for a moment, then collected herself.

"Second example," Bianca said, discreetly fanning herself, "you stare a lot."

Kraven stared.

"Like that," Bianca pointed out. "And you hide in your cabin all the time."

"I don't hide."

"Then what are you doing in there?"

"I don't have to tell you that."

"See? Ambiguous."

"If you were capable of picking up on non-verbal signals," Kraven sighed, "you would have noticed my many attempts to..."

"Didn't you tell me the other day to stay away from you?"

Kraven bit his lip. Then he threw the bag of peanuts at Bianca.

"I thought," Bianca said, dumbfounded, "you wanted to feed chipmunks."

"I'm not the type," Kraven snarled.

***

With the bag of peanuts clenched in her fist, Bianca brisk walked down a worn dirt path. Kraven was walking in a huff beside her.

"Are you following me?" Bianca chuffed.

"No," Kraven rumbled.

"I thought you wanted nothing to do with me."

"Our cabins are next to each other," Kraven explained haughtily. "I have to walk in this direction to get back to my cabin."

"I need some time alone," Bianca said. "Can you please just give me a head start and walk back to your cabin in a few minutes?"

"You need time alone and I'm the hermit."

"Be elsewhere."

"Literary vocab. Sexy."

"Stop."

"Did you learn to talk like that in Toronto?"

"Kraven…"

"Being a literary city."

"Kraven!"

Why can't he just get off my butt?

Dammit. Now I'm thinking about his butt.

Is he thinking about my butt?

Bianca! Yeesh! What are you? Twelve?

A chipmunk – arguably the cutest chipmunk in the world – suddenly began scampering behind Bianca, right at her heels. She quickened her pace, eyeballing the chipmunk with growing concern.

Kraven smirked. "Are you afraid of that chipmunk?"

"Absolutely not."

"Then why did you suddenly start walking faster? With your cabin key protruding from your fist like a potential weapon?"

"No reason."

"He's cute," Kraven dimpled.

"It's a rodent. Rodents carry diseases."

"What kind of weird chipmunks do you have in Toronto?"

"I've never actually... seen one."

"Wow. You're sheltered."

"Make it go away."

"He wants your peanuts."

"Make it go away."

Stopping abruptly, Kraven grabbed the peanut bag from Bianca while she whimpered like a bichon frise. Kraven ripped the bag open and poured a few peanuts into his hand. Cupping his hand gingerly, Kraven squatted and presented his offering to the chipmunk.

Bianca cocked her head in wonderment.

Chipmunks? Really?

What is up with this guy?

Bianca's eyes glossed with wonder when the little chipmunk waddled right into Kraven's hand, picked a nut up with his ridiculous little fingers, cramming the entire thing into his cheek. Kraven scrounged another peanut from the bag and held it between his thumb and index finger. The chipmunk stood on his hinds with his little hands poised in a begging gesture. He chattered gleefully. With a coy dimple, Kraven rewarded the chipmunk with the coveted peanut. He nuzzled the chipmunk's stuffed cheeks with the crook of his pinky finger.

Kraven became aware that Bianca was watching him smiling childishly at the chipmunk. The smile crept back into its hiding place. He cleared his throat conspicuously and lumbered back into his cabin, hands elusively in his pockets.

Bianca squinted intensely as he disappeared into the Wolf Den.

I will never figure that guy out.

CHAPTER TWENTY-FIVE
(DAY 8 IN ALGONQUIN PARK)

"I understand, Dear," Trudy said into a rotary phone which was yellowed with antiquity. "Good day, Mr. Grosswater."

There was a forlorn expression etched on Trudy's face when she hung up the phone in the ramshackle, little hut. She kept her hand on the receiver as it sat in its cradle for a lingering moment. Her eyes were closed. She inhaled deeply with her forehead squishing into a worried torsion.

From the water taxi, Tucker waited anxiously for Trudy to return. "Well?" he squeaked as Trudy tottered into the canoe and took her place at the bow.

"Tucker, my boy," Trudy exhaled like a dreary wind, "it's beyond me how our Bianca lasted as long as she did before she blew a gasket. That man... oh, that man..."

"What did Grosswater say?"

"Oh, he droned on about being busy and being important," Trudy said, shaking her head in utter disbelief." And how he was busy doing important things and how important the things were that he was busy doing. And how the busier you are, the more important you are. And how important it is to be busy. I told that old sock that if he was so busy being important, why was he spending so much of his important time telling me how busy and important he is? Shouldn't he be getting to the point if he had so little time to spare? I said that to him, Tucker. I said it with my mouth."

"And Bianca?" Tucker asked, paddling into the lake.

"Bianca must have the patience of Job," Trudy replied. "Working under the thumb of that task master for as long as she did. If you ask me, she would be better off never going back to that horrible place."

Tucker perked up. Then his face sagged when he stated the obvious. "Bianca loves her work."

"I can't imagine why," Trudy sighed. "Her boss has the personality of a sturgeon. I can only imagine the toxic work environment that poor girl has had to endure. It's enough to make anyone chew on their arm and ramble on about squirrels. But you're right, I suppose. Bianca's work does seem to mean a lot to her. We should respect that."

"But what did Grosswater have to say about Bianca's... I don't know... trial?"

"Tucker, I love Bianca. You and I both. But I think it's as clear as a sober man's head that Grosswater is setting her up for failure. I believe in her, Tucker. I do. But the pressure he's putting on that poor girl..."

"Do you think..." Tucker said, lowering his head, "...that she'll lose her job? Maybe she wouldn't have to go back or..."

"That would just crush the poor girl," Trudy snuffed. "She's an executive through and through.

Tucker nodded silently.

"But we have to do what we can," Trudy nodded optimistically. "Bianca is a strong-willed little thing. If she is determined to keep her job…"

"What are the odds that will happen?" Tucker asked dismally.

"Don't know, Kiddo," Trudy sighed. "But if we love her, we need to…"

"You love her?" Tucker looked up, glossy-eyed.

Trudy's face melted into a maternal pudding. "I know it's silly. Getting attached to a guest who we'll likely never see again after September. I just can't help myself. The heart loves who it wants to. We don't get a say in it, do we."

Tucker carefully considered his next words. "She… she reminds you of… someone. Doesn't she?"

Trudy pursed her lips emotionally. "She does, Tucker. She does. That black bob hair. Those eyes." Trudy's eyes brimmed with tears. "The feisty personality. Which, by the way, I can see right through. That girl can't fool me. She's a corporate teddy bear, I just know it."

"You're a good mom, Trudy," Tucker said bashfully. "That's why Gemma went to Mumbai."

Trudy squeezed her eyes shut as tears escaped down her sunburned cheeks. "She's doing important work, there.

Meaningful work. Doesn't earn enough to come back and visit her mom..."

"Trudy..."

"I guess she doesn't need me."

"Because she's strong and independent," Tucker offered. "That's on you, Trudy."

"You're a good boy, Tucker," Trudy sniffled happily, patting Tucker on the hand. Then she hoovered her emotions back inside. "So regarding Bianca..."

"What do we need to do..." Tucker swallowed, "to help her remain employed?"

"We need to put a little *wild* into that girl."

"How?"

Trudy smirked mischievously. "Tucker, upon our return to the lodge, put Bianca's name on the list. Our girl is participating in the advanced level hike."

CHAPTER TWENTY-SIX
(DAY 9 IN ALGONQUIN PARK)

"No," Bianca said firmly as Trudy positioned a backpack on her.

"It'll be fun, Dear," Trudy said, brimming with enthusiasm.

"The map says this hike has an above average level of difficulty," Bianca argued.

"Advanced," Trudy chimed. "Only the best for our little overachiever."

"But Trudy. It's *me,*" Bianca urged. "I'm in a toxic relationship with Mother Nature. I won't survive out there."

"Tucker will keep you alive, Dear," Trudy said, fitting Bianca with hiking boots. "We wouldn't send a guest on the advanced hike without a guide. That would be irresponsible. Consider the gorge."

"Gorge?"

"Also the bears."

"Bears?"

"Bears, wolves," Trudy guffawed. "It's a giant forest. Who knows what you'll find out there? But don't worry. Tucker watched the training video. He's certified."

"Don't you mean *certifiable?*" Bianca muttered.

Trudy sprayed Bianca with a very wet laugh. "You have a rapier wit, you little jester, you."

"Wouldn't it make more sense to start me off on the beginner hike? Seeing as how I'm completely devoid of experience? And how my muscles have been conditioned to do little else than sit at a desk all day?"

"You're fit," Trudy said, surveying Bianca up and down. "Girls like you have gym memberships, don't they?"

"When am I going to have time for a gym?" Bianca squinted. "Between meetings? During the lunch break that I never take? Or perhaps during my connecting flights at the Dusseldorf airport?"

"At work do you take the elevator?"

"Stairs."

"Good enough," Trudy gushed. "You're plenty trained for the advanced hike. Now since you need to get an early start, I've packed a nice breakfast-on-a-bun in your backpack with a thermos of grapefruit juice. You'll also find one of Jedd's famous cheese and cucumber sandwiches for lunch. That should keep you fed until dinner, which you'll have here at the lodge. If you're back before dusk."

Bianca stiffened.

"Stay close to Tucker, you hear?" Trudy said, wagging a maternal finger. "He knows the way. And no matter how pretty it looks on the precipice, don't get too close. We don't want you falling into the gorge. We love you."

"I'll try to control myself," Bianca said uncertainly.

***

"I have to pee," Bianca called to Tucker, who was walking a good thirty paces ahead of her.

"Okay, go for it," Tucker huffed from the exertion of climbing up a rocky crag. "I'll cover my eyes."

"What are you talking about?" Bianca asked, raising an eyebrow.

"So you can pee."

Bianca looked around, seeing nothing but dense thickets of trees and a bird that seemed to be disapproving her life choices. "Where's the ladies' room?" she asked obliviously.

Tucker blinked.

"Tucker," Bianca said, crossing her legs indiscreetly. "I'm serious. I really have to go."

"We're in the middle of Algonquin's remote interior," Tucker said slowly for fear of being berated.

"Are you saying..."

"I thought it would have occurred to you..."

"There's no flushable toilet?" Bianca squawked in horror.

"There's no toilets in general," Tucker shrugged sheepishly. "Flushable or otherwise."

"You're joking," Bianca warbled nervously. "Because I'm new. You're playing with me right now."

Tucker's mouth moved around silently, grasping for words.

"No," Bianca said flatly. "Not in a million years."

"We have about five hours left of the hike so…"

"I can hold it," Bianca said with a look of agony.

"For five hours?"

"I've had meetings longer than that," Bianca said semi-honestly. "If I can hold it during one of Tommy Fung's long-winded power point presentations, I can hold it for a few more kilometers."

"But your dainty, little bladder…"

"*Don't* talk about my urinary tract, Tucker. That's inappropriate."

"Okay, but…"

"Tucker, the less we talk about pee…"

"Right. Focus on other things," Tucker nodded submissively. "Other. Things. Oh look! I found deer tracks!"

"Deer?" Bianca quavered.

"You're afraid of deer too?"

"What do you mean *too?*"

"I mean you're afraid of a plethora of things." Tucker looked proud that he finally found an opportunity to use the word *plethora* in a sentence. "Bears, for example. Canoes. Chipmunks. Mosquitos. Peeing outside. Intimacy. Slowly descending into madness. Possums..."

"Wait, what?"

"Possums?"

"No, before that."

"Slowly descending into madness?"

"What makes you think I'm afraid of intimacy?"

Tucker suddenly paled. More. "Well I... you know."

"I don't actually. Educate me."

"There are two examples I can think of offhand," Tucker said, nervously running his twitching fingers though his mousy hair. "But for the sake of decorum, I will skip the first example..."

Bianca squinted at Tucker.

"Kraven," Tucker said flatly.

"What about him?" Bianca said, squinting even more.

"Um... the two of you?"

"I don't follow," Bianca said, her insides sinking like a boot after the spring thaw.

"The shirt," Tucker said with subtle resentment. "The *unbuttoned* shirt."

Bianca felt hot, as though mercury was rising to her face. "That..." she stammered, "...had nothing to do with... Kraven and I."

"See what you're doing right now?"

"I'm not doing anything," Bianca said defensively.

"Exactly," Tucker said. "You never do anything. Whenever someone tries to connect with you..."

"Are you pegging me as some kind of social recluse?"

"No... I don't know... In a sense... Maybe... Yes. I mean no."

"It is perfectly normal," Bianca said, making herself taller for some reason, "for me to feel a disconnect..."

"I can tell you like him."

"Kraven?"

"I saw the way you look at him," Tucker sulked.

"With revulsion and at times, fear?"

"With desire," Tucker sniffled.

"That..." Bianca grasped. "... that is insane!"

"And he's trying so hard..."

"To torment me?"

"To connect with you," Tucker sighed.

"No he... how can you tell?"

"He never bothers with anyone," Tucker shrugged. "I've been working here for three summers so far and I've never once seen that guy talk to anyone. Engage. Even make eye contact. But you. He never stops looking at you."

Something flapped around anxiously inside Bianca's ribcage.

"There's clearly an energy between the two of you," Tucker said morosely.

"Negative energy," Bianca said feebly.

Tucker shook his head. "No," he said. "It's not negative."

A beat.

"You're crazy," Bianca nervously laughed.

"Maybe," Tucker shrugged.

***

I REALLY have to pee.

How much longer is this hike?

The terrain was getting more challenging as Bianca and Tucker approached the fourth hour of the hike.

"Are you sure you don't want to stop for lunch?" Tucker hollered back to Bianca who was trailing far behind.

"Not a chance," Bianca puffed. "I just want to finish this thing..."

"That's the determined girl we all love!"

"So I can use the toilet."

Tucker cocked his head. "You should really..."

"Nope."

"Bianca..."

"I pee in a toilet or not at all."

Tucker winced.

"Tucker," Bianca panted as she wedged her hiking boot into a protruding rock and pulled herself up a steep bluff, "do you hear something?"

Tucker cocked his ear.

"You hear it, right?" Bianca said, pushing her palm down on another rock in an earnest climb. "Something snorted."

"Did Kraven follow us here?" Tucker asked, looking around.

"Shhh," Bianca hissed. "Listen."

A distinct snort in the trees caused the two hikers to stop in tableau. Bramble rustled and the vibration of heavy paws vibrated in the ground. More snorts. Whatever was foraging in the shrubs was clearly suffering from a daytime form of sleep apnea.

"What is that?" Bianca stage whispered.

Tucker shrugged. His face was ashen.

"What do you mean you don't know?" Bianca quavered. "You're the guide. You watched the training video."

"It could be anything," Tucker warbled. "Hopefully it's Kraven."

"It's not Kraven!" Bianca hissed.

"How do you know?"

"I would just know if it was him."

"Because your souls vibrate at the same frequency?" Tucker challenged.

"Don't be daft," Bianca spat. "Because it doesn't smell like Kraven."

"You've memorized his fragrance?"

"Jasmine blossoms... Why am I even explaining this?... I usually know when he is approaching because the aroma gets stronger the closer her gets."

"Jasmine blossoms?" Tucker said quizzically. "That's a new one. He usually just smells like campfire smoke and bug repellent."

"Must be a new aftershave or cologne or something," Bianca said.

"When did he start wearing cologne?" Tucker squinted challengingly at Bianca. "In a forest no less?"

"Tucker, stop," Bianca said, using her hand to shoo away Tucker's nonsense. "There's something over there in those trees. It snorts. And I'm ninety-seven percent sure it's not human."

"Then what..."

Shocked, Tucker abruptly stopped when a glossy, black bear lumbered out of the woods.

"Tucker?" Bianca said hoarsely when she saw that Tucker had lost his ability to move.

"Don't make a sound," Tucker warbled. "Just... run."

"What is it?"

"Run, Bianca!"

"But... Bianca said, realizing she was still climbing up the rocky bluff. Her left hand and right foot were securing her. Any sudden moves would cause her to lose her footing and possibly plummet to her demise. "Tucker?"

The crunch of limestone beneath rubbery soles indicated that Tucker had run for his life. Bianca clenched onto the rocks, increasingly aware that she was alone. The snorting became louder and breathier. Looking up, she saw the face of a black bear, peering down at her, licking his chops.

Don't move.

Or run?

Good god, it has two mouths!

No, wait.

Just the one mouth.

And teeth!

Holy hell, the teeth!

What am I going to... do?

The bear licked his chops with more relish. Bianca felt her clothing moisten with sweat. She could feel hot tears streaming down her face. She squeezed her eyes closed, unable to look directly at the potential eater of Bianca. She could hear the bear snuffing loudly.

He's sniffing.

Like fervently sniffing.

Do I really smell that delicious?

Wait...

My backpack.

There's food in my backpack.

That's what he wants.

Swallowing hard, Bianca freed one hand and maneuvered the backpack off her shoulders. After unzipping the bag with her teeth, she hastily tossed the backpack as hard as she could in a random direction. Instantly, the bear dashed hungrily in pursuit of the bag.

Bianca used this opportunity to complete her ascent of the steep bluff, scraping the palms of her hands and twisting her ankle in the process. She ran. In her mind she ran with astonishing speed but who are we kidding? She was stumbling clumsily on a twisted ankle over treacherous terrain of protruding tree roots and random rocks.

Looking over her shoulder she ran. Bianca saw the bear in the distance, ripping her backpack open and snarfing her cheese and cucumber sandwich, cellophane wrap and all. If he could figure out how to use a thermos, the bear would be ready to party.

Run, Bianca.

Just run.

Just...

And that is the moment when everything went black.

CHAPTER TWENTY-SEVEN

"BIANCA FELL IN THE GORGE!" Tucker screamed, flailing his arms ridiculously as though he was made of rubber.

Out of the lodge bolted Trudy, Jedd and Lizbeth, each with urgent concern carved into their face.

"What are you saying, Lad?" Jedd asked gravely.

"Bianca!" Tucker wailed. "She fell in the gorge! Oh, the horror!"

"Tucker," Trudy said stoically. "Slow down. Tell us what happened."

"Is she okay?" Lizbeth asked after swallowing her gum.

Tucker stared in disbelief at Lizbeth. *"She fell in the gorge!"*

"Shhh," Trudy said, flapping her hands around to achieve some order. "What happened, Tucker. Come on now. Tell us."

"We were on the advanced hike," Tucker said, holding his chest and catching his breath. "About four hours in she had to pee..."

"Show some decorum, Son," Jedd nudged.

"She was climbing up a bluff," Tucker said, trying to collect his thoughts. "I was way up ahead. She was struggling a bit. Then we heard a snort."

"A bear?" Lizbeth said, wide-eyed.

"A snorting bear," Tucker nodded. "I told her to run."

"Then what?" Lizbeth begged.

"I ran," Tucker chuffed. "I ran hard. Because there was a bear. I thought Bianca was behind me. If I knew, I wouldn't have left her behind!"

"You left her behind?" Trudy shrieked.

"Not on purpose," Tucker panicked. "As soon as I realized she wasn't with me I turned back. Bear or not, I couldn't just leave her there alone. I couldn't find her for a while. I guess she wrecked her ankle or something because she was hobbling. But then I saw her silhouette. Right up by the precipice. I heard a scream..."

"Lord Jesus, take the wheel," Trudy sobbed, holding her heart.

"I saw her fall..."

"Into the gorge," Lizbeth said with a stunned numbness.

"Why!" Jedd screamed, falling to his knees, shaking his fist towards the sky. "Why did you have to take her from us? She was so... well, out of place. But she was a lovely girl! Have mercy on her!"

"What's going on?" the male honeymooner called, running alongside his new bride. As it turns out, their names were Logan and Cheryl.

"It's a dark day," Trudy said mournfully. "We lost Bianca."

"Bianca?" Logan asked. "You mean the weird girl?"

"From the city!" Cheryl piped up, holding up the index finger of epiphany.

"She fell in the gorge," Tucker moaned.

Logan and Cheryl winced.

"Afternoon, mortals," the morbid teenager said casually. "Is something up?"

"Bianca," Jedd said with his face in his hands. "She's up in Heaven."

"Gorge," Lizbeth said despondently, now chewing on a new piece of gum.

"Well…" the teenager said dryly. He was surprisingly crestfallen. "Why… is nobody out trying to find her?"

Everyone looked at each other.

"I'd do it myself," the nameless teenager added. "But I'm a minor. I'd need supervision."

"Hey." The monosyllable emerged from deep in Kraven's throat as he lumbered towards the lodge.

Everyone stopped in tableau.

A long silence ensued as everyone gaped at Kraven's imposing figure.

"Something's wrong," Kraven rumbled.

"That Toronto girl fell into the gorge," the teenager said. "And apparently it didn't occur to anyone to retrieve her remains. Or you know. See if she's still alive."

The group studied Kraven's face which was morphing into an indecipherable expression. Even more indecipherable than usual.

And just like that, Kraven Kane was gone.

***

"Toronto!" Kraven's voice boomed through the dense forest. It echoed in endless ripples, bouncing off every surface and tree. "TORONTO!" he thundered even louder. His voice assumed the texture of a gravelly, country road. His reverberating footsteps caused every woodland creature within a reasonable proximity to flee. "If you can hear me..." he screamed, "just... just say something!"

Nothing.

Kraven crumpled to the ground and put his face in his hands. After a few moments of agonizing silence, he removed his hands, revealing his rapidly reddening eyes.

"TORONTO!" he screamed with a crack in his voice.

"That's me!" he heard a faint voice in the distance. "I'm Toronto!"

Kraven buckled with emotion, mashing his teary eyes with his palms. "I'm coming!" he screamed. "Just... Just keep talking! I'll find you!"

"Kraven?" Bianca's faint voice quavered.

"I'm coming!" Kraven yelled.

"I'm here!"

"Toronto?"

"Here!"

Kraven followed Bianca's voice, which led him to a precipice. He looked down...

No gorge.

"What are you doing down there?" Kraven asked, rolling his eyes.

"I fell," Bianca said defensively. She was lying, awkwardly mangled on the ground. She had fallen about five feet. "I think I blacked out for a bit... Wait, are you crying?"

"I could throttle you right now," Kraven said, climbing down the shallow bluff.

"I hurt my ankle," Bianca pouted. "Be nice."

"We thought you fell down the gorge."

"Who told you that?"

"Tucker. He said he saw you fall."

"And he just left me here? So much for us all being family."

"He was hysterical," Kraven said, offering his hand to Bianca. "He panicked and just ran."

"What are you doing?" Bianca asked, eyeballing Kraven up and down.

"Rescuing you."

"Because your mom raised you to be a gentleman?"

"Something like that."

Kraven yanked Bianca to her feet. She yelped when her ankle buckled, and she crumpled back onto the ground.

"Let me see that," Kraven said, grabbing Bianca's ankle without permission.

"OW!"

"Sprain," Kraven said, examining the increasing blueness of the bulbous muscle. "Hopefully not a fracture."

"Why did they send you?"

Kraven shrugged. "You're not walking on that."

"Then how am I..."

Before Bianca could get a say in the matter, she was abruptly grabbed and draped over Kraven's rocky arms. "What are you..."

"I said," Kraven barked, "You're not walking on that ankle."

Bianca wriggled for a bit, but soon found a way to position herself comfortably into the crook of Kraven's arms. He was warm. A little sweaty. She inhaled the jasmine scent that was clearly wafting from behind his left ear. She closed her eyes and relished the aroma.

I don't hate this.

But it's Kraven.

Still don't hate this.

He doesn't have to know that I don't hate this.

CHAPTER TWENTY-EIGHT

Scratching her head, Trudy perused some paperwork on her desk with Lizbeth, Tucker and Jedd looming behind her.

"I don't understand it," Trudy said, perplexed. "I don't see it anywhere."

"She doesn't have an emergency contact number?"

"I can't imagine why," Trudy sighed. "Her employer said he filled out her forms in full."

"Everybody has an emergency contact number," Lizbeth shrugged.

"There must be some kind of mistake," Trudy said. "Tucker, would you mind paddling over to the hut and calling Mr. Grosswater? Tell him Bianca's forms are incomplete and we need to contact the person closest to her. Next of kin, friend."

"But..." Tucker trailed. "What do I say happened to her?"

"Don't say anything until Kraven gets back and we know what's going on," Trudy instructed. "We can't tell Grosswater anything until her next of kin has been notified."

"She must have some family close by," Jedd offered.

"Or a best friend," Lizbeth added. "Partner."

Trudy pursed her lips.

"Kraven's back!" Logan announced, followed by a very exuberant Cheryl. "He has Bianca!"

Trudy, Jedd, Tucker and Lizbeth dashed outside, hoping for the best, dreading the worst. They saw Kraven in the distance with Bianca draped over his arms. They all held their breath simultaneously until Bianca lolled her head to look at them and smiled sheepishly. Then everyone exhaled simultaneously.

"Bless my soul!" Trudy cried, waving her hands in the air religiously.

"Our girl!" Jedd gleamed, smiling with his signature overbite.

Everyone swarmed Kraven and all started bantering at once.

"Where was she?"

"Is she dead?"

"Of course she's not dead! Her eyes are open!"

"It's a miracle!"

"Is she okay though? Is anything broken?"

"Does she have amnesia? Internal bleeding? Emphysema?"

"Get her some water!"

"Whisky! Whisky heals everything. I'll go get some."

"Get that girl into bed!"

"We love you so much, darling girl!"

"What was it like falling off the gorge?"

"She didn't fall into the gorge," Kraven snarled, looking directly at Tucker.

Tucker reddened. "I need to paddle to the hut so…"

"Stay put, Son," Jedd said. "It's more important that we are here to support Bianca emotionally."

"And see to her needs," Trudy added. "What do you need, darling girl? Anything. It's yours."

"I'm fine," Bianca insisted, wriggling from Kraven's clutches.

"She fell five feet," Kraven grunted.

"It was more than seven feet," Bianca argued. "Perhaps you didn't see my ankle's particular shade of blue."

"Purple."

"Blue. Cobalt, to be more specific. The color of agony."

"It's a sprain," Kraven exhaled.

"I was unconscious," Bianca snapped.

"For like twelve seconds," Kraven said.

"How would you know…" Bianca began.

"Tucker," Trudy said, looking intently at Bianca's injury, "we need ice."

"I thought I was supposed to paddle to the hut and call Mr. Grosswater," Tucker said, scratching his head.

"This is more urgent."

"Wait," Bianca interjected. "Why is Tucker supposed to call Mr. Grosswater?"

Trudy, Jedd and Lizbeth looked at each other knowingly and with concern. Bianca quizzically cocked her head at them.

"I suppose," Trudy said, "since you're alive, conscious and to the best of my knowledge, of sound mind we might as well just ask you instead of troubling Mr. Grosswater."

"What?"

"We were just wondering," Trudy said gingerly, "why you don't have an emergency contact number."

Bianca paled.

"I hope we aren't being too intrusive," Trudy added quickly. "It's just that when we thought you fell in the gorge, we had nobody to call. There was no contact number in your paperwork, so we had no idea…"

"I'm fine," Bianca said sharply. "You don't need to contact anyone."

"I understand," Trudy replied. "But for future reference…"

"Do you anticipate I'm going to have a fatal accident?" Bianca asked defensively.

"Well," Trudy stammered. "No. It's just... well, Dear, in only nine days you've managed to fall out of a canoe, also a tree, get lost in a forest, take a pretty serious fall, sprain an ankle..."

"Also, she had a standoff with a bear," Tucker added.

"Seriously?" Kraven asked.

"He just wanted a cucumber sandwich," Bianca said. "There's no need to declare an emergency."

"We need a number here, Dear. It's our policy."

Bianca blinked.

"I..." she said, barely audible.

Kraven stared at Bianca with a laser focus.

"Um..." she said again, her voice cracking.

"Leave her alone," Kraven growled.

"Kraven, Dear," Trudy said, "We are just trying to..."

Without another word, Kraven hurled Bianca over his shoulder and carried her firefighter style back to her cabin.

CHAPTER TWENTY-NINE

Startled, Bianca fell backwards onto her bed. She looked up in disbelief at Kraven who had just tossed her onto the bed like sack of onions. The springy mattress objected with a boing. Kraven loomed over her, casting a shadow twice his size on the wall. Bianca cowered a little. Her ankle throbbed. Her heart thrummed like a nervous rhythm guitar.

Bianca and Kraven looked at each other for an awkward amount of time.

"You're welcome," Kraven grunted as he turned to leave.

"Wait," Bianca said a little more urgently than she had intended.

Kraven turned to face her. Agitated, he shifted from side to side as his eyes roamed the room.

"Why did you do that?" Bianca asked.

"What did I do this time?"

"Did they send you into the forest to look for me?"

Looking down, Kraven shrugged.

"You came looking for me."

"It was the decent thing to do."

"You were crying."

"Allergies."

"You removed me from an uncomfortable situation back at the lodge."

"You're hurt. You had to come back..."

"Why though?"

"Don't read into things, Toronto."

Bianca pursed her lips.

A beat.

"Later, Toronto."

The screen door shrieked shut as Kraven thumped out of Bianca's cabin.

CHAPTER THIRTY
(DAY 19 IN ALGONQUIN PARK)

There was a crack in the cabin ceiling that resembled a platypus. Lying flat on her back for ten consecutive days, Bianca had analyzed the crack thoroughly. She had little else to do while she waited for her ankle to stop throbbing. Even short hobbles to the toilet were challenging.

Bianca had been adequately cared for by the *Whispering Beaver* staff during her bout of bed rest. Ice was left for her at the door every morning. A covered tray with lukewarm food was left for her at mealtimes. Her ankle was complaining a little less now. The cobalt blue bruise was fading to a more attractive magenta tint. Regardless, it was still painful to put any weight on her wobbly ankle.

One would think that Bianca would be contented with the break from Algonquin Park's naturalistic horrors. But along with her ankle, Bianca's brain throbbed with worry about how this idle passage of time would affect her ability to prove her worthiness to Arthur Grosswater. Already she had flunked the canoe tour and the advanced hike. She could not even stay on good terms with the woodland creatures. And she was losing precious time with each day she convalesced. With Trudy reporting back daily to Grosswater regarding Bianca's progress, Bianca furrowed with dread at the possibilities of what could be in store for her come September.

I am SO fired.

But I can't be. I've been employed since I was seven years old and licked envelopes on a contract basis for various local businesses.

I don't know how to be unemployed.

It's simple. I just can't let it happen.

I have to prove to Grosswater that I can rise to the challenge.

Says the girl lying in bed with a sprained ankle after having lost her cucumber sandwich to a slobbery bear.

How am I going to do this?

With a sprained ankle?

And no survival instincts?

I miss my pungent city.

The porch creaked under timid Tucker feet right before Bianca heard a rap on the door.

Not now Tucker.

I'm not up for this.

Whatever it is, why can't he just leave it on the porch like a rational person?

"Bianca?" Tucker called feebly as Bianca groaned and rolled over in her funky sheets. "I have an item for you that is both practical and meaningful."

"Enter," Bianca moaned, while Tucker was already letting himself in. She looked up queasily at Tucker who seemed to be gleaming with an alien glow. Also, he was holding a walking stick. Bianca squinted at it, wondering if she was really being gifted with a stick or if something trippy was going on with her anti-inflammatories.

"It's a walking stick," Tucker said, proudly showcasing all his yellowish teeth.

Bianca blinked.

"It's from Jedd," Tucker gushed. "Isn't is swell? Look, the handle is carved from real basswood."

Accepting Tucker's meek offering, Bianca examined the walking stick, on which was a handle, masterfully carved into the likeness of a bear. Bianca's face turned into a mason jar of split pea soup.

"A bear?" Bianca said nauseously.

"Unfortunate irony, I know," Tucker said. "But it's pretty special, don't you think? Jedd's great grandfather made it with his own hands. Jedd wants you to have it. You know. To help you hobble around."

Bianca's heart melted like a piece of milk chocolate on a warm tongue. She ran her fingers over the intricate carvings, musing on the effort and soul that went into the craftmanship.

"I..." Bianca stammered. "I've never had anything like this before."

"So you like it?" Tucker bounced like a jumping bean.

"I'll return it as soon as..."

"I don't think you understand," Tucker interjected. "It's for keeps. Jedd wants you to take it home with you when you go. You know. Back to Toronto."

Bianca gaped. "I couldn't..."

"You have to," Tucker insisted. "Jedd would be heartbroken if you turned down his gift."

"But his great grandfather..."

"You don't like it," Tucker said with a rapidly sagging face.

"I do! I... I do. It's just... why me?"

Tucker shrugged.

"Also," Bianca added, "why didn't you just leave it on the porch like you did with all the other stuff?"

"I don't understand," Tucker blinked.

"The ice. The food."

"What are you talking about?" Tucker asked, shaking his head in befuddlement.

"For the past ten days," Bianca explained. "You've been leaving things on my porch so I can stay off my feet."

"Things?"

"Things!" Bianca said, spiraling into a state of confusion. "Ice bags. Ibuprofen. Lukewarm tuna melts and an iffy casserole…"

"I didn't leave those things," Tucker said solemnly.

"Tucker…"

"I didn't. I swear."

"But before." Bianca was getting flustered. "The tuck shop clothes. The clams. You keep showing up at my cabin with gold, frankincense and myrrh…"

"I stopped bringing you food and other essentials because you seemed annoyed," Tucker shrugged. "I only brought you the walking stick because it's special and Jedd wanted me to describe your reaction."

"Then who…"

Tucker shrugged.

"Trudy?"

"I don't think so," Tucker said. "I've only seen her leave the lodge when I paddle her over to the telephone hut."

"Jedd, Lizbeth?"

"We all just thought you were choosing not to join us for meals," Tucker squeaked. "Probably because of your ankle."

"You thought I was going without food for ten days?"

"I thought maybe you city folks have like a meal replacement pill or something. For when you don't have time to eat."

A sudden *plunk* reverberated on the porch outside.

"Someone's out there," Bianca said, craning her head. Using Jedd's walking stick, she wobbled towards the screen door and looked outside.

"Who is it?" Tucker asked.

Bianca looked around. "Whoever it was," she sighed, "he's quick like a ninja."

"Gone?"

Bianca nodded. She then spotted a new covered tray, waiting patiently on the porch. Lifting the lid, Bianca found a bowl of carrot soup with a basket of warm, cheddar biscuits.

"Who left this?" Bianca asked.

"Beats me," Tucker said. "It obviously wasn't me. Jedd and Lizbeth are busy cleaning up the lunch mess in the kitchen... there's cheese everywhere... and prepping for dinner..."

"Warm cheddar biscuits," Bianca mumbled, her eyeballs lolling towards the Wolf Den.

No.

It couldn't have been him.

CHAPTER THIRTY-ONE

A metaphorical electric eel wrapped itself around Bianca's ankle and squeezed tightly when she took her first step outside on the hard earth. She buckled and fell to her knees with a yelp. Stabbing Jedd's walking stick into the dirt like a bayonet, Bianca courageously pulled herself up, steadying herself. Then compensating for her injured appendage, she doddered awkwardly along like an uncoordinated praying mantis. As she began the impossible hobble towards Kraven's cabin, she heard the squeaky wheels of a rusty golf cart approaching. Lizbeth was driving carelessly with fresh towels neatly stacked in the back of the cart.

"Hey Girl!" Lizbeth hollered from the cart, slowing to a halt. "What are you doing on your feet?"

"I'm okay," Bianca said stoically, squinting in a deep focus at the finish line of her quest.

"What in the world..." Lizbeth said, leaping from the cart to assist. "You can't walk around like this. Sprains take up to fifteen days to heal!"

"Lizbeth…"

"Where are you hobbling to anyhow?"

Bianca gaped.

"No," Lizbeth, said, smacking her gum. "You can't go over there."

"How do you know where…"

"Kraven made it clear he did not want to be disturbed."

"I never said I was going…"

"When Kraven goes on one of his stints, there's a solid week, week and a half, when we can't disturb him. We can't even change his sheets."

"Again, what makes you think… stints?"

"He works in there. And he needs to focus. It's dire."

"What does he do?"

"Nobody knows," Lizbeth said, eyes widening with mystery. "Just locks himself in there. Days at a time. Never says a word. Only showed up at the lodge to pick up his covered trays…"

Bianca triangulated her left eyebrow.

"Hasn't eaten at the lodge in ten solid days," Lizbeth shrugged.

"He's been taking his meals out for ten days?" Bianca gulped.

"Tuna melts. Jedd's special casserole…"

"Warm cheddar biscuits…" Bianca said ominously.

"With the carrot soup, yeah," Lizbeth nodded. "That's real sweet, you remembering his favorites. Say! Are you sweet on him?"

Bianca swallowed hard.

"I wonder sometimes what that guy even does for a living," Lizbeth said day-dreamily. "Hidden away in that deep focus of his."

"May I get a lift to the beach?" Bianca interrupted.

"Secretive, whatever it is," Lizbeth continued. "Possibly eccentric. Illegal…"

Bianca hopped into the golf cart alongside Lizbeth, who instinctively began driving towards the beach – still lost in the throes of imagination.

"Nice day," Bianca said in a lame attempt to change the subject. "I've been cooped up in my cabin…"

"I thought maybe he could be a secret service agent," Lizbeth continued. "On account of him being so solitary and suspicious. On the other hand, he could be trying to dodge the secret service. He is a little dodgy."

"Thought it would be nice to sit by the water," Bianca added. "Veg. Take it all in. That's what people do on vacations I've heard."

"Actuaries are generally quiet people," Lizbeth pondered. "Or he could be a mad scientist. He has the hair…"

"You know we're going to the beach, right?"

"Once there was this guest," Lizbeth said nostalgically. "I don't recall his name. So let's call him Dave."

"Where are you driving me right now?" Bianca asked nervously, gripping the sides of the golf cart. They passed the beach a couple of ramblings ago.

"Dave kept mostly to himself. Much like Kraven. We wondered and wondered about that one. It nearly drove us to distraction. Turns out, he studied turbots. He was really private about it too."

"We're off the main path…"

"Do you think Kraven studies turbots?" Lizbeth asked.

"I somehow doubt it."

"Yeah, you're probably right. He's more likely to be the yeast supplier for an extremely private bakery."

"Stop the golf cart," Bianca ordered, snapping Lizbeth out of her storytelling trance.

The cart screeched to a halt.

"What's wrong?" Lizbeth panted. "Did I hit a squirrel?"

"You missed the beach."

"I did?" Lizbeth said, looking around. "Gosh, how'd I manage that? Let me turn this thing around."

"So… when Kraven ordered all those trays of food…"

"Are we still talking about him?"

"Did he say anything at the lodge?"

"About what, Hun?"

"About anything."

"He doesn't really talk much."

"Did he mention where he was going?"

"We all presumed back to his cabin," Lizbeth said, scratching her head. "Are you angling? I don't catch your drift."

"He just took the food. And left?"

"That's generally how take-out works."

"And there was no mention of where he might be going with the food. Other than his cabin."

"What are you talking about?"

"Me!" Bianca warbled exasperatedly, pulling strands of her hair. "Did he say anything about *me?*"

Shaking the tizzy of confusion from her head, Lizbeth replied. "I don't follow. Why would..."

"Forget it."

"I can't forget it now," Lizbeth said. "You've got me thinking. Why would Kraven talk about... you?"

"Obviously he wouldn't," Bianca muttered.

"Something tells me you weren't taking those city slicker meal replacement pills this week."

"Oh my god."

"I thought you looked too nourished and rosy-cheeked…"

"Lizbeth…"

Snapping her fingers startlingly in Bianca's face, Lizbeth stated, "He brought you food."

"I have no idea who brought me food."

"It was him," Lizbeth said, smacking her lips smugly. "I just know it."

"I have no proof."

"He's sweet on you too," Lizbeth said with epiphany.

"Too?"

"It's obvious to everyone here that something's brewing between the two of you."

"That's not a thing."

"Oh, it's a thing alright."

"Turn this cart around," Bianca said queasily.

"The two of you are going to do it in a canoe. I have this feeling."

"Lyme Disease," Bianca said flatly. "The feeling is Lyme Disease."

"Oh my gosh!" Lizbeth warbled. "To think it all started at our modest, little resort…"

"I'm out," Bianca said with finality as she stumbled out of the golf cart.

"I thought you needed a lift to the beach," Lizbeth called as Bianca limped away.

CHAPTER THIRTY-TWO
(DAY 25 IN ALGONQUIN PARK)

"Comfy, Dear?" Trudy asked perkily as she seated herself next to Bianca in an adjacent Adirondack chair by the shimmering waterfront.

A squirrel was eavesdropping.

"Why can't I just talk on the phone with Arthur Grosswater myself?" Bianca asked, favoring her healing ankle.

"I don't understand the man's reasoning," Trudy said, shaking her head. She produced a ball point pen from the pocket of her apron. The apron had pinecones all over it, in case you were wondering. "He insisted on corresponding with me."

"He's already reassigning my duties," Bianca exhaled. "I can feel it."

"Or this could be his way of ensuring that you disconnect entirely from the office," Trudy offered. "He is one of your biggest stressors, wouldn't you say?"

"That's an optimistic way to look at it," Bianca said, massaging her throbbing ankle. It was periwinkle today. Quite an improvement. "You don't know Grosswater like I do. You are assuming he has a smidgeon of empathy. His mind doesn't work that way. If he's blowing me off, it means he's hatching an evil plot."

Trudy smiled stiffly and nodded in a circular way. "Well then. Let's review your activity logbook, shall we?" Trudy clicked her pen with an enthusiastic blink. "What have you been up to since our last little powwow?"

"Five days ago," Bianca said, tapping a pen on an item in her logbook, "I couldn't put any weight on my ankle. So despite my ambitions of trying out the paddleboards, I resorted to building a sandcastle."

Trudy furrowed into a French bulldog of worry.

"I can see by your expression that you question the athleticism and nature theme of this task," Bianca said in her best corporate voice. "But I assure you that I applied my signature determination and perfectionism to this sandcastle. Drawing on the inspiration of nature, I did not build a medieval, architectural structure. Rather, I sculpted the likeness of a beaver. Possibly a whispering one. Behold..." Bianca produced a polaroid photograph of her creation of sand.

Trudy grasped her heart and scrunched her face emotionally. "You figured out how to use the camera."

"First I had to figure out that it WAS a camera," Bianca said, rolling her eyes. "At least you allow some semblance of technology around here, regardless of how primitive."

"It's a magical beaver, Dear."

"Sure," Bianca said, inching her Adirondack chair a little further from Trudy. "So four days ago," Bianca continued, "I drummed up the nerve to float around the lake on a raft and observe waterfowl."

"I'm so proud of you!" Trudy gushed maternally.

"I figured I wouldn't have to strain my ankle doing so."

"Genius," Trudy gleamed. "Did you find any feathery treasures?"

"I followed some ducks around for a while," Bianca said. "And I freaked out a loon. I may have interrupted his mating ritual."

"It was his own fault for not being more discreet," Trudy said, putting a reassuring hand on Bianca's shoulder.

"Three days ago," Bianca continued, trying not to be phased by Trudy's bizarre nurturing instincts, "I attempted the beginner's hike." Bianca held up a calming hand to hush Trudy's excited squeaks. "It was embarrassingly simple, really. Those toddler twins from the Muskrat cabin passed me on the trail. But I did see a woodpecker which was different. I hobbled the whole way with Jedd's stick. Unfortunately, I think I overdid it. My ankle was buzzing afterwards."

"Two days ago?" Trudy said, nodding and writing something down.

"I was feeling brave, so I attended the weekly midnight Wolf Howl with a few other guests."

"Oh!" Trudy bubbled. "How exciting! Did you hear any wolves howling?"

"No," Bianca replied. "Only Tucker was howling. But he wasn't very convincing. He didn't attract any wolves. He sounded more like a defective car alarm."

"Mr. Grosswater doesn't have to know that," Trudy said, writing something secretly mischievous. She put her finger to the side of her nose knowingly. Bianca did not get the innuendo. "What about yesterday? It was raining. I didn't see you at the rainy day crokinole tournament."

"I dug in the moist soil for dew worms," Bianca blinked, matter-of-factly.

Trudy blinked.

"I did it like a boss," Bianca defended herself. "Right out there in the rain. In a poncho."

"Worms?"

"Worms are aspects of nature," Bianca clarified. "Don't you people use them as fishing bait? Let's pretend I'm going fishing."

"Maybe you actually could go fi..."

"No," Bianca said firmly. "So today I was thinking I could..."

"Maybe you could just take it easy today," Trudy suggested.

"Why?" Bianca asked, twitching her left eye.

"Oh, I don't know," Trudy said, lolling her eyeballs innocently up at a chickadee on a branch. "You should be resting your ankle..."

"It's almost better."

"You wouldn't want the injury to recur."

"I'm running out of time," Bianca persisted. "I have to prove to Arthur..."

"We need you at the lodge promptly at 5:00..."

"My job is on the line, Trudy."

"... for dinner."

"Time is slipping through my hands like a live, wet fish."

"If you're out and about in the wilderness you might not be back in time..."

"For what?"

Trudy blinked. "Dinner."

"So pack me something in case I'm not back."

"I'm going to have to insist..."

"What is so important..."

"Pork."

"What?"

"Jedd is making pork," Trudy said, reddening. "He's trying his hardest too. If you don't show up for dinner tonight, he will be absolutely heartbroken."

"I didn't realize pork means so much to Jedd."

"Oh it does, Sweet Pea," Trudy said, nodding gravely. "It really does. And he's making a special dessert tonight."

"I avoid carbohydrates."

"He knows that. Which is why he is preparing a carbohydrate-less treat that you are bound to like. With seasonal fruit."

"I don't understand."

"Listen," Trudy pleaded. "If you would just take it easy today and stick around close by the lodge, I'll write here in the logbook that you went fishing today. With those worms of yours. And caught yourself a nice, chubby bass. It will look so good on you."

Bianca squinted at Trudy with perplexity.

***

The lodge was eerily quiet as Bianca approached. The gingham curtains were pulled shut and the lights were dim. Bianca grunted as she trudged up the river rock walkway. All that yammering from Trudy about a weird pork emergency, and the dining room was not even open yet.

Bianca tried the door. It screeched open like an obnoxious monkey. She heard whispers and hushes all around the dark room.

"The hell?" Bianca said, grinding her teeth with frustrated curiosity.

Temporarily blinded by a sudden burst of light, Bianca found herself dodging a flurry of people wearing conical party hats and screaming things like *"yay Bianca"* and *"are you surprised?"*

Before she could stop it from happening, Bianca was being squeezed senseless by a sentimental Trudy and having her hair mussed by a glowing Jedd with his celebratory overbite. Tucker was bouncing around doing whatever it is that Tucker does at parties. Lizbeth was taking way too many Polaroids.

"The hell?" Bianca said again, this time in shock and bewilderment.

"Look!" Tucker bubbled. We decorated your table with biodegradable trinkets and organic confetti made from hole-punched sugar maple leaves! And there's no balloons because we have a moral problem with balloons! Oh my god! We love you so much!"

"Thanks for that, Tucker," Bianca said half-heartedly.

"I made pork!" Jedd boasted, wriggling proudly.

"I don't even know what to say," Bianca said, smiling politely.

"Sit," Trudy coaxed, pulling a chair out for Bianca. "We are so excited to celebrate you, Dear."

"Why are you celebrating me?" Bianca asked, tentatively taking a seat at table nine.

"I'll get the cake!" Lizbeth squealed school-girlishly before bounding through the saloon doors into the kitchen.

"Cake?" Bianca asked, alarmed.

"Pork first," Jedd said, pointing a lecturing finger at Bianca. "I worked really hard on the sauce."

"Could somebody please just tell me what's going on?" Bianca said, raising her voice to be heard over the gaggle of fishermen singing a barber shop quartet version of *"Holiday"* by Madonna.

"Before or after you open presents, Dear?" Trudy asked obliviously.

"Why am I being gifted?" Bianca asked even more obliviously. "I don't understand the context of this cake. And why does that sculpture of mashed potatoes look like me?"

"That was my contribution," Tucker said bashfully. "Do you like it?"

"I'm not a carbohydrate person," Bianca said.

"Damn," Tucker winced.

"August the 2nd only comes once a year," Trudy said gleefully.

"Most days only come once a year," Bianca squinted.

The festivities suddenly stopped in tableau. Every head in the room turned to gape at Bianca.

"You..." Trudy said softly, "... you really don't know what day it is?"

Bianca shrugged. Her eyes slowly widened, wondering if something obvious was swooshing right over her head.

"Today marks the day..." Tucker swallowed. "...of your birth."

The artichoke of awkwardness suddenly lodged in Bianca's throat. She briefly lost the ability to speak.

Trudy gasped and put her hand to her mouth. "I... I don't think she knows it's her birthday."

"Seriously?" Tucker asked.

"Maybe they don't have birthdays in Toronto," Lizbeth shrugged.

"Hogwash," Trudy said. "Torontonians have birthdays all the time. I have proof."

"Does this mean she's not going to eat the pork?" Jedd swallowed emotionally.

"Oh, she's going to eat the pork," Trudy said affirmatively. "We're all going to eat the pork."

"I don't 'get it," Tucker said, scratching his head. "How could she not..."

"I forgot, okay?" Bianca said defensively.

The din in the room dissipated. Everyone was looking at Bianca again. She felt as conspicuous as a giraffe in an inflatable wading pool. She wished she could crawl into a hole and hibernate for a yet-to-be-determined amount of time. How was she supposed to explain this? How could she stop the rapid flow of blood that was rushing to her face before she passed out in front of everyone? Could she *seem* any more eccentric in front of all these dirty-fingernailed bumpkins?

"Never mind that," Trudy said after coughing some subject-changing phlegm. "The gathering is what's important. And we have a whole evening prepared to celebrate your special light, Dear."

"I don't know if I really want..." Bianca stammered.

"Pork!" Jedd said triumphantly, pointing a finger in the air as he ventured into the kitchen.

"This may not have been how you had planned to spend your evening, Dear," Trudy said confidentially to Bianca. "But we all put a lot of thought and heart into this shindig so please try to have an open mind."

Bianca held her breath involuntarily.

CHAPTER THIRTY-THREE

The pork was passable. The cake was more of a chocolate pudding than a cake, wobbling as it was cut into triangular slices. Jedd really did do his best. A few unwrapped gifts adorned table nine: A hand-knit toque with a furry pompom from Trudy. Organic, lemongrass goat soap from Lizbeth. Handpicked, wild daisies from Tucker. A limited-edition reference book about wild mushrooms from Jedd. Jitterbug fishing lures from the gaggle of fishermen. A handmade card with a skull from the undead teenager. Expired birth control pills from the centenarians. She even got a secondhand romance novel from Cheryl and Logan — but mostly Cheryl.

A scratchy rendition of *'Catch a Falling Star and Put it In Your Pocket'* had been playing on a psychotic loop for the past hour and thirty-five minutes but Bianca had conditioned herself to block it out as white noise. She twitched awkwardly in her uncomfortable, wooden chair as dozens of people slow danced on a makeshift dance floor. Her glassy eyes meandered around, soaking up the image of each pair, including the elderly couple who were surprisingly spry and busting some pretty epic ballroom dance moves.

"Erm…" Tucker choked, awkwardly loosening the collar of his shirt.

Looking up, Bianca discovered Tucker who was beginning to resemble a nervous Maritime lobster.

"I don't suppose…" Tucker gulped, "… you'd want to… I don't know…"

"I can't dance," Bianca said feebly.

"Because of your ankle," Tucker nodded glumly. "I guess you're off the hook then."

"No," Bianca replied. "I actually *can't dance*. Like at all."

"Oh," Tucker breathed. "I thought you were blowing me off. As it happens, I can't dance either. Want to go out there and look like idiots together?"

Bianca sprayed laughter all over table nine.

Tucker's mouth curled into a bashful smile.

"Why the heck not?" Bianca said, getting up and yanking a startled Tucker onto the dance floor.

"I didn't think you'd agree to this," Tucker said, scared to put his hands anywhere on Bianca's body. He eventually settled one hand on her shoulder and the other on her ribcage. "How come you can't dance? I figured a classy lady like you…"

"No time," Bianca said, trying to be mindful of where she put her feet. "I work seven days a week and I don't get home until well after midnight. I don't have time for recreational activities or idle play."

"Jeez," Tucker said, wincing after a misstep. "When do you have time to... I don't know. Live?"

Bianca erected her posture. "My work is fulfilling. I have a lot in my life that I'm proud of."

"What about..." Tucker swallowed hard. "You know. Relationships?"

"I have many," Bianca said corporately. "Professional ones."

"That's not what I mean."

"Not all relationships involve exchanging saliva," Bianca stated.

"Doesn't it get sad sometimes?" Tucker squeaked. "Being alone?"

"I am a strong, independent woman."

"Sure, but you're also an emotionally complex human."

"I don't want anything getting in the way of my success."

"But companionship..."

"That would be distracting."

"I'm just... worried."

The starch in Bianca's proverbial shirt unstiffened. "Tucker..."

"How come you don't have an emergency contact number?"

"Tucker, come on…"

"Don't you have anyone? Like at all?"

"I have plenty of…"

"I just don't understand how someone as smart and as beautiful as you doesn't have…"

"Stop."

"You deserve to be adored."

A hiccup of emotion caught Bianca off guard. She pursed her lips, trying to squeeze back a wave of tears that was insolently trying to gush from her eyes. "I am respected," she said in a wobbly voice while trying to remain poised. "I am highly respected in my field and that is enough. I don't need to be coddled by some…"

A throaty growl suddenly caused both Bianca and Tucker to startle. Kraven glared challengingly at Tucker who whimpered and dashed away, quick like the shade. Bianca blinked away all evidence of emotion and fluffed herself up like a confident puff pastry. Before she could refuse, she was abruptly scooped into Kraven's imposing arms, dancing with him. Bianca uttered a guttural objection.

"What kind of a circus freak forgets her own birthday?" Kraven grunted.

"Shut up," Bianca grunted back.

"What is up with you, Toronto?" Kraven said, squinting his left eye. "Are you so out of touch with reality that you don't remember the birthday of literally the only person in your life?"

"That's insulting," Bianca said, giving Kraven the stink eye. "My life is extremely full."

"Of yourself?"

"Be nice," Bianca pouted. "Apparently it's my birthday. I think there might be a rule."

"Do you normally not observe?"

"Parties are frivolous and counterproductive."

"You can't take one evening a year to spend with..."

"Maybe I have religious reasons. Did you consider that?"

"You're not religious."

"How would you even know that?"

"Someone with such a narrow scope of the universe?" Kraven said breezily. "How could you be capable of believing in anything?"

"I believe..." Bianca stammered. "I... I believe in myself."

"That's hardly enough."

"Someone has to believe in me..." Bianca trailed.

Kraven cocked his head.

"Why are we dancing right now?" Bianca writhed. "I don't remember consenting to this."

"You don't seem to be putting up much of a struggle," Kraven smirked.

"What are you even doing here," Bianca sulked. "Shouldn't you be hidden away somewhere, studying turbots?"

"What?"

"Isn't this the forbidden window, during which time you hunker down and indulge in your covert moiling?"

"What are you even talking about?"

"Your special time," Bianca said with a scrutinizing squint. "When you hide in your cabin like a clam. Demand privacy. And don't change your sheets."

"You're making no sense right now."

"What do you even *do?*"

"Excuse me?"

"Are you violating some kind of universal code of morality?" Bianca interrogated. "Are you a hacker? A corrupt political lobbyist? Do you deceive people with a bogus air duct cleaning service?"

"Toronto," Kraven breathed. "You need to chill." He gripped her shoulder, causing a tendon to sear like barbecued meat.

"There's... There's people watching," Bianca stammered.

"All you city girls care about is your image," Kraven rumbled. "How things appear."

"Don't put me in a box, Kraven. I'm a very complex individual."

"In what sense?"

"You are a stranger. I don't need to tell you that."

"Stranger?" Kraven said with his eyebrows lowering with indignation. "Wow."

"You are essentially a stranger, yes," Bianca said, swooshing her hair to the side for no reason. "I know virtually nothing about you. Other than you are the brooding type. You smell okay. And your marble eyes are filled with a thousand secrets."

Kraven eyes turned into slits of mystery as Bianca lolled her eyeballs to the side, choosing to fixate on a flickering gaslight sconce on the wall.

"You consider me a stranger," said Kraven with his voice shredding like a Janis Joplin impersonator.

"Let's just say if you offered me candy, I would go limp and scream *'this is not my daddy.'*"

"We spent the night together," Kraven smirked. "Shirtless."

"That doesn't count."

"Bear," Kraven said, counting on his fingers, "capsized canoe, piggy-back ride, campfire, lack of pneumonia, Douglas fir, evil chipmunk, another bear, ankle..."

"I don't need to be rescued."

"Oh, Toronto."

Bianca blinked. "So you bring me some cold, gummy food for a few days and now we're on familiar terms? Is that how it works?... Thank you for that, by the way."

"You think I brought you food?" Kraven said elusively.

Bianca blinked again. "Process of elimination. It must have been you."

"Why would I do something like that?" Kraven asked, tilting his head mysteriously.

"Well... I don't know. You must have..."

"That's a little presumptuous, don't you think? Assuming I would bring you food?"

Kraven's intense, alien-green stare permeated through Bianca. He yanked her closer to his body, his hands possessively encasing her ribcage. Bianca could feel his heart thrumming. His breath was roasting the back of her neck.

Frig. I can't move.

Why can't I move?

Why don't I hate this?

Bianca's head suddenly felt swimmy. With difficulty she swallowed what felt like a ghost pepper meatball moving much too slowly down her throat and esophagus. She forgot to breathe for an eternity, as this bizarre moment was suspended in time.

Oh my god, what's happening?

Without a word, Kraven grabbed Bianca's head with both hands and rapaciously smushed his lips hard against hers. Letting out a mousy whimper, Bianca writhed around ridiculously as everyone else in the room gasped and burst into applause.

A loud smack silenced the room.

Gasping for breath, Bianca wiped her mouth with the back of her hand, smearing her red lipstick across her cheek like a failed Nike swoosh. Shaking, she backed away from Kraven who was rubbing his tingling face. A red impression of Bianca's hand was embossed on his left cheek. Kraven looked back at Bianca with a punctured expression.

"Nope," Bianca squeaked as she collected her dignity like a basket of farm-fresh eggs and breezed out of the lodge.

CHAPTER THIRTY-FOUR

Panting, Bianca slammed the screen door behind her as she found refuge in her cabin. Her lips were still numb and tingling. She made a beeline for the bathroom and saturated a hemp washcloth, scrubbing the shame – and possibly communicable germs – from her face and mouth. She whimpered with revulsion as she goggled at herself in the mirror to see if she looked slightly less virtuous than she did a couple of hours ago. Or if somehow a piece of her soul had been extinguished. What she saw was a version of herself with an ambiguous glow.

Jaysus, Bianca. Stop glowing!

Bianca became suddenly aware of the persistent chill in the room. A cold front was coming through, sucking some of the oppressive humidity from the air. Having bad circulation and feeling the blood draining from every extremity in her body, Bianca foraged for a wool blanket. Out the window she noticed wisps of smoke swirling from cabins along the shoreline.

She turned her head skeptically towards the neglected fireplace in the corner. A look of emotional indigestion occupied Bianca's face. A fire would be so warm and cozy, somewhat like a flannel shirt. But she had never done anything so primitive as starting a fire. How would she even do that?

Biting her lip in contemplation, she spotted some matches on the mantle. She lit the kindling sticks which were triangulated into a teepee in the cindery pit. She scraped a match against one of the jagged stones that framed the fireplace, skinning her knuckle in the process. The persnickety flame singed her finger. She winced and dropped the match quickly into the fireplace. The teepee reddened from within and little tufts of smoke curled out of the kindling. Hardly the comforting blaze she was hoping for.

Foraging around the room for something combustible, Bianca opened a wicker hamper in the bathroom and discovered a treasure trove of toilet paper. Unravelling a roll, she ripped off squares of the recycled tissue and tossed it cautiously into the little fire. She gasped and lunged backwards when a sudden flame flared dramatically like an old-timey camera flash.

"The hell?" Bianca shrieked at nobody in particular.

The fire instantly dwindled, and Bianca scrambled to reignite it. The toilet paper seemed to be even more effectively combustible than wood. If three squares of toilet paper could produce one theatrical flame, surely the whole roll would make a fire that would crackle warmly for the entire night. Bianca unraveled an arm's length of bathroom tissue and tossed several streamers of the stuff into the fireplace. Each time she did so, the fire swelled theatrically. Then little, flaming plumages wafted through the air, threatening to land on the pine floor and curtains.

"Crap!"

***

Kraven awakened to find a coon cat attached to his face. A rusty meow and some persistent claws alerted Kraven that whatever he was dreaming about would just have to wait. Pulling the coon cat from his face, Kraven grunted and blinked the sleep from his eyes. It took him only a moment to notice an eerie, orange glow radiating through his window. He sniffed the air and jolted, pushing the coon cat out of his way as he darted towards the window. Outside he saw an inferno where Bianca's cabin used to be.

"Dammit, Toronto!" Kraven barked hoarsely as he urgently pulled on some pants.

CHAPTER THIRTY-FIVE

A shrill whistle pierced through the obscure silence. Bianca's ears protested with ringing that was surely audible to all the curious squirrels, watching tentatively from their trees. Bianca was standing on her porch like an idiot, blowing the damn cris s whistle. Flames had engulfed the rickety porch steps and the surrounding railing, stranding her in her own personal, circle of hell.

She stopped in mid-whistle to cough. The noxious smoke was making her feel woozy and strangling her lungs. She hacked and hacked, shielding her mouth and nose with an arm. She scoured her surroundings, hoping someone heard the whistle. By now it was almost 10:00 p.m. and as usual, the absolute worst things always seemed to happen to her after 9:00.

The moments were brief but seemed like an eternity for Bianca, who was feeling like she was being swallowed by fire. Very soon, vague murmurings started emerging from the shadows. She could hear gasps and a few hysterical screams. Some tender soul called for help. Had Bianca's eyes not been stinging from the heat, she would have seen the worried guests forming an audience from a safe distance.

"Is nobody going to get her?" the creepy teenager warbled existentially.

"How do we get to her?" Logan asked when Cheryl nudged him forward.

Suddenly, Bianca felt a hand slap kidnap-pishly over her mouth. She muttered a muffled scream as she was thrust over someone's shoulder and ushered heroically through the flames. Gasps of horror and wonder could be vaguely heard through the sound of angry fire. Bianca was too paralyzed with shock to object.

Bianca was thrust onto the ground with a squeak as an umbral shadow loomed over her. As she went into a ridiculous coughing spasm, she found a human yurt forming around her. Familiar faces were looking down at her with concern, each face glowing from the fiery orangeness behind them. Bianca squinted up at them in a shock-induced stupor.

"Who..." she stammered.

"For god's sake, Toronto," a familiar voice heaved.

***

"Toilet paper?" Kraven exhaled. "Really, Toronto?"

"Shut up," Bianca grumbled.

Kraven put a wool blanket around Bianca as she shivered under an elm. "You realize there was a pile of precut firewood piled next to the left exterior wall of your cabin."

"I did not know that."

"Also, you had the option of knocking on my door if you needed assistance."

"I don't need your help."

Kraven triangulated an eyebrow right before he used his thumb to remove a smudge of soot from Bianca's face. Bianca reddened and looked away.

"All my presents were in there," Bianca mused as she watched the Fox Hole disintegrate into a glowing pile of embers. "Everyone put so much thought into..."

"Toronto..."

"And..." Bianca faltered emotionally with her lips trembling, "the stick."

"The stick?"

"Jedd's walking stick," Bianca said, her eyes brimming with tears. Her face scrunched into a quivering, sobbing, snotty mess. "I left it in there."

Biting his lower lip, Kraven slid to a sitting position under the elm, next to Bianca. He put a tentative hand on her trembling shoulder blade.

"Are you okay?" Kraven quietly croaked.

"Fine."

"What do you need?"

No reply.

"Toronto?"

With every nerve ending in her body buzzing, Bianca grasped for a segue. "How did you walk through flames without so much as a singe on your feet and lower legs? Are you a vampire?"

"My boots are fire retardant."

"You just happened to have fire retardant boots?"

"They are multipurpose wilderness boots. I like to be prepared."

Pulling the wool blanket more tightly around her body, Bianca stared glassily at the glowing embers. Kraven watched her for a lingering moment, his face melting into a pile of empathetic slush.

"Come on," Kraven said casually.

"What?" Bianca asked, bewildered.

"You're not going to sleep under this elm, are you?"

"You don't seriously mean…"

"Where else do you expect to stay?"

"Anywhere except…"

"I asked around," Kraven interrupted. "Logan and Cheryl want their privacy during this special time. The centenarians said the same. The family with the toddlers already have four people in their bed. The fishermen have a similar problem. The teenager diagnosed himself with social anxiety..."

"No."

"You are required to be here for the rest of the summer," Kraven argued logically.

"Trudy and the others will be back in the morning," Bianca nodded determinedly. "They'll come up with a solution."

"First off," Kraven rumbled. "you're not sleeping out here all night. That's obtuse. You're stuck here for the summer. The place is booked. I'm the only one with the flexibility..."

"Absolutely not."

"I am your only reasonable option and you know it."

"Be that as it may," Bianca resisted, "it is beyond inappropriate."

"In what sense?"

"You... you just had to go and snog me."

"Dammit."

"So you admit you made a colossal mistake?"

"No, I knew what I was doing."

"Oh my god," Bianca moaned, nursing her head.

"You know as well as I do it was only a matter of time before one of us went for it."

Agog, Bianca huffed. "And you expect me to feel safe? With you? In a cabin? Alone? I'd rather bunk with a saltwater crocodile."

"Your call," Kraven shrugged, ambling back to the Wolf Den.

Bianca chuffed, looking back and forth between Kraven and the smoldering foundation of her cabin. As bent and awkward as his proposition was, the thought of being alone that night made Bianca throw up in her mouth a little bit. Whimpering, she collected herself and followed Kraven resentfully back to the Wolf Den.

CHAPTER THIRTY-SIX

The Wolf Den smelled like Kraven's shirt. Bianca eyeballed the room as she lurked inside, afraid to touch anything, gape too long at any one object, or step on too many creaky floorboards.

"I'm plugging in the kettle," Kraven announced. "Want some tea? Instant cocoa?"

Bianca's mouth moved around a bit, but no words came out.

"I'm not going to poison you, Toronto."

"Sure," Bianca said, shaking her head as though trying to rattle an image out of her addled brain. "Cocoa. Please."

"Sit," Kraven ordered, nodding towards a tweed, moss green couch.

Bianca obeyed like a frightened puppy-in-training. The awkwardness was palpable. Although there was only one Kraven in the room, to Bianca, it felt like there were dozens of him. Kraven's essence was filling the cabin like a conspicuous custard. Bianca felt smothered in Kraven-ish energy. Returning Kraven's concerned ogle would be unbearable so Bianca chose to zero in on an unusual painting on the wall.

"Group of Seven," Kraven said, following Bianca's eyes towards the painting.

"Group of seven *what?*" Bianca asked obliviously.

"It's a group of Canadian artists," Kraven explained. "That's *Pic Island* by Lawren Harris."

"Is she famous?" Bianca shivered obliviously.

"*She's* a dude. And yes, he is very famous."

There was a pause as Bianca sat primly on the couch, trying her best to behave. "Why does it look like that?" Bianca squeaked.

"His style is inspired by French Expressionism," Kraven sighed. "It's supposed to look like that."

Bianca began to slither into the couch as humiliation squeezed one of her vital organs like a supple, Florida orange. She knew nothing about art. Why would she choose art as a subject of conversation meant to abate the suffocating awkwardness? Now she was steeped in a cesspool of art criticism, beyond all hope. She scrambled to redeem herself. "It's simplistic."

"That's the point," Kraven said, pouring water from the whistling kettle into speckled, aluminum mugs. "People tend to overcomplicate things. Life is meant to be enjoyed, not endured."

Bianca felt the couch cushion bounce as Kraven took a seat next to her. She felt a tingling sensation on her left side, where

Kraven was sitting mere inches away. After an excruciating pause, Bianca blurted, "I don't get it."

"You don't have to *get* it, Toronto. You just have to just *feel* it."

Bianca gaped at Kraven who was blowing on his steamy cocoa, making delicate waves in the mug. So Kraven was one of those artsy-farts who feels paintings and probably smells music. With each passing nanosecond she felt herself drifting farther and farther out of her element.

Kraven's eyeballs lolled up from his beverage. "Are you doing okay?" he asked. "Your hands are shaking."

Bianca steadied her hands on her mug, suddenly realizing the turbulence she had created in her cocoa.

"I can still smell the smoky embers," Bianca quavered. "It's all over me. I stink like a smoked herring."

The silence that followed gave Bianca indigestion.

"Want to take a shower?" Kraven muttered.

Agog, Bianca choked on her cocoa.

"Not together," Kraven said exasperatedly. "Jeez!"

Bianca curled tightly into a ball, hugging her knees.

"Look," Kraven sighed. "I'm doing my best here."

"I know, but..."

"I don't often have company," Kraven apologized, running his fingers nervously through his hair. "Plus, you literally just experienced a trauma..."

"It's just weird," Bianca interjected.

"You're just going to avoid showering for the rest of the summer? Because it's weird?"

Bianca blew some conflicted bangs from her forehead. The idea of hot water pelting down on her face, slowly saturating her hair, washing away the panic...

A white, fluffy towel suddenly percussed Bianca in the face.

"Don't hog all the hot water," Kraven advised as he stepped outside on the porch. "I'm next."

Bianca blinked. She gaped stupidly for a moment, watching Kraven's lumbering silhouette outside, finding a seat in a rickety rocking chair. She tentatively approached Kraven's bathroom, peeping through the open door like a suspicious tarsier. There was indeed a shower in there, beckoning her. She lurked into the bathroom, letting her sooty clothes fall onto the floor. Discreetly allowing herself into the shower, she cranked the water to maximum heat.

The water pressure was pathetic. She turned her face upwards towards the showerhead like a yearning sunflower, only to be repeatedly spit in the face by ridiculous globs of water. Sooty puddles formed on the tiles beneath her, blending with rivulets of soap swirling around her ankles. She whimpered as the throbbing pelts of water slowly washed away the distress of that horrible night.

From the next room, Beckett pawed something clunky off a surface, sending the clunky whatsit clambering to the floor.

Bianca jolted.

Bianca peered from behind the shower curtain.

No Kraven.

She breathed.

***

Wrapped demurely with a towel, Bianca beheld her newly showered self in the bathroom mirror. Her mussy hair was casually towel dried and her eyes were reddened from shampoo, exhaustion and tears. She squinted at the medicine cabinet, fighting the urge to open it.

Nope.

None of my business.

On the other hand, it's perfectly within reason to find out a bit about the person I'm sharing a cabin with.

What if he's hiding something in there?

Illegal narcotics.

A live huntsman spider.

The souls of those who have displeased him.

Bianca quickly opened the medicine cabinet and exhaled with disappointment. Behind the mirror was merely evidence of an unremarkable, yawningly average man. A tube of fluoride toothpaste. A soft-bristled hairbrush. Floss. Fingernail clippers. Suddenly, a sleek bottle caught Bianca's eye. Upon closer inspection, she discovered that the bottle contained cologne. The label sported a postmodern jasmine blossom. Impulsively grabbing the bottle, Bianca raised an eyebrow at the label which read, *Raw Masculinity.* Bianca instantly reddened and pursed her lips.

An abrupt rap on the door startled Bianca, causing the cologne bottle to slip from her fingers and smash on the floor.

"My turn," Kraven droned from the other side of the door.

Eyes widening with panic, Bianca beheld the cologne pooling on the pine floor, trickling between shards of broken glass.

"Ugh…" Bianca gasped. "Hold on!"

The room was quickly infusing with the overpowering aroma of jasmine blossoms. She desperately tried to sop up the pungent potion with a hemp washcloth, her nose scrunching with revulsion.

"What's going on in there?" Kraven asked.

"I'm…" Bianca panted while carefully removing the intricate shards from the floor, "I'm… shaving my legs."

"Are you okay?"

"Of course I'm…" Bianca yowled when she cut her finger on broken glass.

The door quickly opened, and Kraven found toweled Bianca sucking on her pinky finger. She squeaked with embarrassment and reinforced her towel.

"You're bleeding," Kraven observed. He was suddenly punched in the face by an oppressive blast of jasmine. Grimacing, Kraven shielded his nose with his arm.

"I..." Bianca stammered. "I... was looking for some ibuprofen?"

"Ibuprofen," Kraven said, unconvinced, eyeballing the potent mess on the floor.

"Ibuprofen," Bianca nodded, making brave eye contact with Kraven. "I have no interest in your raw masculinity."

Kraven smirked. "Put on some clothes, Toronto."

***

The cabin was eerily silent, save for the running shower in the bathroom where Kraven was currently becoming a soapier version of Kraven. Bianca scanned the empty room, curdling with curiosity. Foraging uninvited in his closet, Bianca discovered a row of identical plaid, flannel shirts. She inhaled the scent of a random shirt before noticing a desk sitting challengingly in the corner. Atop the desk was a plethora of pencils.

Why does he need a plethora of pencils?

A scrap of loose-leaf paper peeped out from a locked desk drawer. Quickly she tried to free the paper, but it was veritably wedged in the drawer. She rattled the handle, but the drawer stubbornly remained locked. Poking a particularly sharp pencil into the keyhole, she probed and jostled, but to no avail. The pencil snapped in half at the same moment that Kraven emerged from the bathroom.

"Hey," Kraven said casually as Bianca abruptly played innocent. "What's going on?"

Bianca was not sure how long her mouth was hanging open like a stunned Muppet. But her tongue instantly dried up when drippy Kraven stood before her with his wild, wet, shimmering locks of hair cascading down his shoulders. Her eyeballs wandered down to his hips where he had meticulously wrapped a towel.

"Agah..." Bianca choked.

"What's wrong?" Kraven asked as he discreetly dressed in the closet.

"This is a big mistake."

"What do you mean?" Kraven asked, now appropriately pajama-clad. Even his boxer shorts were buffalo plaid.

"I don't think I can stay here."

"You have nowhere else to go."

"You don't understand."

"Is this about what happened at the lodge?"

"I don't know."

"Look, I honestly thought you wanted to..."

"Nope."

"You keep giving me these mixed signals," Kraven explained. "You stare a lot. You inhaled me…"

"It's not my fault you're a talented kisser."

"Do you want me to say I'm sorry?"

"Are you?"

"… No," Kraven mumbled.

Rapidly pinkening and pursing her lips, Bianca looked yearningly at the door.

This is where you run, Bianca.

Run.

Why am I not running?

"Please just try to trust me," Kraven urged. "You can't sleep outside by yourself. Not after everything that happened tonight. Besides, you don't do so well outdoors and I'm really too exhausted to save your life again."

"Ugh…"

"It'll be fun," Kraven smiled, putting a reassuring hand on Bianca's shoulder. He expected her to flinch, but her rhomboid muscles surprisingly relaxed like pasta softening in boiling water.

He did just walk through fire for me.

So there's that.

"I'm not admitting to anything," Bianca said reflexively. "This does not in any way mean that I'm into you. Just to be clear."

Kraven did a *hands-off* gesture with his palms.

"Good," Bianca yawned. "So we're on the same page."

"Tired?"

"No," Bianca lied. She stared gravely at Kraven's bed, her eyes widening with anxiety.

"Take it," Kraven said with a jerk of his head.

"What?" Bianca said, swerving her head around to face Kraven.

"The bed," Kraven replied. "I'll take the couch."

But that's the bed Kraven sleeps in.

What if he sleeps naked?

They haven't been changing his sheets.

"I don't think so," Bianca said, shaking her head.

"Why not?" Kraven exhaled.

"In some cultures, wouldn't that mean we're married?"

"Who the hell cares? It doesn't mean a damn thing in our culture."

"Fine," Bianca huffed, pulling down the musky comforter. Underneath she was startled to find Beckett, glaring judgmentally at her. "Christ on a cracker!" Bianca shrieked. "You have a raccoon?"

"Cat," Kraven corrected as Beckett leaped into his arms, seeking refuge and squinting back at Bianca resentfully.

"You have a cat," Bianca said sickly.

"What's wrong with cats?"

"Nothing," Bianca said, trying to shake something troubling from her mind.

"Meet Beckett," Kraven said, nuzzling the cat's head.

"You named it?" Bianca asked.

"Of course I named him," Kraven's chuckled. "He's my friend."

"Don't get out much, huh Kraven?"

"And *you do?*" Kraven teased, crossing his arms.

"I travel the world on a weekly basis," Bianca pouted.

"Fascinating," Kraven said with teasing intrigue. "So what's your beef with cats?"

"I can't go into any details about that," Bianca shrugged. "I signed a confidentiality agreement at work."

Kraven blinked.

"I'm tired," Kraven changed the subject, arranging a blanket on the couch for himself. He summoned Beckett who curled up lovingly on Kraven's chest.

"Alright then," Bianca said, gaping. After an awkward pause, she climbed into Kraven's bed and cocooned herself in his funky sheets. She felt strangely hugged. She inhaled the unique scent of the bedsheets, memorizing them.

"Are you sniffing my bedsheets?" Kraven droned sardonically.

Dammit!

"No," Bianca lied. "That's dumb."

"Go to sleep, Toronto."

"I can't," Bianca whimpered. "I almost became a toasted marshmallow. My heart is still thumping."

"You're safe now," Kraven assured her.

"I know but it's dark and there's..." Bianca gazed at the moon outside that was currently illuminating Kraven on the moss green couch. "... a cat."

"I'm so tired, Toronto. Saving your life is exhausting. I know this because it's become a routine part of my day at this point."

Bianca's eyes meandered the moonlit room. She squinted at the slanted desk in the corner, adorned with pencils. "What's all that for?" she asked.

"We don't need to talk about that tonight," Kraven yawned.

"We do, actually. I won't be able to sleep unless I know why you own so many pencils."

"It's complicated."

"Do people even use pencils anymore?"

"I do."

"What for?"

"You tell me why cats traumatize you and I'll tell you what I do with pencils."

"I barely know you."

Kraven let out a slow, guttural exhale. "Do you read, Toronto?"

"Of course."

"What do you like to read?"

"*Like* to read?" Bianca asked, scrunching her nose.

"You don't like to read?"

"I read."

"Okay."

"I read content."

"That's ambiguous."

"Documents," Bianca continued. "Emails. Power Point presentations. Status reports..."

"Do you read for fun?"

"Why would I do that?"

"May I go to sleep now?" groaned Kraven as he rolled over in a subject-changing kind of way.

"Almost," Bianca said. "I need to know where you're from."

"Would you please just go to sleep?"

"Kraven," Bianca pleaded, "I... I don't want to close my eyes. I'm afraid."

There was an empathy-drenched pause. "Okay," Kraven said softly.

"Thanks, Kraven."

"I was recently sprung from Kingston Penitentiary."

"I'm out," Bianca said, getting out of bed.

"Get back in bed, Toronto. I'm from Huntsville. Jeez."

"So you're from the sticks?"

"Town. It's a town."

"Describe it, please."

"The town?"

"Please, Kraven," Bianca quavered, "I just need you to keep talking until I fall asleep."

Kraven crooked his neck to catch a glimpse of Bianca who was hedgehogging into a vulnerable pouch of blankets. His face softened like melting cheese. "Sure," he coughed. "So it's a smallish town. Compact. Friendly. A little bit touristy during high season. It's basically got everything you need like any regular town. Lots of live bait shops. A general store with an ample supply of firewood."

"Is there a blacksmith?"

"No blacksmith."

"That's disappointing."

"It's not that kind of town."

"Sorry, I misunderstood."

"No worries."

"Do you like Huntsville?"

"Sure. Do you like Toronto?"

"It's my whole world."

"What's it like?"

"Busy."

"What else?"

"What else is there?"

"What do you mean?"

"I like being busy," Bianca sighed. "I don't know how to be anything else."

Silence.

"Do you think I'm weird?" Bianca asked quietly.

"You know I do," Kraven smirked.

In a huff, Bianca buried her head under the comforter.

CHAPTER THIRTY-SEVEN
(DAY 26 IN ALGONQUIN PARK)

The fervent knock at the door did not awaken Bianca. Spot-lit by the pale, yellow, morning sunlight, Bianca lay in bed with her arms splayed like a postmodern sculpture. A strand of hair stiffened from last night's saliva strung through her open mouth. Kraven's bare arm lay protectively over her body like fallen timber as he slept with his face buried in her mop of black hair.

The knock became louder.

After a tense pause, the door was shouldered open and into the cabin burst Trudy, Tucker and Lizbeth. They all gasped melodramatically when they saw Bianca and Kraven entwined in a pretzel of sleep. The gasp startled Bianca who awoke with a screech when she discovered Kraven's arm draped over her. The screech suddenly woke Kraven who instantly jolted into a sitting position. Bianca reactively pummeled Kraven in the face with a pillow, causing feathers to explode everywhere.

"What in the hell are you doing in my bed!" Bianca screamed shrilly at Kraven, who was spitting feathers out of his mouth.

"It's my bed!"

"We had an arrangement!" Bianca squeaked, pointing an accusing finger in Kraven's face. "You violated the arrangement!"

"Would you calm down?"

"What's with the arm, Romeo?" Bianca demanded. "I can press all kinds of charges for this!"

"I instinctively splay my arm over the pillow to my left!" Kraven defended himself with a growl. "I can't be held accountable for what my arm does while I'm asleep!"

"What were you doing in the bed in the first place?" Bianca asked, pulling the covers securely around her collarbone.

"You were twitching and whimpering in your sleep!"

"My reasons for that are none of your business!"

"How could I just let you lie there when you were clearly distraught?"

"Did I *say* I was distraught?" Bianca said, lunging. "Did I imply in any way that I wanted your arm on me?"

"You were crying in your sleep!" Kraven lunged back. "Crying about cats!"

"People don't cry about cats!" Bainca argued. "That's not what they do!"

"You clearly needed comfort, albeit unconsciously!"

"Unless I literally cried out to you for help..."

"You did actually."

"What?" Bianca said with a confused squint.

"You said my name," Kraven explained. "Sobbing. Several times."

"I would never..."

Bianca and Kraven discovered Trudy, Tucker and Lizbeth blinking at them intensely from the foot of the bed.

"Oh my god," Bianca moaned.

"Are we interrupting something?" Trudy asked politely.

"What are you all doing here?" Kraven asked, quickly putting on a shirt.

"We've been looking everywhere for you," Trudy quavered, collecting Bianca in her arms. "Ralph, Larry and Sid – those are three of the fishermen, in case you're unaware - were waiting for us at the water taxi first thing this morning and told us what happened last night. We knocked on all the cabin doors, trying to find you, Dear. Are you okay? Let me check you for injuries."

"I'm fine," Bianca said, repossessing her elbow from Trudy's inquisitive hands.

"What happened?" Tucker asked. "The Fox Hole is completely gone."

"I don't want to talk about it," Bianca said, limply waving the question away with her hand.

"How did um..." Tucker mumbled, nodding towards the bed, "*this* happen?"

"It makes no sense for her to stay anywhere else," Kraven explained curtly. "I'm the only singleton around here, minus the spawn of Vincent Price two doors down."

"The two of you," Tucker said numbly, "... are..."

"I don't have a lot of options," Bianca complained.

"Folks are telling us Kraven here saved your life," Lizbeth said, smacking her gum nervously.

Bianca blinked at Kraven.

"The important thing is you're safe," Trudy said, wiping her brow with a lacy handkerchief. "Cabins can be replaced but..."

"Where's Jedd?" Bianca asked, looking around. "The four of you always go together like extremely wholesome, apocalyptic horsemen."

Trudy, Tucker and Lizbeth all looked at each other, faces drooping like those of basset hounds.

"He's outside," Trudy choked. "At the Fox Hole."

***

Wrapping herself in one of Kraven's flannel shirts, Bianca traipsed outside and found Jedd, standing by the ashen foundation of the Fox Hole cabin with his hands in his pockets. He was expressionless and did not appear to be blinking. Bianca tentatively approached and put a hand on Jedd's shoulder. He stood motionless like a numb statue.

"Jedd..." Bianca tried.

"It's all gone," Jedd said, finally blinking.

"Oh Jedd," Bianca's voice cracked.

"I..." Jedd stammered. "I just can't believe it."

"I can't tell you how sorry I am," Bianca said, fluttering tears away with her eyelashes.

"It was the very first cabin my daddy built, seventy-one years ago," Jedd said, wiping his nose with his sleeve. "I was six. Maybe seven years old..."

Bianca pursed her lips tightly.

"I helped him," Jedd continued with teary eyes. "In my way. I handed him the nails. Brought him lemonade on the hot days. He gave me a little paintbrush so I could help him paint the logs. That's why the low spots were a little messy."

"I did notice that, actually," Bianca sniffled.

"Great Grandpa carved that bear inside."

"He did?" Bianca asked sentimentally.

"Auntie Myrtle painted the moose on the wall," Jedd said with his voice cracking. "She was a raw talent, she was. Never even had one art lesson. We were so proud of her."

Bianca squeezed her eyes shut.

"There was just..." Jedd said, lowering his head reverently, "there was just so much of *me* in there, you know? My daddy. My identity. Gone. Poof. Just like that."

"Maybe we can fix it," Bianca tried feebly.

Jedd slowly turned his head to face Bianca, stared at her for a lingering moment before chuckling despite of himself. "You are a treasure."

"I really am sorry."

"It wasn't your fault," Jedd said, pulling Bianca in for a hug.

"It was, sort of."

"Hmm?"

"I accidentally toilet papered the teepee."

Jedd blinked.

"I didn't know," Bianca insisted.

"I'm not sure I want to know what you're talking about, Dear," Jedd said with a brave smile. "But I'm sure it was just an accident."

"It was my own stupidity," Bianca said. "I was cold. I was too proud to ask for help. So I..."

"You are not stupid," Jedd said, gripping Bianca's arms and looking directly at her. His eyes were moist and red with emotion. "You are a good girl," he said firmly. "A little lost and confused sometimes. But you have a good heart and that's what counts."

Bianca's lips parted. "I... I don't know..."

"Nobody is blaming you for the fire."

"But..."

"You listen here, girl," Jedd said in a grandfatherly tone. "When we got word that your cabin suddenly burst into flames, we were worried to death that we lost you…"

"Jedd…"

"When we came running to find you this morning, the cabin was the last thing on our minds. We just wanted to hug you so bad."

Bianca's face crinkled with emotion. She shook her head. "I don't deserve…"

"You do."

"Jedd, I…"

"Shhh, none of that matters."

"Jedd," Bianca sobbed into Jedd's chest. "I… I lost your walking stick. With the bear. The one your great grandfather…"

"No," Jedd croaked soothingly.

"What?"

Jedd pulled out the walking stick from seemingly nowhere.

"How?" Bianca asked, cocking her head.

"I found it in the debris," Jedd winked.

"But…"

"Figures, don't it," Jedd smiled toothily. "This here stick survived a tornado, a couple of wars, a random sinkhole, three and a half basement floods, an outbreak of basswood fungus, an accidental trip to a dump in Haliburton, an infestation of termites, the infamous blizzard of 1966, an unfortunate septic mishap and one very determined beaver. Now it survived a fire. You know what I think?" Jedd winked. "I think this here stick brings with it, good luck."

"Jedd..."

"Take it," Jedd insisted.

"I shouldn't be trusted with something so special," Bianca snuffed. "I accidentally set things on fire."

Jedd put the stick firmly in Bianca's hand and gleamed. "It's for you."

CHAPTER THIRTY-EIGHT

Gripping the intricate handle of Jedd's walking stick, Bianca ambled towards the main lodge, not in any great hurry for breakfast. She was neither hungry nor unhungry. She was merely listless. Having lost track of Kraven after her talk with Jedd, Bianca felt a tugging dread of being alone. Narrowly escaping Dante's inferno will do that to a person.

It wasn't until she approached the now familiar lodge that she realized something. The one downside to seeking company would be facing the meddlesome faces of folks who were most likely discussing Bianca's lapse of judgment concerning toilet paper. Not to mention the swirling gossip that was sure to be filling the lodge after discovering herself and shirtless Kraven in a questionable contortion that morning.

Barely inside the lodge door, Bianca's cheeks were smooshed between the hands of Trudy who was cupping her face like an indulgent mother.

"You are so loved," Trudy said evenly.

"I'm fine, Trudy," Bianca said in a squishy voice, feeling somewhat like a panini sandwich.

"We are all here for you," Trudy added.

"I know," Bianca replied. "May I please just..."

After liberating herself from Trudy's overzealous squish, Bianca avoided eye contact with literally everyone in the room as she headed for the table. She winced when she heard Lizbeth's gum smack in a more empathetic way than usual. She swerved to avoid Jedd when the kitchen's saloon doors squeaked open. No doubt everyone would want to make her feel better about the fire, but Bianca was not feeling up to such emotional banter. It took all the nerve she had to show up for breakfast in the first place.

Suddenly, a cold, bony hand gripped Bianca's wrist tightly as she passed table four.

"Did you see it?" the cadaverous teenager said ominously.

"What?" Bianca asked, bewildered.

"Death," the teenager whisper-hissed.

Bianca shook her head in a way that was both circular and interrogative.

"Last night," the teenager pleaded. "In the fire. Was it coming for you? Did it emerge from an ambiguous portal? Was it carrying a sickle? Did you fear it or were you oddly compelled? Was it gendered? Did it tell you its name? I always imagined its name to be Arnold. Did it mention me at all?"

"No death," Bianca said. "Sorry."

"Dammit, Arnold," the teenager pouted as Bianca shook herself free of his grasp.

Exhaling like a relieved balloon, Bianca hastily took a seat at Kraven's table with Jedd's walking stick still gripped tightly in her hand.

Kraven's eyebrow triangulated, his mouth stopping mid-chew.

"That was intense," Bianca breathed, feeling around the tabletop for a menu. "What's on today? Saskatoon berry pancakes?"

Kraven blinked.

"Did you see this?" Bianca asked obliviously, showcasing Jedd's walking stick. "Jedd found his walking stick in the debris."

"Unreal," Kraven droned ethereally.

"Right?" Bianca said, feeling the intricacy of the bear carving. "It's some kind of deranged, rural miracle. I felt absolutely sick about... well, everything. So many things that were lost in that cabin weren't just *things,* you know? It honestly hadn't occurred to me how much this place means to Jedd and the others. I thought it was just a gross little shack."

Kraven squinted curiously.

"Look at it though," Bianca said, thumbing the bear's detailed fur. "Someone made this with their hands. Jedd wants me to have it, despite... He thinks it brings good luck. Why do you suppose he thinks I need good luck?"

"You're sitting at my table," Kraven suddenly stated the obvious.

A sudden silence swallowed Bianca as she realized every eye in the room was bulging like a ping-pong ball and goggling at her. Every fork had stopped in tableau.

Bianca blinked. "I... I am fully aware."

"What does this mean?" Kraven asked.

"It means nothing," Bianca laughed nervously. "I just... forgot myself for a minute."

Kraven leaned back in his chair, relishing.

"Look," Bianca said primly. "This morning has all been kind of a blur. I didn't want to be accosted by people feeling sorry for me today. And I didn't want to talk to anyone about the events of last night..."

"So you sat at my table and started talking to me," Kraven observed sardonically.

"I'm delusional, okay? I almost died."

"Your table is over there if you'd rather eat alone."

Bianca bit her lip.

"You don't want to be alone," Kraven said, squinting his left eye.

Bianca slowly shook her head.

"Understandable," Kraven sighed before loading his mouth with a forkful of pancake.

"I can't just get up and move to my table now," Bianca stammered. "It would seem conspicuous."

"Nobody said you had to," Kraven shrugged.

Bianca nodded awkwardly. She had become so accustomed to defending herself, she was unsure of how to communicate with Kraven when he was being agreeable. She gawked stupidly for an awkward amount of time.

"People are staring," Bianca finally blurted.

"Meh," Kraven said.

"You don't care what people think?" Bianca asked. "About us sitting together? Finding us together this morning?"

"Let them think what they want," Kraven shrugged. "Besides, what would you care? You're just stuck here for a few more weeks before you disintegrate into the city, never to be seen again. I, on the other hand, return every summer."

"Disintegrate..."

"Come September, you're never going to see these people again, Toronto. Why does their opinion of you matter?"

A stinging tear surprised Bianca. She mashed it back into place with her palm.

"What's going on with you, Toronto?"

"My eyes are still irritated from the smoke..."

"Are you starting to like it here?"

"Shut up."

"Maybe there's an Algonquin girl hiding in there somewhere."

"Eew."

"A little fresh air never hurt anyone."

"I am genetically predisposed to inhale toxic fumes."

"Seriously?"

"Fresh air gives me anxiety attacks."

"Fresh air," Kraven said, making his fingers walk across the table before cupping Bianca's hand in his. "*That's* what gives you anxiety?"

Bianca pulled her hand away frantically as though she had just stuck a wet finger in an electrical socket.

Kraven smirked.

"You are so awkward," Kraven observed.

Bianca stiffened indignantly. "I have more social graces than everyone here combined."

"Do you even have any friends?"

"Yes!" Bianca announced with a raised index finger. "I do! Would you like me to list them?"

"Other than at the office."

Bianca silently swore but then perked up, clapping her hands together in revelation. "I do!"

"Name?"

"Brenden."

"Really."

"I'm not making him up."

"Who is Brenden?" Kraven asked, using air quotes.

"He's... this guy in my building," Bianca explained. "My neighbor. He's lived next to me for over five years. We. Talked."

"Tell me about him," Kraven said expectantly, resting his chin on his hands.

"He... has a cat."

"I thought you had a thing about cats."

"I do."

"Then how can you and this Brenden character be friends?" Kraven challenged. "You have an irrational fear of cats."

"I've... never actually met his cat."

"*Why* do you have an irrational fear of cats?"

"It's not an irrational fear. I just... have negative associations with them."

"That makes no sense."

"It does though! Ugh! Okay, look," Bianca hissed. "That's why I'm here, okay? I fell apart a little. Everything fell apart. I was managing a VR project at work. Spent a solid three years on it. We were developing software for cats to use."

"Wait, what?"

"You can't peep a word of this to anyone or I could be banned from the industry indefinitely."

"Software," Kraven blinked. "That *cats* can use."

"Yes."

"Like autonomously."

"Pay attention, Kraven. We were just about to launch a brand of technology..."

"So they use their little paws to manipulate the software by themselves."

"It's cutting edge," Bianca insisted. "Virtual feline companionship."

"Oh my god," Kraven said, trying painfully to suppress laughter. "So like..."

"Yes," Bianca nodded seriously. "It's for cats who have trouble meeting other cats."

Kraven unexpectedly sprayed laughter across the table.

Stoically, Bianca wiped the mist of hilarity from her cheek.

"So it's like *Kitty Tinder*," Kraven joked.

"Don't be daft," Bianca corrected professionally. "The cats aren't pursuing IRL relationships…"

"*IRL relationships,*" Kraven squeaked with laughter.

"The companionship is *virtual.* There is no commitment involved. It's meant as an elaborate enrichment activity."

"Toronto, how are you able to say all this with a straight face?"

"Are you making fun of me?"

"*Cats who have trouble meeting other cats.*"

"It's not funny!" Bianca pouted. "Our competition beat us to it a few days before we were supposed to launch."

"More than one company thought this would be a good idea?" Kraven howled.

"Please take this seriously."

"I'm trying to imagine the series of events that led you to believe that cats would want virtual relationships."

"It was a natural transition," Bianca explained. "My company has been manufacturing virtual companions for seven years."

"For humans?"

"Yes."

"Who would come up with such an asinine…"

"Me," Bianca said smally. "It was my idea."

"Oh," Kraven said, reddening. "Why though?"

"People get lonely, Kraven. It's hard for some people to get out and meet..."

"How does virtual romance even work?"

"It's nuanced."

"No kidding."

"The user gets to program their ideal lover."

"What happens when the user eventually wants some action?"

"It's not all about sex, Kraven. There's a deeply emotional aspect..."

"So a person can emotionally connect to someone who's not real?"

"Some people..."

"What if the hologram wants babies?"

"Obviously you don't want to understand," Bianca said, flustered. "You're not even trying."

"I'm trying very hard, actually."

"You are making jokes about my career," Bianca stammered. "My entire reason for existing."

"But the cats."

"Cats have feelings too!"

"Beckett has feelings," Kraven shrugged. "You haven't gone out of your way to be his friend."

"What reason would I have to..."

"You're bunking with him for the rest of the summer."

Bianca paled.

CHAPTER THIRTY-NINE

"Beckett," Bianca said evenly.

Beckett sat menacingly in an Adirondack chair on the dock, glaring cattishly at Bianca.

"I was going to sit in that Adirondack chair," Bianca said, challenging the cat to a staring contest.

Beckett meowed like a slow, low-pitched fire engine being played on the wrong speed.

"Apparently we have to be friends," Bianca said curtly. "That goes both ways."

The ensuing meow sounded more like a foreboding moo.

"You," Bianca exhaled, "are a cat. You can literally rest your cat butt anywhere. I, on the other hand, need that Adirondack chair. Chairs are human constructs and are therefore redundant to cats."

If cats could grimace, that is exactly what Beckett would have done in that moment.

Looking around paranoidly, Bianca got down to the cat's level and hissed, "Listen, I am trying really hard to love you…"

Unbeknownst to Bianca, Tucker appeared behind her with a rusty, red wagon piled with various items from the tuck shop.

"You have to meet me halfway, you terrifying little weirdo," Bianca continued. "I can't be the only one trying here. We have to make this work, understand? Don't ruin this for me."

Tucker silently cocked his head.

"Don't give me that look, Beckett," Bianca continued. "I didn't plan any of this. I especially didn't plan for *you*. There is no room in my life for a cat right now, but I am willing to make some concessions for the sake of…"

Beckett stretched theatrically, very intentionally showcasing his cat butt in Bianca's direction.

"Wow," Bianca said, shaking her head in disbelief. "That was *subtle*. I figured I could appeal to you, adult to adult about this. I see now that I am the mature one."

Fidgeting agitatedly, Tucker watched Bianca's futile attempts to shove a very obstinate cat from the Adirondack chair. Her grunts systematically made Tucker wince.

"You are completely overreacting," Bianca continued. "Nobody is trying to steal your Kraven… Don't look at me like I'm being irrational. *You* are clearly the irrational one here. I just want… Well, I don't really know what I want because I'm thoroughly bewildered right now. But Kraven… Can you just learn to blend like a normal cat? I'm not trying to replace you. I just want... Kraven is just so..."

Tucker awkwardly cleared his throat.

Bianca spun around, her stomach sinking like quicksand.

"You are having a two-way argument with a cat," Tucker observed dryly.

"Tucker..." Bianca said breathlessly.

"What's going on with Kraven?" Tucker said, tousling his mousy hair.

"What do you mean?"

"The cat," Tucker said, nodding towards Beckett. "You were arguing with a cat over your respective roles in Kraven's life."

"That's not what I was doing," Bianca said stiffly with widening eyes.

"Is that Kraven's cat?"

"Do cats really *belong* to *anyone?*"

"Why is that cat's opinion of you so important?"

"It's not," Bianca stammered. "Obviously."

"Do you want to be that cat's... new mommy?"

"Tucker!"

"I don't know how I feel about this," Tucker mumbled.

"What are you doing here?" Bianca asked quickly, leaping to her feet.

"I was given instructions to offer you ample supplies from the tuck shop," Tucker began, "without being too imposing or overwhelmingly sympathetic about the fire. Because, you know. Triggers."

"Thanks," Bianca said uncertainly. "I'll reimburse you later today."

"No need," Tucker said, raising a hand. "We are here to take care of you... Because of our outstanding customer service policies. Not because of our failure to recognize boundaries."

"Tucker, I should take responsibility," Bianca said. "I should replenish the essentials I lost."

"You lost everything you brought with you to the resort," Tucker said, trying much too hard to stiffen with professionalism. "Everything. You probably don't even have a fresh change of underpants. Your comfort is our responsibility."

"Tucker. Sit," Bianca said, nodding towards the dock, sitting and dipping her feet in the water. Tucker decompressed a little, removed his tattered sneakers and copied her.

"You can't help being imposing and overwhelmingly sympathetic," Bianca offered.

Tucker looked up at Bianca woefully. "How come you're not with Kraven?"

"He locked me out of the cabin," Bianca answered.

Tucker became visibly agitated. "He did what now?"

"Relax, Tucker," Bianca said, teasingly pushing him in the arm. "He didn't release me into the wild to fend for myself. He's just working."

Tucker lolled his eyes upwards towards Kraven's cabin. "Curtains shut? Door locked?"

"Yup," Bianca replied, making ripples in the lake with her toes.

"And you don't mind?" Tucker asked. "Him just leaving you out here? With his weird-ass cat?"

"That's what he came here for," Bianca shrugged. "He's doing me a favor here. I shouldn't just demand his attention. Nor do I need his attention," she added quietly.

"Did you figure out what he's doing in there?"

"How could I possibly know that?" Bianca asked.

"You were in there," Tucker breathed. "In his lair."

"*Lair,*" Bianca chortled. "Knock it off, Tucker."

"What was it like in there?" Tucker asked, nodding towards the Wolf Den.

Bianca shrugged.

"Was it dreary?" Tucker asked ominously.

"Not so much."

"Was there a foul odor?"

"Musky. But otherwise, unremarkable."

"Was it... haunted?"

"Tucker!"

"Did he do anything nefarious?" Tucker pleaded.

"Honestly?" Bianca said. "It was just an underwhelming cabin. Disappointingly average, actually."

"And Kraven?" Tucker said intensely, leaning into Bianca's personal space.

"He was okay."

"Okay?"

"He did his best," Bianca nodded. "Had passable manners. Boring toothpaste. Odd cat. Shirts."

Tucker pursed his lips in disappointment.

"What's going on with you?" Bianca asked. "You're acting weirder than usual."

"I'm good," Tucker twitched.

"Tucker..."

"I'm not supposed to..."

"I won't tell anyone," Bianca promised.

Tucker gulped.

"Summer's halfway done," Tucker shrugged. "Soon things will be changing again."

"In what sense?" Bianca asked obliviously.

Tucker blinked at Bianca. "The days will be getting shorter. The Fox Hole is gone now. Summer guests will be leaving and... getting on with their *real* lives..."

"I'm sure the autumn guests will be..."

"But they're not..." Tucker swallowed.

"Tucker..."

"...you," Tucker finished. "I really get the sense that you are less repelled by me than you once were. I'm growing on you, like a boil. An awkward yet strangely adorable boil."

"Tucker, come on..."

"I'm never going to see you again," Tucker squeaked. "I know everything is dependent on your boss and your ability to acclimate to the outdoors. But you're so feisty and badass. Despite the fact that you've nearly met your demise an alarming number of times, you're going to fight for your job and succeed. Why? Because you're a champion, Bianca. We all know it, me included. We believe in you. And it just sucks, you know? Because the more we set you up for success, the faster you'll slip away from us."

Bianca gaped.

What is he getting at?

Did Tucker actually think I would...

"So much is about to change..."

"Tucker, nothing has changed much around here in seventy-one years."

"That's why it's so scary."

"What are you talking about, Tucker?"

"I... I'm not supposed to talk about it," Tucker winced. "Trudy said so."

"Something's going on," Bianca nodded wisely. "What's happening, Tucker? Is the *Whispering Beaver...*"

"I can't say until we know more."

"... in some kind of trouble?"

"I don't know what's going on," Tucker whimpered. "I honestly don't. It's all happening so fast."

"But everyone here seems so happy."

"We are," Tucker sniffled, "happy."

"If you're struggling..."

"Please don't make me talk about this," Tucker begged. "I'm going to get in trouble."

"Maybe I can..."

"Please," Tucker quavered as he rose to his feet. Lake water dripped down his wan legs, making puddles on the dock. "Trudy's trying really hard to keep a smile on her face. Jedd, it's even harder for him. But we can't let on, see. The other guests – all our regulars – they have no idea. So please just..."

"Tucker, I just want to..."

"You can't," Tucker said, ambling up the hillock without looking back. "You just can't."

CHAPTER FORTY

There was a narrow slit where the green, tweed curtains nearly met in the center of the window. Exploiting this fact, Bianca squinted through the slit, focusing on the murky silhouette of Kraven inside. He was crouched at the desk, his body jerking and fidgeting as he did something ambiguous with an intense fixation.

What is he doing in there?

Behind her, Beckett was gingerly strutting across the porch railing with the finesse of a trapeze artist. Uttering a rumbling meow of warning, the vigilant cat leered disapprovingly at Bianca.

"Shhh," Bianca shushed the cat. "You're going to blow my cover.

Disgruntled, Beckett bopped a flowerpot off the porch railing for no reason.

"Seriously?" Bianca hissed as she made a futile attempt to grapple the stealthy cat from the railing.

Beckett repeatedly slipped from Bianca's pathetic grasps, eventually leaping like a ninja into the air. Bianca looked around stupidly for the cat before falling on her face when Beckett started weaving around her legs.

"For the luvva!..."

FWUUMP!

"You did that on purpose," Bianca whimpered at the cat who clearly did not care.

The screen door suddenly screeched open, revealing a perturbed Kraven. Bianca and Beckett simultaneously looked up at him, doe-eyed and startled.

"Your cat is trying to kill me," Bianca pathetically defended herself.

"What are you doing?" Kraven exhaled.

"Trying to rationalize with your cat," Bianca said, un-mangling herself from the deck. "He clearly takes after you," she mumbled.

"My privacy is nonnegotiable," Kraven said evenly.

"You were in there for a weird amount of time."

"Were you trying to..."

"It was Beckett's idea," Bianca said quickly.

Beckett's eyes turned into slits of ire.

"I need to focus," Kraven droned.

"I get that," Bianca panted. "But you can't just leave me alone all day with your cat. I'm running out of things to talk to him about. And I think he's secretly plotting my demise."

"When inspiration hits," Kraven interjected, "you have to jump on it. There's only a narrow widow of time."

"Inspiration..."

"I have no control over when it happens."

"So you were just suddenly pummeled with inspiration..."

"Last night."

"Last..." Bianca stopped. "... night?"

"Later, Toronto," Kraven said as he was about to close the door.

"Wait!" Bianca pleaded. "Why can't you tell me..."

The door shrieked shut.

***

"Fine, whatever," Bianca said to Beckett, who was for some reason, following her to the tuck shop. "He wants privacy? I can respect that. Regardless of how freaky and sinister he is. Lurking around like a deranged recluse. Doing whatever it is that *Kravens* do. In cabins. Alone. Secretive as a looper moth."

Beckett began to weave between Bianca's legs as she walked. More prepared this time, she stealthily avoided collapse with each aptly timed step.

"You know him better than anyone," Bianca said obliviously to Beckett. "You must know what he does for a living. And why he so sketchy and private about it. Can you at least give me a hint? It's making me crazy."

Beckett mewed rustily.

"What do you think he meant," Bianca asked tentatively, "when he said that he was struck with sudden inspiration last night?"

Beckett looked up at Bianca as though she was literally the stupidest, carbon-based lifeform he had ever met.

"I feel like he was implying something," Bianca pondered. "But I don't want to be presumptuous. Am I being presumptuous?"

Beckett did not care.

"And... you don't care," Bianca sighed. "Because you are a cat. I am talking to a cat. An oddly perceptive cat. But still a cat."

Followed by Beckett, Bianca entered the tuck shop – a feeble cabin with the door propped open. Mosquitos swerved drunkly around the shaded entrance. Bianca waved them away as she stepped inside.

"Hello?" Bianca called to nobody in particular as her voice echoed throughout the empty room.

Beckett immediately found a tattered wingback chair in the corner, jumped on it and started nesting with his claws.

The room was loggy and rustic. A citronella candle was flickering on a makeshift counter. Crooked shelves lined the walls, upon which was an eclectic collection of clothing, toiletries, snacks, camping supplies and souvenirs. One entire wall had ceiling to floor shelving, cramped and sagging from the weight of paperback novels. Bianca blinked at the books.

"Do people actually read?" she whispered down to Beckett. "Is that still a thing?"

As though exasperated, Beckett buried his face in a furry ball of Beckett.

Her curiosity, and perhaps boredom, inspired Bianca to survey the rows of book spines, completely lost without hope in a literary jungle. She had no knowledge of books – especially paper ones. The last book she read was on a tablet six years ago and it was purely technical. But these shelves were oozing with fiction. A genre she could neither identify with nor rationalize. She felt like a little girl perusing an antique shop, reluctant to touch anything for fear of breaking or desecrating something sacred. In a sense, she felt unworthy of taking one off the shelf. She ran her finger over the myriad of book spines, pretending like she knew what she was doing.

Bianca's left eyebrow involuntarily steepled as a little gasp escaped. A lime green book caught her attention, upon which was the indisputable name...

"Kraven Kane?" Bianca mouthed.

Her fingers worked faster than her brain as she unwedged the lime green book from the airtight shelf. In a frenzy, she thumbed through it, the words whirring together like a fuzzy tornado of letters.

"Seriously?" Bianca stage whispered to Beckett.

Bianca suddenly jolted when she heard voices in the next room. There was no door, but rather a campy, plaid curtain offering only meager privacy. She recognized Jedd's mud-crusted boots beneath the curtain, as well as Trudy's obsolete sling-backs. Bianca became deliberately quiet.

"Anything that's in there," Jedd quavered emotionally from behind the curtain, "take it."

"It's not enough, Jedd," Trudy replied stoically. "Besides, you have to consider yourself..."

"This is who I am, Trudy," Jedd said tremulously. His letter S's whistled vulnerably through his prominent teeth. "Whatever it takes..."

"Things were rough before the fire," Trudy said with a crack in her voice, "but now that the Fox Hole is gone..."

Bianca bit her lower lip queasily.

"It's..." Jedd snuffed, "it's my everything."

"I know, Jedd," Trudy replied, "but we have to be realistic here."

"Sweet Jesus, take the wheel," Jedd sobbed.

"Oh Jedd," Trudy sniffled. Her voice suddenly muffled as though she had buried her face into Jedd's chest. "We'll all still have each other. I promise you that."

"My... my daddy," Jedd cried. "Great Grandad..."

"They're up there," Trudy reassured Jedd, "being so proud of you for fighting so hard."

Tears brimmed in Bianca's eyes as she suddenly realized she had forgotten to breathe for a few seconds. The room felt briefly like it was spinning. When the curtain was pushed aside, revealing moist-eyed Jedd, Bianca mashed the tears back into her face and inhaled deeply.

"Bianca," Jedd said, attempting to be jovial.

"Hey, Jedd," Bianca choked. "How are things?"

Jedd blinked, choosing not to answer. Instead, he smiled bravely with his lovable overbite. "What have you got there? A book?"

Discreetly concealing the author's name, Bianca replied, "I'm not much of a reader but I couldn't help but admire your eclectic collection here."

Jedd nodded, pretending to move some papers around the counter.

"Have..." Bianca hesitated, "... have you read any of these books in your inventory?"

"Me?" Jedd chortled. "Nah. My eyes aren't so good. Trudy does all the orders. She knows her books."

Bianca nodded awkwardly. "Is... everything okay, Jedd?"

"Yes!" Jedd said a little too quickly. "Why? Have you heard something?"

"You seem a little off," Bianca said softly.

"We're all a little emotional after what happened last night at the Fox Hole," Jedd coughed.

Bianca bit her lower lip guiltily. "Jedd, if I've caused…"

"Do you have everything you need?" Jedd snuffed, suddenly changing the subject. "Did Tucker swing by with the wagon o'goodies?"

"He did," Bianca replied.

"Did we forget anything?" Jedd asked. "Do you have enough socks?"

"You don't have to worry about me, Jedd."

"If we forgot anything," Jedd added, "just pick out whatever you want from the tuck shop. It's on us."

Bianca swallowed. "I think I should purchase my own…"

"Nonsense," Jedd guffawed.

"Jedd, are you sure everything is okay?" Bianca asked. "I'm sensing that something is wrong and that I might have something to do with it."

Exhaling slowly, Jedd replied, "It's not my place to say."

"What do you mean it's not your place to say?" Bianca persisted. "This whole place is literally yours. This place wouldn't even be here without you. It's more your place to say than anyone else."

"Trudy is taking care of things," Jedd breathed. "She's good at that. Tucker, Lizbeth and I? We're here to take care of you."

Bianca blinked.

"Would you like to take that book?" Jedd asked.

CHAPTER FORTY-ONE

As she ambled back to the Wolf Den, Beckett in tow, Bianca got a glimpse of Kraven rummaging through the rusty wagon of merch. Fumbling, Bianca tucked her lime green novel out of sight.

"What's all this?" Kraven called over to Bianca. He raised an eyebrow at Beckett who was following Bianca pertly with his tail in the air.

"Tucker brought it," Bianca called back. "Are you finally finished colluding evildoings in obscurity?"

"For today," Kraven said dryly, examining a cured sausage he scavenged from the wagon. "Why did he bring cured sausage? And underpants?"

"Because of the fire," Bianca explained. "They wanted to replace the things I lost."

"You lost your cured sausage?"

"And my dijonnaise potato salad, apparently."

Kraven pulled out a checkered picnic blanket. "They thought of everything, didn't they?"

Bianca shrugged.

"Do you feel like eating at the lodge tonight?"

Bianca fidgeted.

"What's going on, Toronto?"

"I don't know," Bianca said quietly. "Nobody will tell me anything."

"What?"

Bianca shrugged.

"Okay, you're being weird," Kraven began, "so I'm going to make an executive decision and do up a picnic with all the perishable items in this wagon."

"A... picnic?"

"Do you have an aversion to picnics, Toronto?"

"No, it's just..." Bianca trailed off as she noticed a sorbet colored sunset illuminating Kraven from behind. He looked magical. Which gave Bianca flu-like symptoms.

But the picnic blanket had already been spread across the pine-needled ground.

***

Things got weird. As Bianca stared at Beckett licking mustard from Kraven's knuckles, she had a wrenching feeling. Kraven was a writer of fiction. A prolific one, as indicated by the scads of Kraven Kane books in the tuck shop inventory. For some deranged reason, Kraven was going to ridiculous measures to prevent Bianca, or anyone else for that matter, from finding out about his occupation. Why? Why was it such an elaborate secret? Bianca struggled with the fact that she knew something she shouldn't know. Should she say something? Would he freak out? Bianca wasn't sure how long she could endure the tugging sensation she had in her chest. It seemed devious to keep this from Kraven. She could almost taste the dishonesty in her mouth. It tasted like curdling chocolate milk.

"You come here every year?" Bianca finally said before awkwardly forking a mound of potato salad into her mouth.

"Yep," Kraven replied after taking a substantial swig of hibiscus lemonade. "Easier to work out here where it's remote and quiet."

Bianca nodded greenly. "Easier to focus, no doubt," she added.

"Much," Kraven said. "I'm thinking about making a permanent move here. Live here year-round."

"Really?" Bianca said, pretending to be engrossed in the ambiguity of his career.

"This cabin has a good energy," Kraven explained. "Much more inspirational than my flat above that sketchy strip plaza."

"You… talk a lot about inspiration."

"Everyone needs inspiration," Kraven shrugged. "I'm much more productive here. Might as well make this my official home."

"Have you..." Bianca began, giving pause before finishing. "...looked into whether or not there will even be a cabin for you after the summer?"

"They always keep the Wolf Den free for me," Kraven shrugged. "I'm a regular. They give regulars priority."

"Right, but maybe the Wolf Den won't be... available."

"What do you mean?"

Bianca inhaled deeply. "Have you heard anything about what's going on with Jedd and the others?" she asked quickly.

"*What do you mean*?" Kraven asked, suddenly shifting with concern.

"Something's happening," Bianca said. "They don't want to tell me, but I just know."

"Toronto..."

"Tucker was rambling about things changing. Jedd and Trudy were getting all emotional behind the curtain..."

"I haven't heard anything."

"Yes, but you're antisocial."

Kraven narrowed his eyes.

"I think the fire is causing them more problems than they are letting on," Bianca quavered.

"Are you sure?"

"I can't stand it," Bianca said, squeezing her eyes shut. "I'm really struggling with the fact that I may have... They are the closest thing to a..."

Kraven's eyes widened.

"... I've never really had a real..." Bianca tried again.

"Is your family not close?" Kraven asked boldly.

"What?" Bianca asked with a look of indigestion.

"Did you all drift apart after you mom passed?"

"Wait, what?" Bianca asked. "My mom's not dead."

"Oh..." Kraven said, perplexed. "I thought you said... that time by the campfire..."

"You misunderstood."

"Sorry," Kraven said, rapidly blushing.

"It's just... I'm overwhelmed by how intense everyone is around here."

"They are deeply caring people."

"I know," Bianca said, flustered. "They are just so... involved. It's making me question..."

"What's the deal with your family?"

"Why do you keep talking about my family?"

"Let's see," Kraven said, stroking his chin stubble ponderingly. "You talk about your mom like she's dead, but she's not. You have no emergency contact number. You are thoroughly confused when people genuinely want to help you..."

"I can take care of myself," Bianca said primly. "I always have. That's how I was raised. To be self-sufficient."

"It all makes sense now," Kraven nodded. "Why your birthday dropped off your radar."

"Stop it."

"Nobody has ever made you a birthday cake."

"Carbs," Bianca said defensively. "Because I don't consume carbs."

"Does your family even know you're here?"

Bianca silenced, gaping at a devilled egg in a stupor of denial.

"They sound like a-holes."

"You don't understand," Bianca pleaded. "My family are not bad people. They're just busy."

"Busy."

"I come from a family of professionals," Bianca explained. "We are an I.T. family. We understand that each of us has demands on our time."

"So they don't have time to be a family?"

"You're not paying attention. We love each other. We just express it differently."

"Where was your family when you unraveled at work after the cat catastrophe?"

"I... I don't know."

"Oh my god."

"Don't read into things!" Bianca said desperately. "I know it probably looks bad, but we support each other in our way."

"Just not in the form of actual support."

"We support each other by not imposing on each other's time."

"Because you're busy."

"Now you're getting it."

"So your mom raised you to believe that being busy is a badge of honor, and that a person's worth is measured by how little spare time they have?"

"My mom... didn't raise me," Bianca said with her voice drifting away like a gentle breeze.

"What the actual f..." Kraven began, shifting in preparation to defend Bianca from an imaginary assailant.

"Don't judge her," Bianca scolded. "She had to make a decision."

"Did she walk out on you?" Kraven said with a rumble of thunder deep in his chest.

"It's not like that," Bianca explained. "I can understand her reasoning. She was just so busy..."

"Too busy to be a mom?"

"You don't understand. Having my brother Chad was a real blow to her career. See, I wasn't planned. So when I came along..."

"She walked out on you."

"Stop saying that!" Bianca quavered. "You're making me question my entire childhood and sense of normalcy."

"Jaysus, Toronto. You didn't even have a fair chance to be a normal person."

"I know but... what's that supposed to mean?"

"This explains why the notion of being loved traumatizes you."

"That's a gross exaggeration," Bianca argued. "It's just that I'm not used to the way things work around here. I'm not used to being taken care of. Accepted. Having everyone so invested in my happiness and success. I think I might like it a little and that confuses me."

"Oh Toronto..."

"I'm just starting to question everything, you know?" Bianca sniffled. "I thought I was a confident, poised and eloquent professional. But being here has made me realize that outside of my office context, I'm nothing but a cumbersome misfit, devoid of any veritable social skills. It's humbling. And utterly humiliating. I've lost myself."

Kraven swallowed conspicuously. "We're all misfits around here. I think that's why everyone at the lodge empathizes with each other so deeply."

"They are possibly the only people who have ever understood me," Bianca moaned. "And I think I may have decimated their lives."

Kraven's facial features softened as he watched Bianca blink her pinkening eyes. He edged his way closer to her on the picnic blanket his arm was touching hers. Bianca looked up at him, her eyes pooling with tears.

"It was an accident," he crooned sandpaperishly.

"I think I've thrust them into some kind of financial calamity," Bianca sniffled. "Do you think it's possible that I singlehandedly took out the *Whispering Beaver*?"

"You're being awfully hard on yourself," Kraven offered.

"They are such kind people," Bianca heaved.

"They are," Kraven droned softly.

"And I've ruined them," Bianca heaved. "My stupidity astonishes me sometimes."

"Hey," Kraven said, lifting Bianca's chin and directly locking eyes with her. "Nobody said you were stupid."

"Tell that to my..." Bianca stopped herself abruptly, biting her lower lip until it whitened.

"You have an intriguing mind," Kraven droned, placing a stray lock of black hair neatly behind Bianca's ear.

"Right," Bianca snuffed sarcastically. "You said yourself my idea for virtual cat companionship was daft."

"Maybe I just don't understand your brand of genius."

Bianca sprayed out a sudden, explosive laugh. "You're laying it on a bit thick there, Krave."

"I like you," Kraven said evenly.

"No you don't."

"Why would you say that?"

"For starters, you refuse to call me by my actual name."

"Because you've never told me your name."

Bianca blinked.

All this time and I've never once told him my name?

Dammit.

"Bianca," Bianca said almost inaudibly. "It's Bianca."

Kraven mouthed the word *Bianca*.

CHAPTER FORTY-TWO
(DAY 27 IN ALGONQUIN PARK)

Her eyes were still shut. But Bianca could sense the early morning sun through her closed eyelids. Her sleep had been deep, but it swirled with trippy dreams about her teeth falling out, freefalling while naked, being chased by a homicidal cassowary, Kraven saying that he likes her and being slowly eaten alive by worms.

He likes me.

What does that even mean?

Apparently, Bianca did not know what this meant. Kraven told her directly that he was fond of her. It made sense, really. Seeing as how he ran into a fire to save her. Ventured into the wilderness in search of her mangled body when he thought she fell in a gorge. Caught her when she fell flailing from a Douglas fir. Saved her from drowning when the canoe capsized. Anonymously took care of her for ten days when she injured her ankle. Took her in when she had no place to go. I mean honestly, the fact that Kraven even had to directly declare his fondness seemed a little redundant in retrospect.

Okay, I get it.

He likes me.

He... likes me.

So why am I so afraid to open my eyes?

Pretending to be asleep was feeling more and more awkward the longer Bianca laid there in Kraven's bed. She was feeling just a little too secure, wrapped in the tangle of sheets. The cabin was eerily silent. What could Kraven be doing? Sleeping? Silently undressing? Using the toilet? Staring at her like a psycho while she slept?

Opening only one eye, Bianca remained completely still and eyeballed the room. No Kraven. Stretching cattishly, Bianca scoured the room. Kraven was slumped, sound asleep, facedown at the desk. He was impossibly still. Curious, Bianca emerged from the bed and lurched towards the desk, noticing scads of paper, askew. Scrunched-up paper adorned the desk, strewn everywhere like forgotten snowballs. Bianca gingerly picked up a paper ball and tried to un-scrunch it, but the crinkly sound made her reconsider.

Beneath Kraven's sleeping head was a piece of paper, scrawled with frantic writing. Bianca angled her head to get a glimpse of what Kraven had been scribbling. She could only see the upper, left corner of the page as the rest was weighted down by Kraven's cementlike jaw. But the one thing that caught Bianca's attention that was indisputable, was her name. Obscured only vaguely by a puddle of sleep drool, the word *Bianca* was etched shamelessly on the page. It was written on the page several times, in fact.

A squirt of adrenaline surged through Bianca's body as she desperately tried to read the other, less conspicuous words. The only way she could see what he wrote about her would be to somehow unwedge the paper from under Kraven's rugged jaw. Without waking him of course. She gave the paper a little tug, but Kraven's stubborn head kept the page anchored in its place. A second tug tore the paper. Bianca startled, silently waving her hands in a futile attempt to shush the paper.

In the corner, Bianca spotted Beckett batting around a scrunched-up ball of paper. He rolled onto his back, fluttering his paws around the ball and using his teeth to unravel it. Bianca's eyes widened.

"Beckett," Bianca stage-whispered. "Give me the paper."

Beckett kept the ball of paper firmly secured with his teeth and front paws, kicking his back legs in a flutteringly playful way.

"I'm serious, Beckett," Bianca hissed quietly. "Give. Me. The. Paper."

Suddenly possessed by the spirits of his hunter ancestors, Beckett viciously attacked the ball of paper, sinking his teeth into it like a thirsty vampire bat. His pupils were frighteningly dilated as he clawed psychotically with all fours. Satisfied that his kill was successful, Beckett flattened his floofy cat body atop the paper, claiming his prey. Or perhaps suffocating it for good measure.

"Beckett," Bianca pleaded while pulling the paper out from under the obstinate cat. "I'm pretty sure it's dead now. Just give it."

With a rusty mew of objection, Beckett unwillingly surrendered the paper to Bianca, who read the tattered page with a thumping heart.

She paled.

Her jaw dropped.

Oh my god. It's...

"Hey!" Kraven bellowed.

Gasping, Bianca spun around and found Kraven giving her the *lumberjack death stare.*

"I didn't..." Bianca stammered, pointlessly hiding the paper behind her back.

"That's private!" Kraven roared, grabbing the paper from a very startled Bianca. "I told you, my privacy is nonnegotiable!"

"I know..." Bianca tried. "It's just... I saw my name?"

"No, you didn't," Kraven groaned, tearing scads of paper into shreds.

"Kraven, stop!"

"I ask you for one thing!" Kraven quavered. "I do *everything* for you and the only thing I ask in return is your respect... that you respect..."

"Kraven, I know you're a writer!"

"You... you do?"

Bianca sheepishly revealed the lime green novel she was hiding under her pillow. "I found it in the tuck shop. I found about a dozen of your books there."

Flustered, Kraven plunked onto the couch, tangling his fingers anxiously through his hair.

"Are you famous?" Bianca asked guiltily.

"Extremely," Kraven said with his face in his hands.

"Why on earth would you want to keep this a secret?"

"This is the only place I can go where people leave me alone," Kraven said, his voice muffled from behind his hands. "I just come here and disappear for a while. I'm recognized everywhere I go. Even in Hunstiville I'm ambushed. I'm a local celebrity and everyone there is damn proud to have a homegrown writer. Here, I just keep a low profile and up until now, I've avoided being recognized."

"Kraven..."

"I just want some peace," Kraven moaned. "I don't like being famous. It's a colossal imposition on my privacy. I want to be normal."

"So nobody around here knows who you are?"

"Trudy knows," Kraven explained. "She's been doing her best not to blow my cover. Jedd doesn't read. Lizbeth isn't really the literary type. Tucker isn't too bright so it's not hard keeping a secret from him. I had a decent run for a while. But I guess the beans were bound to spill sooner or later."

"Are you writing... about me?"

"That's personal," Kraven grunted, frantically scavenging paper from around the room."

"You snogged me," Bianca argued. "You keep rescuing my ass like a freaking superhero. You haven't exactly been discreet this whole time about how you feel..."

"This is different," Kraven snarled. "You can't see this until...the writing process is raw..."

"What did you say about me?"

Kraven twisted in agitation.

"Did you say anything defamatory?" Bianca asked nervously. "Am I naked? Oh god, I'm naked in the book aren't I."

"See, this is why I didn't tell you..."

"You really should have asked for my permission Kraven. Especially if I'm naked."

"What kind of an off-color book do you think this is?"

"I don't know!" Bianca squeaked. "You won't tell me!"

"It's not literally you," Kraven sighed. "It's a literary adaptation of you?"

"Why though?"

"I couldn't help it," Kraven muttered. "I was stumped this year. My publisher wanted a manuscript submitted by September and I thought I was toast. The ideas just weren't flowing the way they used to. Then when you showed up..."

"You became obsessed with me."

"Inspired," Kraven grunted. "The word is inspired."

Bianca squinted interrogatively.

"When you're around," Kraven inhaled, "I get pummeled with ideas. Thousands of them. I can't explain why. It just happens."

Bianca reddened.

"Then yesterday when you told me your name," Kraven exhaled, "it was like *BAM.* That's it. That's the detail my new story was missing. The rhythm. The cadence. The word just fit so perfectly and poetically in the story."

Bianca gaped.

"I don't know what to say," Bianca said softly. "I'm not really sure what I did to deserve..."

"Everyone deserves to be loved," Kraven said evenly.

Bianca swallowed hard.

Love?

Is that what this is?

Holy sh...

CHAPTER FORTY-THREE

It was slightly less awkward eating breakfast with Kraven at the lodge that morning. To switch things up a bit, they decided to eat at Bianca's table this time. Best not to risk getting stuck in a rut. By this time, they had grown accustomed to the whispers and giggles from surrounding tables, along with the voyeuristic stares. Honestly, you would think nobody had ever seen a man and a woman eat chocolate chip waffles together.

Wait a minute, waffles?

"Since when do you eat carbohydrates?" Kraven asked, liberally pouring local maple syrup over his waffles. "I thought you avoided carbohydrates."

"A girl can change her mind," Bianca said, carving a delicate triangle from the corner of her waffle.

"I thought carbs didn't agree with you."

"It was more of a matter of *me* not agreeing with *them*," Bianca explained. "As it happens, I find carbohydrates surprisingly unoffensive. Maybe it's true what they say about riboflavin."

When Lizbeth approached, she was all smiles and moist eyes. Bianca noticed that she smacked her gum with slightly less verve.

"Want me to go ahead and top up that maple syrup Mr. Kane?" Lizbeth quavered bravely.

"Lizbeth?" Bianca said hoarsely.

"We have blueberry sauce if you prefer," Lizbeth muttered emotionally as she started for the kitchen. "How's about I just go and get some?"

"Lizbeth, wait!" Bianca pleaded.

It was too late. Lizbeth had already swooshed through the saloon doors into the kitchen. Without hesitation, Bianca dashed into the kitchen behind her. Bianca grasped her wrist as Lizbeth attempted to sob into the sink.

"What's going on?" Bianca asked.

"Everything's good!" Lizbeth said cheerily with tears and snot gushing from every orifice in her face.

"Something is going on around here," Bianca said assertively. "And all of you suck at hiding it from me."

"I've been given my orders..."

"When is someone around here going to be honest with me?" Bianca squeaked. "Lizbeth, I know you guys are struggling and that it's all my fault. Can you just..."

"Did I ever tell you about the time Leonard Cohen stayed in the Shimmering Otter cabin?" Lizbeth said stoically. "He was a barrel of monkeys, he was."

"Lizbeth, please knock it off with the nostalgic tangents," Bianca begged. "I really need to know what's going on. Maybe I..."

"Or was it Gord Downie?" Lizbeth pondered. "It was an iconic, Canadian singer, either way..."

"Lizbeth!" Bianca shrieked.

Lizbeth exhaled and looked around the kitchen suspiciously. "Okay. I don't see any moles so it should be okay."

"Who in the world would be spying on you right now?" Bianca moaned.

"No," Lizbeth explained. "I mean actual moles. Those ugly little critters freak me out. They're always sneaking into the kitchen and violating our health and safety code. One time I found one wallowing in a bag of cornstarch. And sometimes we find their little footprints in the margarine."

Bianca repeatedly thwacked her head against a countertop in frustration.

"*The Elusive Moose!*" Lizbeth blurted, right before gasping and covering her mouth.

Bianca squinted at Lizbeth, dumbfounded.

"I've said too much," Lizbeth said gravely. "I must go now."

"The only thing that is elusive around here..." Bianca argued.

"Fine, okay," Lizbeth warbled. "I'll spill. But you have to promise not to tell the others I told you, eh?"

Bianca nodded certainly.

"'Kay, here goes," Lizbeth swallowed. "See, there's been talk about a massive, luxury resort opening up across the lake."

"The Elusive Moose?"

"Shhhh," Lizbeth hissed. "Don't let anyone hear you say that. I'm not supposed to tell you about this. Anyhow, *The Elusive Moose* is still in the planning stages, but it's been on our radar for a couple of years now. Thing is, we don't turn much of a profit around here. *The Whispering Beaver* only has nine cabins and they've never been updated. We just scrape by with the loyalty of our regulars. And since we lost the Fox Hole... well, that's one less cabin and we just can't afford to lose the revenue. And the cost of rebuilding is just not realistic for us."

"Oh my god," Bianca choked.

"We work so hard to keep our doors open every year," Lizbeth continued. "We've been surviving on passion, faith and well, each other I guess. All of us here, we live for this place. It's our world. I don't know what's going to happen to us when..."

"You're worried you won't be able to compete with a monster resort," Bianca guessed.

"They'll squash us," Lizbeth warbled. "Like a harmless and freakishly cute spider. They're talking about making the place twenty stories high with a jacuzzi tub on every balcony. Luxury suites. Room service. Full-on spa. Three onsite restaurants featuring international, Michelin chefs. I mean, Jedd may not be so good with flavors, but he puts a lot of heart into his casseroles. It's not even fair."

"But what about your brand?" Bianca offered.

"Sorry, our what?"

"Your brand," Bianca explained. "This place has history in its favor. It's eco-friendly. Is this other place off the grid?"

"No way," Lizbeth said, earnestly shaking her head. "That horrible place will suck up all the electricity from here to the Kawarthas. Especially if they follow through on that flashy casino they're talking about building. It'll undo all the efforts we've been making over here, reducing our carbon footprint."

"I just think you guys have a legitimate brand that is bound to resonate..."

"I'm sorry, girl," Lizbeth said, perplexed. "I don't know what you're talking about when you get all corporate like this. I just work hard and try to be kind to people. That's all I know about business."

"But *The Elusive Moose*..." Bianca began.

"How does she know about *The Elusive Moose?*" Jedd said with surprising gruffness as he stood prominently in the kitchen doorway.

"Oh gosh," Lizbeth said nervously. "Jedd, it just kind of slipped out. Bianca here can be very persuasive."

"Yes," Jedd nodded gravely. "Persuasion is one of our girl's finest talents. But we had an agreement."

"I know Jedd," Lizbeth said, forlorn. "I just couldn't stand it anymore. Pretending like nothing is wrong. Keeping a smile on my face. It feels dishonest. I don't want to lie to people. It's not my way."

"Jedd," Bianca interjected. "Don't blame Lizbeth. I exploited her blatant lack of filters."

"Thanks, girl," Lizbeth said, dimpling proudly.

"What a mess," Jedd said, shaking his head in dismay. "The whole point of you being here is to relax and escape. We never meant for you to be dragged through all this..."

"I feel responsible," Bianca interrupted. "I feel like I've exacerbated everything."

"That's not how we want you to feel," Jedd insisted.

"I know," Bianca said. "But we have to keep it real, Jedd. *The Elusive Moose...*"

"Lord have mercy," Trudy said gravely while clutching her chest.

The heads of Bianca, Jedd and Lizbeth instantly swerved in Trudy's direction. Nobody noticed her padding softly into the room.

"She knows?" Trudy wept.

"I was weak," Lizbeth said feebly.

"We agreed not to let this leak," Trudy said, wagging her finger.

"I'm sorry Trudy!" Lizbeth beseeched. "I can't help being leaky!"

"She really can't," Bianca vouched.

"Bianca," Trudy said maternally, gripping Bianca's shoulders intensely, "you must not internalize this. *The Elusive Moose* has been an impending threat long before the fire."

"Yes," Bianca argued, "but because of me…"

"It's not your fault," Trudy said firmly, "that some wasteful, nature-squelching trillionaires decided to build a ginormous, concrete eyesore in the middle of the remote wilderness. That's the real headache. Not you, Dear."

"Maybe I could…"

"There's nothing you can do," Jedd said defeatedly. "Is there…" he reconsidered, lolling his head towards Trudy, "something she could do?"

"Nope," Trudy shook her head with finality. "*The Elusive Moose* has money on its side. Once they break ground, we'll just have to admit defeat."

"But environmental awareness is a major commodity," Bianca persisted.

"Oh Sweetie," Trudy said maternally. "You are adorable. But tell me the truth. If *you* had a choice between staying in a rustic shack or a glamorous castle with all the bells and whistles…"

Bianca's heart plunged into a sinkhole of guilt. She would definitely choose a luxury resort over a shabby cabin. No question. Because she was pampered. Spoiled. Vain. People like Bianca with their entitled taste for convenience were the reason these good people were in for the struggle of their lives. The weary and defeated looks on the faces of Trudy, Jedd and Lizbeth were more than Bianca could bear.

CHAPTER FORTY-FOUR

The two neon slits that Kraven also used as eyes were penetrating Bianca, who was standing vulnerably on the dock. He had been glaring like that for seventeen agonizing seconds. Beading with sweat, Bianca mentally begged him to say something, her eyes pleading. This was the worst part, Bianca thought in a state of utter, psychological torment. Waiting for his reply.

"Kraven?" Bianca tried feebly.

And still, Kraven glared.

"Say something," Bianca begged. "Please."

There was a nauseating pause.

"Get in the canoe," Kraven finally droned with a jerk of his head.

"What?" Bianca asked, startled.

"You. The canoe. Be in it."

"But every time I get in a canoe, something bad happens."

Before Bianca could have any say in the matter, she found herself scooped up and casually carried to the canoe.

"Put me down," Bianca squealed, wriggling ridiculously in protest.

Without a word, Kraven plunked her into a canoe adorned with scratchy, red paint. He then plunked himself in his usual spot in the back, intently grabbing a paddle.

"Why?" was the only thing Bianca could think of to say.

Ignoring her, Kraven paddled with a purpose.

"I get that you're upset," Bianca grumbled. "That's totally understandable but... where are we going?"

Still, Kraven paddled with intensity.

"You're not going to murder me or something?"

Kraven grunted.

"I told you something was going on with the lodge," Bianca persisted. "I just didn't know how serious..."

"This is bad," Kraven grunted.

"You would have found out about the fate of *The Whispering Beaver* sooner or later," Bianca insisted. "I just thought I should fill you in on the extent of it. Since you were making plans for a permanent move. I knew you'd be mad, but damn."

"You can't possibly understand what I am about to lose," Kraven rumbled.

"If it's just a matter of finding a quiet place where you can concentrate..."

"Are you even paying attention?" Kraven snarled. "I hate being famous. Everywhere I go, I'm treated like a version of myself that's not even real. Everyone thinks they know me. They don't know me. They don't know anything about me. And do you know why?"

"Because you're antisocial?"

"Because nobody ever really *knows* a celebrity," Kraven droned. "I've become a concept. A symbol. A graven image. I don't do this for a living because I want attention or publicity. I just want to tell my damn stories. Around here, that's what I can do. I can just be myself. Nobody worships me for the purpose of making themselves seem more intellectual. They love me for being Kraven."

"I'm not sure that it's love, so much as fear."

"You're missing the point, Bianca."

"For the trillionth time, my name is not... no, wait. That is my name, actually. Carry on."

"You had a hunch something bad was about to happen," Kraven groaned. "I thought you were overreacting. Again."

"Maybe there's something we can do..."

"Bianca, this is not *Atticus & Blart*. You can't just rewrite some code or call in a corporate favor. This is not an easy fix, no matter how smug an executive you are."

"If you please, I can do anything I set my mind to!"

"You can't control everything, Bianca!" Kraven said, his voice cracking emotionally. "As hard as this pill is to swallow, you are *not in control* right now!"

"You can't just paddle away from your problems, Kraven!" Bianca shrieked, gripping the sides of the canoe, white knuckled.

"Watch me."

Feeling like a scolded schoolgirl, Bianca sat primly in the canoe and tried her best to behave. Who knew that such a seemingly innocent roll of toilet paper could have caused the worlds of so many people to unravel? The people to whom she was growing emotionally dependent. She had never been emotionally dependent on anything in her life except the espresso machine in the *Atticus & Blart* lunchroom. Kraven was right. For the first time in her life, Bianca was not in complete control. And it stung like the word's nastiest rug burn.

Suddenly, Bianca cocked her ear like a curious cocker spaniel. She heard strange sounds emitting from Kraven as he paddled laboriously and cathartically. Trembling snuffs. He shielded his eyes with a flannelled arm as his shoulders heaved with each sob. Without having any say in the matter, Bianca's lower lip started to quiver.

"I'm not crying," Kraven lied.

"Stop it," Bianca whimpered. "Now I'm crying."

"Shut up," Kraven sniffled.

"I can't help it," Bianca quavered. "I saw you... the tears started... this is all involuntary."

"Knock it off," Kraven said, trying to blink away his tears. "If you start then I'll start."

"Don't pretend like you didn't start this, Kraven."

Hiding his face and swearing into his hands, Kraven took deep cleansing breaths. Bianca watched him intently, her eyes glossing with tears. Less than a month ago, she perceived him to be a hardened wilderness man, incapable of human emotion or sentiment. Now look at him. He had more dimensions than a quantum physicist's theories. His pensive eyes, which had seemed so foreboding a few weeks ago, now seemed deeply human and intuitive. He looked so vulnerable over there, mashing his teary eyes with his palms. Blinking the sting of despondency from his pinkening eyeballs. Indelicately wiping snot with his sleeve. Swallowing an impending cry-ball. Pursing his lips to seal in any unexpected waves of emotion. His humble posturing implied that he craved comfort.

Damn. He is so hot right now.

So you can understand why Bianca felt the need to impulsively jump Kraven at the moment, like an amorous puma.

The last thing Kraven expected was to be ambushed by a fervidly lustful version of Bianca. He toppled backwards in the canoe, eyes widening, as Bianca ravished him with abandon. The boat wavered unsteadily in the wake of what looked like the world's most bohemian mating ritual.

Paying no mind to where she placed her hands, Bianca started spontaneously swatting Kraven on random parts of his body. He yipped like a Yorkshire terrier as he was mercilessly smacked on his chest, hip, butt, shoulder and exceptionally hard on his left cheek. Then after unexpectedly biting Kraven's nose with notable verve, she mashed her lips aggressively against his while Kraven was in the process of asking her what the hell was going on. Running out of air, Kraven struggled to pry Bianca's face off his own, writhing for his freedom. Then he turned his head just in time to be licked sloppily on the left side of his face.

Panting for breath, Kraven looked up in utter shock at Bianca, whose eyelids were drooping lustily. "The hell?" he gasped.

Abruptly stopping, Bianca realized that the stunned and possibly frightened look on the face of the man beneath her, was an indication that her technique was not good. Paling with mortification, Bianca crawled off Kraven and cowered back to her corner of the canoe.

"Oh my god," said Bianca emptily, curling into a ball of disgrace.

"That was..." Kraven began. "... different."

"I was terrible, right?" Bianca quivered. "Oh my god. I'm a circus freak."

Kraven's mouth moved around a few times, trying to be ultra-conscientious with his next words.

"Wow," Bianca said, scrambling to find her dignity. "I'm just going to go ahead and crawl in a hole forever..."

"Bianca..."

"That whole thing played out a lot more erotically in my head," Bianca moaned. "I should have just..."

"I'm sorry, Bianca."

"Why are *you* sorry?" Bianca asked, scrunching her nose. "I'm the one who basically assaulted you in a canoe."

"I didn't realize how little experience..."

"Wait, what?"

"I just assumed... you know... the lingerie... But I shouldn't have assumed that you... I mean, you and *men*..."

"I have experience."

"You..."

"What makes you think..."

"I mean, the nose thing was a bit..."

"It's been a while," Bianca stammered. "I haven't had time for men. That's not to say I've never been with one."

"I didn't mean..."

"Glenn," Bianca interrupted. "His name was Glenn."

"Glenn liked to be slobbered like a St. Bernard?"

"Very much."

"Sounds like a special guy," Kraven said, shifting jealously.

"He was basically perfect," Bianca said, trying clumsily to salvage her dignity. "Like a Pennsylvanian Jesus."

"Pennsylvanian?"

"I enjoy men from Pennsylvania."

"That's specific."

"I'm a woman who knows what she wants," Bianca said primly. "And Glenn ticked off all my boxes."

"You have boxes?" Kraven asked, cocking his head eagerly. "Tell me."

"Well," Bianca said, squinting her left eye in contemplation, "Intelligence is a *must*. Can't be too short or too tall. Dimples. Always dimples. He needs to look cute in sweaters. Green ones. Strong hands. Velvety voice. Sexy earlobes. Ironic eyebrows..."

"Glenn was all those things?" Kraven asked, raising an ironic eyebrow.

Bianca blinked. "Yes."

"How incredibly lucky for you," Kraven said uncomfortably. "I'll bet all your other men couldn't measure up to someone who was practically custom-made for you."

"I had no need for any other men," Bianca said evenly. "He was everything I needed. Glenn would show up whenever I needed company. He wasn't too needy. Never complained about my crazy schedule. Never hassled me to have kids or whatever. Laughed at all my jokes. We had all the same favorite television programs."

"Then why did you let him go?"

"There was a bug…" Bianca said, stopping abruptly and swallowing hard.

"Oh my god," Kraven said with his eyes widening. "He got sick?"

Bianca blinked. "Okay."

"Bianca, I am so sorry."

"I mean," Bianca said, suddenly scrambling, "there was bound to be a malfunction sooner or later. Glenn was only… human."

"Bianca…" Kraven said, squinting analytically.

"It's…" Bianca said, stammering awkwardly, "it's probably for the best, you know? Things were getting a bit glitchy between us…"

"Please don't tell me that Glenn was a hologram you programed yourself with your company's virtual reality software."

"Don't judge me," Bianca said, pointing judgmentally.

"Oh my god," Kraven said, thoroughly traumatized.

"I am a woman with very little free time," Bianca said as rationally as she could manage, "and I have a right to feel loved like any other woman."

"But it wasn't *real*," Kraven said, curling his lips around the word for effect.

"But it *felt* real... That sounded really psychotic just now, didn't it?"

"You are so screwed up," Kraven said, inching his way closer to Bianca's side of the canoe on his knees.

"Are you going to write in a book about what a bad kisser I am?" Bianca asked as she eyeballed a suddenly approaching Kraven. His eyes were targeting her intensely.

"We'll see how it goes," Kraven answered saucily.

"I don't think this is prudent," Bianca said, arching backwards ridiculously to avoid Kraven, who's face was now dangerously close to hers."

"Meh," Kraven shrugged.

"You don't want..."

"Yes, I do."

"But I'm weird."

"*I like weird,*" Kraven breathed into her ear.

Following Kraven's lips like an over-conscientious robin zeroing in on the world's most disturbing worm, Bianca's eyeballs slowly lolled downwards until she was cross-eyed. She dared not close her eyelids in case he did something cagey. Bianca pursed her lips tightly when Kraven attempted to kiss her and she arched her back further and further the more he leaned in. The canoe began to tip sideways from the weight of Bianca's backwards tilt, until the whole thing capsized.

After being submerged for a few nanoseconds, Bianca and Kraven eventually came up to the surface, next to their upturned canoe.

"Bad things!" Bianca spluttered, gasping from the chill of the lake water. "I told you only bad things happen in canoes!"

"We're not in a canoe," Kraven smirked.

And that is the moment that Bianca Mumford was properly kissed by an actual man who was not in any way algorithmic.

CHAPTER FORTY-FIVE
(DAY 50 IN ALGONQUIN PARK)

"Jedd, get down from there," Trudy said crossly as she hoisted her floral housedress to avoid soiling it from her muddied steps.

"They're over there," Jedd rasped, staring intensely from atop a cabin roof with a pair of binoculars.

"What are you doing up there with those binoculars?" Trudy panted as she trudged more briskly towards the Wolf Den.

"If a man wants to stand atop a roof with binoculars, that's his own business," Jedd said stubbornly.

"Get off the Wolf Den, Jedd," Trudy ordered. "Give those poor kids in there some privacy."

Across the lake, half a dozen corporate looking narcissists, (according to Jedd's mental analysis) were swaggering around the idyllic, naturalistic grove of trees that once served as scenery for the *Whispering Beaver* guests. These suited ruffians were measuring things and gesturing towards random trees that would soon sacrifice their lives to the *Gods of Avarice.*

"Those sneaky little sidewinders," Jedd whistled through his oversized teeth. "They're across the lake right now, doin' Lard knows what."

"They're not breaking ground yet?"

"Nah," Jedd huffed. "Just a bunch of suits sniffing around. Shaking hands. Closing a deal, no doubt. Can't believe it's easy as that."

"Jedd," Trudy pleaded, "please come down. You're torturing yourself watching this all unfold."

"Across the lake," Jedd said, shaking his head. "Of all the darned places to build their concrete atrocity. I'll bet it'll look real institutional. Like an insane asylum."

"Try not to dwell on it, Jedd," Trudy said reassuringly. "We'll do all we can to stay open until..."

"All them motorboats zipping around the lake," Jedd huffed. "I can't understand how they wormed their way around the lake regulations. We promised our guests a calm lake. Tranquil. A quiet and stress-free hideaway. That'll all be a bust now. *The Elusive Moose* will attract the rowdy types, with all their jet skis and drunken parties. They'll drive away whatever business we'll have left. If we survive the year, we'll have to change our name to *The Screaming Beaver*."

"No, Jedd," Trudy said, assertively wagging a finger, "no screaming beavers."

"This land is supposed to be protected by the provincial government," whined Jedd. "This must be illegal."

"This lake borders the park limits," Trudy sighed. "That land across the lake is technically outside Algonquin Park. I'm afraid it's fair game."

"Nothing is sacred anymore," Jedd said, wiping his sweaty brow with a hanky.

"Why is Jedd standing on the Wolf Den?" Tucker asked, approaching obliviously.

"Central view of the scoundrels," Jedd said, gripping the binoculars fervently to his ocular cavities.

"What are Bianca and Kraven doing in there?" Tucker asked ominously.

"Tucker..." Trudy said, limply slapping his arm with the back of her hand.

"What if they're doing something weird?" Tucker persisted. "They've been skipping breakfast for over three weeks."

"They have curtains," Jedd said, not budging the binoculars from his face.

"They could be doing literally anything in there," Tucker said, looking a bit feverish.

"For the love of Pete, Tucker," Trudy scolded. "Would you just mind your own business?"

"But it's Kraven," Tucker said with a warning tone. "He's a dark figure. Maybe he lured Bianca into some form of demonic sacrament."

"Oh Tucker."

"I have a bad feeling," Tucker said queasily. "Since Bianca's been shacking up here with *The Ambiguous Wonder,* she's been pretty tight-lipped about what Kraven does in his cabin."

"Because there's likely nothing to say," Trudy exhaled.

"You seem pretty confident that Kraven has not introduced Bianca to a secret life of crime or other underhanded deeds," Tucker said, triangulating an eyebrow.

"Kraven is harmless," Trudy said, furrowing her brow.

"You seem quite sure of yourself," Tucker squinted.

"Tucker," Trudy sighed. "I am sure that whatever Bianca and Kraven are doing in the Wolf Den is completely legal and consensual."

***

"I did not consent to this," Bianca said, eyeing the freshly caught, large-mouth bass with farcical horror.

"You agreed to go fishing with me," Kraven reminded her.

"I feel as though I was emotionally manipulated," Bianca said, reviled.

"All I said," Kraven sighed, "was that if your career depends on impressing your boss out here, it's kind of ridiculous that you haven't tried fishing yet."

"But now there's a dead fish," Bianca said sickly.

"That's kind of how fishing works," Kraven smirked. "Now are you going to help me clean him now? Or are you worried you'll soil your smooth, little model hands?"

"Hey," Bianca said defensively, "that's what I mean about being emotionally manip…. *Model hands?*"

***

"The curtains are closed," Tucker stage whispered, with his ear pressed up against the Wolf Den cabin. "But I think I hear them in there."

"Tucker!" Trudy scolded. "That is unseemly! Please stop!"

"Don't tell me you're not even a little bit curious about what's going on in there," Tucker pouted. "I mean, it's Kraven…"

"Shhh," Jedd said, putting his ear to the shingles, "I think they're talking."

"Oh, you two," Trudy said, putting her hands on her hips.

Bianca's muffled voice was easily audible from inside the cabin. "Oh my god!" Bianca screamed. "He's still alive!"

"Jesus Lord," Trudy gasped, "let me hear some of that. Move over, Tucker."

"Would you keep it down?" Kraven shushed, muffled from inside. "Do you want the whole damn resort to hear you?"

"He's moving!" Bianca shrieked. "Kraven, he's still moving!"

"Jaysus, Bianca!" Kraven hissed, "Lower your voice! Someone's going to call the frickin' police!"

"I thought you thwacked him on the head first!" Bianca sobbed. "I can't look at this! It's grotesque!"

Tucker, Trudy and Jedd simultaneously gasped.

"Would you calm down," Kraven barked, "and give me a hand with him? He's slippery!"

"Oh my god!" Bianca whimpered with horror. "He's bleeding through the face!"

Tucker, Trudy and Jedd simultaneously winced when they heard a loud TWHACK noise that vibrated the whole cabin.

"There," Kraven said breathlessly. "He's out. Now hand me that fillet knife."

"That's it," Jedd said, sliding down from the roof and rolling up his sleeves. "I'm going in there."

"Jedd!" Trudy yelped. "Consider your loved ones!"

"Some poor soul is in there!" Jedd warbled. "With that ape-man and some newer, sadistic version of Bianca!"

"It's likely too late for that poor wretch," Trudy urged. "We need to hightail it out of here and call the ranger or the O.P.P. or a priest or...!"

"I told you something nefarious was afoot," Tucker squeaked. "I told you!"

Tucker, Trudy and Jedd froze in terror as the screen door opened. Kraven popped his head out and asked if anyone wanted any fish.

Tucker, Trudy and Jedd simultaneously gaped.

***

"Mighty kind of you to share your fish with us, Mr. Kane," Jedd said toothily while roasting his portion of bass by a communal campfire.

Kraven nodded in a way that was strangely both grim and cordial. He had not meant to share his bass with a gaggle of other people. But when Trudy, Tucker and Jedd ambushed his cabin, thinking they were intercepting a grisly crime, what else could Kraven do but divert the drama towards an impromptu fish offering? Kraven's Adam's apple undulated with resentment at the thought of missing out on the hearty meal he had planned on sharing with Bianca. In Kraven's headspace, there was nothing more romantic than large-mouth bass.

Bianca would beg to differ. After witnessing the graphic extermination of a thrashing fish, she would not be converting to pescatarianism any time soon. She writhed with dyspepsia.

Weathered camping chairs were set up in a circle around a blazingly orange campfire by the waterfront. Jedd, Trudy, Tucker, Lizbeth, Logan, Cheryl and Fisherman Sid were creating a din of overlapping chatter as they each gauged a fork in the foil-wrapped bass, which was warming in the embers. Bianca and Kraven exchanged nuanced glances back and forth. They had somehow figured out a way to communicate without actually having to speak.

"You haven't said a word all evening," said Bianca's nuance.

"Low profile," Kraven's nuance replied. Even his essence was curt and to-the-point.

"Because you don't want anyone to know. Yes, I get it, Kraven. But you are making this way more awkward by just sitting there like a mute timber wolf. Would it really matter that much if they found out you're a…"

"You promised you wouldn't say anything."

"I literally didn't say anything. Nobody can hear me right now because I am talking to you with my mind."

"Cute."

With an adorably scratchy chuckle, Jedd dabbed a tear of laughter from the corner of his left eye – an eye that was residually pink from days of emotional struggles. He was bravely joking back and forth with Trudy, both of them clearly grasping for something to be joyful about. They jested mostly about Pog Lake, osprey and moss.

"Look at them, Kraven. They are trying so hard to be brave."

"Grunt."

"I wonder if any of the other guests have figured out what's happening."

"Slightly more empathetic grunt."

"They really only have each other, don't they?"

Suddenly, Bianca felt someone flick her on the shoulder. Ready to bark out a complaint, she refrained when she discovered the existential teenager smirking at her and taking a seat next to her. Sitting on a squeaky folding chair and pulling up his black hood like a funky grim reaper, the teenager coughed out an awkward greeting. The bonfire flames reflected hellishly on his wan face. When Bianca teasingly flicked him back, the youth pursed his lips ironically, which was his version of a smile.

Keeping her eyes centered on Bianca and the dark youth, Trudy nudged Jedd and gestured towards them with a jerk of her head. Jedd's mustached mouth curled into a satisfied grin and he nodded approvingly.

"Want to get out of here?" Kraven's eyebrows gestured to Bianca.

"Wrath just arrived," Bianca's apologetic eyes replied.

"Wrath?"

"The kid."

"Why do you call him Wrath?"

"He likes it."

"I'm sure he won't care or even notice if we…"

"Kraven, it took him all the nerve he has to show up just now," Bianca's pursed lips implored. *"If I leave now, it'll undo any progress he…"*

"I can't believe you named him."

"He doesn't get a lot of validation at home, Kraven."

Kraven's energy softened.

"We haven't seen much of you this week," Tucker said, interrupting the bizarre waves of telepathic energy generating between Bianca and Kraven. "What have you been up to?"

"I...learned to swim," Bianca said.

Everyone blinked.

"That's a big deal for me," Bianca said, suddenly flustered and fidgeting with a loose thread on her camping chair.

"A triumph, Dear," Trudy said, putting down her fish fork and clapping her hands with verve. "We are so proud of you. Aren't we proud, gang?" she continued, urging others to clap as well.

Kraven smirked and elbowed Bianca proudly.

Bianca reddened.

"We'll show that egomaniacal Grosswater what's what," Trudy continued with an indignant harrumph. "I'll bet he didn't think you'd face your greatest fear and learn to swim. Now look at you. A regular Penny Oleksiak."

"I'm not actually good at it," Bianca admitted. "Basically, I can dogpaddle."

"But still," Trudy persisted. "They won't even recognize you when you return to work."

Bianca blinked.

"You'll be a stronger, more robust, spiritual, versatile, rosy-cheeked version of you!" Trudy squeaked. "Not only will you prove your aptitude to Arthur Grosswater, you'll prove to yourself that you have the stamina and determination to take your career to the next level."

Tucker visibly blinked back tears.

Jedd and Lizbeth looked at each other with forlorn grins.

Kraven made a noise that sounded like the growl of a proud Kodiak bear.

Bianca just gaped.

Work?

How could work have slipped my mind for the past...

How many days has it been since I've thought about...

"That's what vacations are for, Bianca," Kraven's nuance interrupted. *"You're supposed to detach from the grind."*

"I wasn't talking to you, Kraven," Bianca's annoyed energy replied. *"I was just musing to myself."*

"You muse loudly," Kraven replied with merely a smirk. *"I couldn't help but interrupt."*

"Kraven, I'm losing my groove."

"No, you're not. Just stop."

"How am I going to integrate back into..."

"You could do that job with your eyes closed."

"You don't understand what's expected of me."

"You'll find your rhythm again."

"How could I let myself…"

"A lot has happened in the past month."

"The pressure though…"

"For God's sake, Bianca. Look around this campfire. Everyone here believes in you. Every single one. (awkward cough) Especially… you know…"

Before Bianca had a chance to mentally reply, every head turned upwards towards a very loud and foreign noise. Headlights of a small jet zeroed in on a clearing, illuminating the confused faces of everyone surrounding the campfire. Ramming into an unassuming Eastern hemlock, the small jet came to a halt and gradually slowed down the engine.

"What in the world…" Jedd said with a look of utter bewilderment.

Wide-eyed, in stunned horror, Bianca mouthed an expletive.

CHAPTER FORTY-SIX

Goggle-eyed, everyone gawked as the hatch of the private jet opened. A sleek woman, seemingly composed of starch and aluminum walked emotionlessly from the aircraft, squinting at her surroundings. She was wearing a designer suit and her pin-straight hair looked like lifeless, synthetic fibers. When she spotted Bianca by the bonfire, the aloof woman swerved robotically and walked towards the fire with a purpose.

Jedd sprung to his feet with a fist of defiance waving in the air. "Scoundrel!" He shrieked.

"Jedd!" Trudy pleaded, trying to tug Jedd back into his seat.

"Look at her in that suit!" Jedd yelped gruffly. "She's one of *them!* Probably come to drive us out! We still got time, Serpent! You skidaddle before I alert the ranger!"

"We still have time for what?" Cheryl asked obliviously.

"Jedd, Please!" Trudy begged. "Not in front of..." she continued, gesturing towards all the confused faces around them.

"Bianca," the tin woman said emotionlessly. "Get in the aircraft."

"Dang," Tucker said in wonderment. "Bianca's an alien."

"Don't be daft," Bianca sighed. "That's Sloane. My dad's personal assistant."

"Are you planning on replacing that Eastern hemlock?" Jedd pouted, crossing his arms.

"I have no idea what that means," Sloane said with aloof piety. "Bianca, I've been given my orders. Come along."

"What's happening?" Tucker whispered nervously to shrugging Lizbeth.

"Our girl has another eleven days with us," Trudy protested.

"We haven't even taken her to the diving rock," Tucker squeaked. "Or mushroom hunting. Or to *Mosquito Gully.*"

"Who are you people?" Sloane said, writhing her shiny, red lips with superior revulsion.

"Her tribe," Jedd said gruffly, still crossing his arms.

"Bianca," Sloane said, nonplussed, "you have caused the family enough embarrassment…"

"How did you even know I was here?" Bianca asked, squinting a suspicious, left eye.

"I picked up your father's messages," Sloane said unsympathetically. "Roughly fifty days ago, you left a cryptic voicemail regarding Algonquin Park and one *Mr. Flooferson.* Clearly, you have taken leave of your senses."

"That's why she's here!" Lizbeth said in a failed attempt to be helpful.

"And you suddenly came looking for me now?" Bianca said with a twinge of vinegar in her tone. "Also, how did you trace me to *The Whispering Beaver?*"

"A tip," Sloane said evenly.

"A tip?" Bianca asked. "Who would..."

"We were alerted that you were suspended from work due to a nervous breakdown," Sloane said with her pin-straight mouth. "You can imagine the disgrace you have brought upon your family."

Kraven snorted.

"This poor girl was under a cruel amount of duress in that toxic office," Trudy said, forming fervid fists. "She just couldn't take it anymore. There's no disgrace in that."

"Mr. Mumford is displeased," Sloane said. "I am required to liberate you from this primitive purgatory."

"*Excuse me?*" Jedd asked, his eyes bulging with indignity.

"I'm not ready," Bianca quavered bravely.

"I don't understand," Sloane said without inflection.

"I'm not in the headspace to return to work," Bianca tried. "I need to mentally prepare..."

"Try to understand, Bianca," Sloane said plastically. "I am doing you an immense favor. Think of what this little stint of sloth and delinquency will do to your reputation and ultimately your career. Do you want this to haunt your professional reputation...?"

"I'm required to be here for an additional eleven days," Bianca reminded Sloane. "Mr. Grosswater is not expecting me back yet. The whole point of me being here is to prove to Grosswater..."

"Do you want to lose everything you've ever worked for?" Sloane asked apathetically.

"But I need to ensure I have a career to come back to!" Bianca fired back. "How is it going to look if I go crawling back to the city nearly two weeks early?"

"Your family is concerned," Sloane said synthetically. "Does that mean nothing to you?"

Bianca blinked. "I... I don't have to go with you. Just because you swoop in here with your orders..."

"But your father..."

"Why didn't he come?"

Sloane blinked. "What do you mean?"

"Why didn't my father come to retrieve me himself?"

Sloane blinked again. "He's busy."

Kraven growled bearishly.

"If he cares so much..." Bianca said.

"There is no need to sentimentalize this, Bianca," Sloane said metallically. "You are idling your summer away when there is work to be done. Impressions to be made. Image. Consider your family's reputation. They have high profile careers, and here you are, grasping for the remaining fragments of your sanity in the boondocks. Have you given any thought to how your idleness and mental frailty is affecting their professional profile? And also yours."

"He didn't have time to answer the damn phone when I..." Bianca seethed, "... when I... needed..."

"He is an important man," Sloane lectured with a manicured index finger. "And important people are busy."

"He could have sent Chad," Bianca said resentfully. "Where's Chad?"

"Dubai," Sloane answered automatically.

Bianca's stinging eyes wildly scanned the faces of the people around her. Their looks of shock and pity wounded her. "Figures," Bianca swallowed.

"You don't belong here," Sloane enunciated condescendingly.

Bianca bit her lower lip hard as way too many concerned faces swerved in her direction.

"Collect your things," Sloane commanded monotonically.

"NO!" Tucker cried.

"Tucker," Trudy whimpered, pulling him back in his chair. "We have to let her go."

"But those people aren't her family," Tucker challenged. "They are not any kind of a..."

"She had a life before us, Dear," Trudy said tremulously. "We have no claim to her."

Jedd comforted Lizbeth, who was sobbing in his arms.

The teenager suddenly looked deader than usual.

Kraven just stared.

Bianca's knees buckled as she stood from her camping chair. She forcibly rammed her emotions back down into the depths of her soul. "Which one of you traitors contacted my father?"

For a terrible, silent moment, every lip was pursed, and every set of eyes bulged.

"I did," Kraven droned as he stood and lumbered into the shadows.

CHAPTER FORTY-SEVEN

"Why?" Bianca barked as she violently lobbed random clothing into a suitcase.

"I thought I was helping," Kraven said, lowering his head.

"You contacted my father?" Bianca squeaked with rage. "What made you think you had the right..."

"Your whole world fell apart and your family didn't even notice!" Kraven insisted.

"It's better that way," Bianca quavered. "My emotions are inconvenient for them. Now everything's messed up. I'm backed up against a wall..."

"You don't have to go," Kraven mumbled.

"This is so humiliating!" Bianca railed, taking her rage out on a green sock. "Being wrangled by my father's personal assistant. Like a toddler."

"Did you hear me?" Kraven croaked. "You don't have to leave with Sloane just because she swooped in with her orders."

"You don't understand."

"No, Bianca. I don't."

"I'm rarely on my father's radar," Bianca explained. "He's watching me now. I have to calculate my next move carefully."

"I can't believe you're complying with this madness!"

"Kraven, this is the most involved my father has ever..."

"Seriously?" Kraven said, taking a step back to get a full view of Bianca's ridiculousness. "You think this is your father's way of telling you he gives a sh..."

"But he's my..."

"I don't want you to go," Kraven said flatly.

Bianca blinked.

"You don't have to get on that pretentious jet," Kraven reinforced.

"You..." Bianca stammered. "You expect me to stay on vacation for the rest of my life? This place is going to be bulldozed in a few months. There won't even be..."

"Then at least stay until that happens."

"I have responsibilities in Toronto."

"Come home with me to Huntsville."

"To live above a sketchy plaza?" Bianca squeaked with disbelief. "Why? So you can continue scrawling secret things about me while I wait outside with some weedy vagrant named Garth?"

"Bianca..."

"What would I even do in Huntsville?" Bianca squawked. "There's nothing to do there. I'd just waffle around, serving no purpose. That would drive me to distraction."

"That's it then," Kraven said, tossing his hands in the air. "You're just going to walk away?"

"I'm a busy lady."

"Too busy for..."

"Yes."

"...me?"

Bianca gaped.

"Do you think living in a rat race with no work-life balance is going to make your family proud?" Kraven croaked. "Because it won't, Bianca. No matter how little free time you have, your family will never be impressed. They are too busy to notice! You're banging your head against a wall for no reason!"

"I have a career, Kraven!" Bianca yelped. "As hard as this is for you to understand, I had a very full life before I met you!"

"So this summer..." Kraven said, forlornly.

"It was fun," Bianca choked. "But I can't give up everything I worked my ass off for..."

"Fun," Kraven droned, shaking his head.

"Kraven, we don't make any sense."

"We do though."

"Outside the context of *The Whispering Beaver,* we make no sense at all. Just look at us! How could we possibly..."

"Just get out," Kraven snarled.

"...What?"

"If I'm that disposable..."

"Kraven, it's not like that. I..."

Bianca shuddered when the screechy screen door slammed. The room conspicuously lacked Kraven. Bianca suddenly felt hollow.

***

The engine of the private jet was droning as Sloane stood impatiently by the hatch like a stark, postmodern statue. She steepled an eyebrow as Bianca approached, moist-eyed and trying her hardest to be stoic. Wordless, Sloane gestured with a jerk of her head for Bianca to enter the plane.

"I need to say good-bye first," Bianca called over to Sloane.

Sloane cupped her ear with a hand, implying that she could not hear Bianca over the rumble of the engine.

"I NEED TO SAY GOOD-BYE!" Bianca called, straining to be heard.

Sloane replied with an irritated look.

The first arms to be wrapped around Bianca were those of Trudy. Following closely behind like faithful shadows were very morose versions of Jedd, Tucker and Lizbeth.

"I've been kind of high maintenance," Bianca choked emotionally.

"It has been our extreme pleasure, Dear," Trudy whimpered bravely.

"Now you behave yourself," Jedd sniffled squeakily, "you hear?"

Bianca nodded, pursing her lips like a pouty toddler, about to give up her most beloved teddy bear. She sheepishly waved Jedd's walking stick as a gesture of thanks. Jedd's eyes brimmed with tears and his lip trembled as he gave Bianca a farewell salute.

After Bianca had been adequately hugged, squeezed and doted on by the *Whispering Beaver* staff, her face was smooshed between the hands of tear-stained Trudy, who was memorizing every detail of Bianca's face.

I... I love you, Trudy.

I love all of you.

Why the hell can't I say this out loud?

"I'm sorry," Bianca said, meaning that on a number of different levels, "I have to leave."

"Dear," Trudy said maternally, "you do what you need to do."

"What about you guys though?"

Sloane cleared her throat impatiently.

"We'll be fine," Trudy squeaked with emotion. "Go on now. Go and be amazing."

Unexpectedly, Bianca felt as though she was being hugged by a clammy corpse.

"Wrath?" Bianca asked, bewildered.

"I've been thinking," Wrath said confidentially, "I'll be eighteen in a month. I can basically do whatever I want then. Maybe I can get a job here," he added with uncharacteristic eagerness.

Bianca, Jedd, Tucker, Trudy and Lizbeth looked at each other, white like ghosts.

"My parents," Wrath continued, "they don't get it. I'm kind of an embarrassment on account of them all being politicians. They don't support or understand my fascination with the macabre. And bats. They think I have a personality disorder. Which could make them unelectable. But I digress. Thing is, here I feel like I'm a part of something. I don't know. Community? Family."

Jedd raised a finger to say something, but Trudy shushed him.

"There's lots I could do," Wrath said. "Dishes. Lug baggage to the cabins. Conduct spider workshops."

"Wrath..." Bianca said sympathetically.

"I think they'd go for it," Wrath said, his eyes popping open like an enthusiastic fruit bat. "I think I might fit in around here. That's a first for me."

"Bianca," Sloane said stiffly. "Time is of the essence."

Bianca lingered in the jet's doorway for a few too many moments, breathing in the essence of that oddball crew of friends she would likely never see again. She took a mental photograph before being yanked into the jet by a very irked Sloane.

***

Why did I get on this plane?

My job.

My career.

The plan has always been to return.

I don't belong in a forest.

But Kraven.

I barely know him.

I met him less than two months ago.

I can't throw everything away for...

A fling.

How is Jedd going to manage without...

What about Tucker? Lizbeth?

Why do I miss Trudy so much?

She's overbearing.

Annoying.

She smothers me.

Like a mom.

I've never had one of those.

And Kraven.

Never had one of those either.

We could talk without... talking.

He...

Forget Kraven.

I'll program myself a more compatible boyfriend.

I'll name him Clive.

And maybe I'll get a cat.

Wait, a cat?

"How could you have let this happen?" Sloane asked curtly.

Bianca shrugged.

"Nearly two months of your life," Sloane added, "wasted. It's a good thing that brazen lumberjack contacted me when he did. Your father will be pleased to hear you've returned when he picks up his messages in Singapore, six, maybe seven weeks from now."

"You mean he's not even going to be there when I get back?"

"Why would that be the case?" Sloane blinked obliviously.

Bianca shrugged.

"You thought this would be some kind of tender reunion?" Sloane said blankly. "That's a little unrealistic, don't you think? Do try to be a tad less selfish."

"He didn't even know I'd left Toronto," Bianca grumbled.

"Who were those emotional people back at *The Dirty Beaver?*"

"*The Whispering Beaver,*" Bianca snapped. "Show some respect."

"Not that it matters," Sloane chuckled dryly. "Let's pretend your little stint of misconduct never happened, shall we?"

Exhaling with exasperation and emotional weariness, Bianca took her seat on the plane. She made a face. She sat on something. Pulling an item out from under her very perplexed butt, Bianca uttered a piercing gasp. In her hands was Kraven's manuscript. The one he had been writing so secretively. The front page, meticulously clipped to a thick chunk of pages touted the title: *Whenever She Gets in a Canoe, Something Bad Happens: An Unlikely Romantic Comedy.* Covering her mouth to shelter a hybrid laugh-sob. Tear drops smeared the front title.

"Open the hatch," Bianca wept.

"We are gaining altitude," Sloane said, matter-of-factly.

"Land the damn plane then!" Bianca shrieked. "I'm getting off!"

"Don't be daft," said deadpan Sloane.

"You can't hold me here against my will!"

"Bianca, sit down and fasten your seatbelt."

"Kraven..."

"What is a *Kraven?*"

"The thing I never realized I needed."

"The only thing you need," Sloane said impatiently, "is to get your life back on track. *No Kravens required.*"

Bianca pursed her lips as she watched *The Whispering Beaver* become smaller and smaller through the jet window.

CHAPTER FORTY-EIGHT

Bianca's pinstripe suit was giving her hives. The sensation in her stomach gave her the illusion that she was plummeting down Niagara Falls in a vintage barrel. Once again sitting in Arthur Grosswater's office was like being suffocated in a vat of molasses. Grosswater was pensively looking at Bianca for way too many excruciating minutes, clacking a pen psychotically against a pad.

"We weren't expecting you back so soon," Arthur finally said.

"There was an urgent family matter..." Bianca began.

"This bungs things up a bit, doesn't it," Arthur interrupted, "with Dirk Thumperson filling in for you during your leave of absence. He was expecting to assume your role for another ten days."

"It was outside of my control," Bianca explained, bravely erecting her posture. "My father's personal assistant..."

"I suppose now is as good a time as any to review your progress," Arthur exhaled. "HR Flannigan is present and will discreetly perform a psych eval in the background."

HR Flannigan saluted Bianca condescendingly with a writing implement.

"Mr. Grosswater," Bianca said assertively, "I think you will be impressed with my accomplishments at *The Whispering Beaver.* I understand you have been in correspondence with Trudy. I trust she has discussed with you my growth…"

"Canoes, fish, waterfowl," Arthur read with his glasses slid schoolmasterishly down his nose, reading his records.

"You will be pleased to know that I also participated in an advanced level hike, during which time I singlehandedly staved off a wild bear with a meager, cucumber sandwich," Bianca professed. "But most importantly, Mr. Grosswater, I went outside of my comfort zone and connected with people vastly different from myself. I feel that I have proven that I can rise to any challenge…"

"This is awkward," Arthur interrupted. "See, things have been going quite smoothly since Dirk Thumperson took over…"

"You're not seriously suggesting," Bianca said, paling.

"He's basically a machine," Arthur said emotionlessly. "No personality to speak of, but he can work twenty-one hours a day without even yawning, which is special."

"But Dirk is an idiot!" Bianca said, lunging from her chair. "He's the one who dropped the ball with the cat software! I can prove it!"

HR Flannigan raised an eyebrow and wrote something down ambiguously.

"I have to think of productivity," Arthur said indifferently. "I mean the office hasn't exactly burst into flames as a result of *not* having you in it. And since Dirk has taken the wheel, there have been a total of *zero* nervous breakdowns in the office."

"But I'm a completely different person now!" Bianca pleaded. "I'm more resilient. Dimensional. Empathetic. Grounded. I have developed a profound sense of community that I assure you, will be invaluable to the company! Didn't Trudy tell you…"

"See, none of these things impress me," Arthur said dryly. "What concerns me is that the company has invested a significant amount of money to send you on a mental health leave. How many mental health leaves are you going to require? Are you on a downward spiral? That, I do not know."

"This is not fair!" Bianca shrieked in her defense.

"Do you need to step out and go to the ladies' room?" HR Flannigan smirked. *"To cry?"*

Bianca gaped.

"Another good point," Arthur said, pointing at HR Flannigan. "Dirk doesn't need *cry breaks* in the bathroom stall. See? *Productivity.*"

"You can't just.." Bianca yipped.

"Bianca, you didn't think we would just mindlessly toss you aside like a sack of dead pigeons, after your seven years of compulsive commitment to *Atticus & Blart?*"

Bianca slowly exhaled.

"No," Arthur chuckled. "We need someone to train Dirk."

"To do my job?" Bianca said in a wineglass-shattering octave.

"We can't think of anyone more qualified," Arthur said, smugly leaning back in his leather chair. "And if you would like to stay on after that, perhaps as Dirk's personal assistant, well, we would be delighted. But of course, that would be your choice."

"Are you Satan?" Bianca asked through clenched teeth.

"Ouch," Arthur said, amused. "HR Flannigan, write that down."

"Stop writing things down, HR Flannigan!" Bianca shrieked.

"Bianca, please compose yourself."

"Did you all set this whole conspiracy up?" Bianca demanded.

"Delusional," HR Flannigan said, writing something down.

"Did Dirk sabotage *Project Cat Companion?* For the purpose of making me go barking mad? As an excuse to get me out of the way? So he could weasel into my swivel chair? Giving you all the illusion of competence? Making me appear obsolete?"

"Unhinged," HR Flannigan muttered, writing something down.

"Don't make me show you how unhinged I can be!" Bianca spat.

"Wow," Arthur said, nonplussed. "This is definitely not something Dirk would do."

"You are making the biggest mistake of your careers," Bianca persisted. "I am the best thing that's ever happened to *Atticus & Blart!*"

"It's not like we're firing you," Arthur pointed out. "Are you saying you are voluntarily resigning? That would save us a bundle in severance, actually."

"If that's what you think," Bianca articulated, "then you don't know me at all! I don't quit! Ever! I don't do anything unless it's with all my heart, soul and gusto! Oh, I'm going to train Dirk alright! I'm going to blow your minds with how well-trained *Idiot Dirk* is about to be! And if I have to be his assistant, which is the most demented twist of irony, then I'm going to be such a mind-blowingly efficient..."

Suddenly, the door burst open, revealing Kraven, squinting with fury.

"Kraven?" Bianca gaped.

Before anyone had time to process the situation, Kraven thrust Bianca over his shoulder and thundered lumberjackishly out of Arthur Grosswater's office. Wriggling and kicking her legs ridiculously, Bianca protested and asked what the hell was going on. As per usual, Kraven ignored her and lumbered through the halls of *Atticus & Blart,* on a mission to get her out of the building.

"Call security!" HR Flannigan yelped, popping his head out of Arthur Grosswater's office.

"Security?" a quavering secretary warbled on the phone, "Bianca Mumford has been kidnapped... Yes, by a sociopathic lumberjack..."

"Kraven!" Bianca yelped, "What is going on?"

"I'll explain later," Kraven droned.

"Put me down!"

"Yeah, no."

"For the luvva...Where are you taking me?"

***

Outside, Kraven's pickup truck was parked illegally by the main entrance. Kraven flopped Bianca into the cab on the passenger side before hopping into the driver's seat and screeching into the ridiculous, Toronto traffic. Dumbfounded, Bianca gaped at Kraven who was weaving aggressively through honking cars.

"Would you care to explain?" Bianca asked, panting for breath.

"I'm saving your ass," Kraven droned, focusing intensely on the road. "Again."

"We are not in the remote wilderness anymore, Kraven! I was in my element! And all things considered, I was handling the situation masterfully. I don't need to be rescued and can't you see that you are completely out of context here?"

"First off," Kraven said, "you're not in your element."

"Excuse me?"

"You are nobody's assistant," Kraven insisted. "You are a leader."

"*Atticus & Blart* is the only thing I know! You had no right to..."

"You'll thank me later."

"Kraven, you literally kidnapped me."

"Would you have come willingly?"

"Well, no. But..."

"Then?"

"Kraven, I'm a high-profile executive! They'll send the police out looking for you!"

"They won't find me where we're going," Kraven said, checking his mirrors before swerving around a corner.

After gawking at Kraven in disbelief, Bianca gasped when she spotted seven of her co-workers, waving at her from the truck's cargo bed.

"Kraven," Bianca quavered, "why are there seven technical specialists in your cargo bed?"

"They wanted to come along," Kraven shrugged.

Bianca's mouth moved around wordlessly.

"You're not the only one who's had enough," Kraven said elusively.

"What are you saying?" Bianca said, squeezing her eyes shut, trying to comprehend. "You sprung them?"

"I met them in the elevator," Kraven said casually. "Nice guys. The freckled one asked if I was lost and I explained to him my motives. They confided in me that they were each grappling with their own sanity, much like you."

"Hey."

"They worried that if the strongest among them – also you – lost her marbles that it was only a matter of time before they also reached a breaking point. The expectations at *Atticus & Blart* are not sustainable for anyone. It's not just you. I told these guys the plan and they begged me to bring them along."

"What plan?" Bianca asked, shaking her head in confusion.

"The plans to revamp *The Whispering Beaver*," Kraven replied as though it was the most obvious thing in the world.

"What?" Bianca squeaked. "What are you talking about? That's not even possible. Kraven," Bianca said impatiently, "you know the lodge can't compete with a resort on the scale of *The Elusive Moose*."

"Not without strong leadership."

Bianca squinted with bewilderment.

"Everything was a mess after you left the lodge," Kraven explained. "Everyone was emotionally all over the place. Weeping. Lamenting. Trudy even swooned."

"I missed you guys too," Bianca said under her breath.

"You made quite an impression," Kraven said, adding softly, "on us all. We've all become kind of emotionally dependent on each other. You were the first among us to move on. It hit us hard."

Tears pearled in Bianca's eyeballs.

"It seemed obvious to all of us at that point," Kraven continued, "that we can't give up on the lodge. It's not just a business, it's a tight community composed of people who really give a crap about each other."

"So you stayed up all night and came up with a plan to save *the beaver*?" Bianca asked sardonically. "Just like that?"

"We have no idea what we are going to do," Kraven admitted. "All we know is that we have to try. And our efforts will be futile without a feisty executive at the helm."

"You're serious," Bianca said, gobsmacked. "You just expect me to wave my executive wand and make *The Elusive Moose* disappear."

"Of course not," Kraven said.

"*The Whispering Beaver* is functionally extinct," Bianca argued. "How to you expect me to salvage an obsolete..."

"Trudy suggested that we convert the little telephone hut by the water taxi into an office for you. That way you can have internet access so you can do all those cyber things that lodge managers do, without infringing on the lodge's environmental policies. Everything on the lodge's side of the lake will still be off the grid."

"But..."

"Lizbeth raised an interesting point," Kraven continued. "She told us about that time you said that the lodge needed a brand. She had no idea what you were talking about..."

"...and told me that working hard and being kind to people was the only thing she knew about business."

"Sounds like a good brand to me," Kraven smirked.

"What?" Bianca asked. "Working hard and being kind to people?"

"Plus, we have environmental awareness on our side," Kraven added. "You told Lizbeth yourself that would be a hot commodity. With some smart PR, we can milk that for all its worth."

"You guys have given this a lot of thought," Bianca admitted. "But that doesn't mean..."

"We want to update all the cabins and add about a dozen or so more."

"Where on earth are you going to get the money..."

"Fundraising."

"But how do you expect to garner attention..."

Kraven swallowed. "Star power."

Bianca gaped. "Are you serious?"

Kraven shrugged.

"But nobody knows."

"I told them," Kraven droned quietly.

"But you hate being famous."

"Everyone's doing their bit," Kraven said, blinking his stinging eyes. "Even Wrath."

"What on earth could Wrath possibly..."

"His dad is trying to get reelected," Kraven interrupted. "The boy went ahead and lobbied his father to declare *The Whispering Beaver* an official historic site and to enforce a sizable, government incentive for off-the-grid facilities."

"How...?"

"He successfully blackmailed his parents into doing whatever he says or else he'll tell everyone that he's their son."

"Smart kid."

"Extremely," Kraven agreed.

Bianca gaped at Kraven for a lingering moment, pondering.

"Alright," Bianca nodded uncertainly, "I see this is a team effort. But realistically, how are we going to make this happen with one executive, a brooding writer, a bumbling gopher, a gum-smacking waitress, an undead teenager, one Trudy and a beaver-toothed chef who can't taste things? What about all the logistics? Online presence? Financials?"

"Any designers in the cargo bed here?" Kraven asked, jerking his head towards the back of the pickup truck.

"Benj is a web designer," Bianca mused, "Clarence is an engineer..."

"Any graphic artists?"

"Raj."

"Bam! He can help design cabins. Yay Raj."

"But what about…"

"Finance?"

"Bob."

"Legal?"

"Horace."

"Marketing?"

"Amos."

"I'd say you're running out of excuses," Kraven smirked.

Bianca stared glassily out the window, woolgathering this surreal turn of events. Less than twenty-four hours after her abrupt exodus from *The Whispering Beaver,* she was being chauffeured back by a surprisingly sexy human/jackal hybrid. She did not seem to mind being abducted from her office like a limp waif being carried off by a cumbersome yeti. Weirder still, was the anticipation she felt about returning the very place that once seemed to be her quintessential hell. Bianca felt strangely as though she was returning home, an utterly unfamiliar feeling.

"Did you read it?" Kraven suddenly muttered.

"The…"

"Yes."

"I did."

Dense silence.

"And?" Kraven finally swallowed.

Grinning with a kind of stupid bliss, Bianca rested her head comfortably on Kraven's shoulder while he drove.

CHAPTER FORTY-NINE

Gravel crackled under the tires of Kraven's pickup truck as he parked crookedly by the lake. Bianca eagerly craned her neck, hoping to catch a glimpse of Trudy, Jedd, Lizbeth or...

"Tucker?" Bianca said, crinkling her forehead with concern.

Standing submissively by the water taxi, Tucker was currently being hectored by a portly, suited man who was towering pretentiously as though trying to seem taller than he actually was. Bianca's eyes narrowed with ire. She could not hear the conversation, but she could hear the staccato of the man's voice and see the corresponding winces on Tucker's face. Bianca was suddenly possessed by the spirit of a protective jaguar as she busted free from her seatbelt.

"What is he doing to Tucker?" Bianca asked through clenched teeth.

"Bianca..." Kraven said, trying to urge Bianca not to pounce too hastily.

It was too late. Bianca was already trotting intensely towards the suited stranger, her eyes simmering with fury. Tucker's eyes widened when he spotted Bianca approaching and he flinched when she stabbed her stiletto heel threateningly into the gravel.

"What is going on here?" Bianca enunciated professionally.

"Bianca!" Tucker warbled.

"Who is this?" Bianca asked assertively. "Is he harassing you?"

"R.W. Stark," the suited man said smugly, scouring Bianca up and down with his eyeballs. "I'm spearheading the *Elusive Moose* project. And you are..."

"Unimpressed," Bianca said, looking down at Stark's extended hand with revulsion. "Why are you menacing Tucker?"

"I only asked the lad if he would paddle me over to the lodge," Stark said with a smoothness of the douchebag variety.

"He wants to bulldoze *The Whispering Beaver* and use it as an overflow parking lot for his absurd yuppie resort."

"You make that sound like a bad thing," Stark chuckled. "Listen, Miss..."

"Don't patronize me," Bianca said without missing a beat. "You are speaking to the senior executive of this establishment. I have more influence in my pinky finger than you have in your entire corporation, so show some respect. In case you are unaware, you are standing on private property. And I have the authority to have you unceremoniously removed. Also charged. Don't think that just because you wallow naked in a bathtub of money that you can assume ownership of something simply by penetrating its boundaries."

"Look," Stark said condescendingly, "let's keep it real. Your pretend little business here…"

"Is a historic, heritage site," Bianca finished firmly. "And is protected by the Government of Ontario. You are violating a plethora of bylaws, not to mention sacred tradition. Your site is outside of the Algonquin Park boundary. As long as you are standing on this property, you are trampling provincially protected dirt. I can also have you forcefully dragged away by the authorities for harassing Tucker. Your money is useless here. Remove yourself."

"And if I don't?" Stark smirked.

"Behind me," Bianca said flatly, "there is a truck containing a furry thug and a cargo bedful of depraved, technical geniuses who can write virtual reality code so graphically odious, it will mess you up. I suggest you run."

R.W. Stark smiled egotistically, but with telltale sweat beading on his sunburned forehead. "You expect me to take this seriously?" he guffawed. "Do you even know who I am?"

"A villainous scalawag!" Jedd said, approaching on a homemade, log raft, waving an ardent fist.

Bianca turned to find the raft approaching, upon which was Jedd, Trudy, Lizbeth and Wrath. Bianca beamed with pride.

"Oh, this is pathetic," Stark said smugly as the offbeat crew anchored the raft and wobbled ashore.

"You should be ashamed of yourself," Trudy said, wagging a finger.

"Parking lot," Jedd spat. "Yeesh."

"I didn't paddle him across," Tucker said with eager angst. "Not even when he threatened me."

"He threatened you?" Bianca snapped.

"Come here, Baby," Trudy said, squashing Tucker in a hug.

"You *threatened* him?" Bianca asked in a voice that was so piercing, Stark had to stick a finger in his ear to stabilize the ringing.

"I merely warned him," Stark sneered, "that if he didn't paddle me across to assess the dimensions of my new overflow parking lot..."

"Horace from Legal will deal with this," Bianca nodded affirmatively.

"Horace from Legal?" Stark repeated, crinkling his nose with confusion.

"We have a *Horace from Legal?*" Jedd whispered to shrugging Tucker.

"If you leave now with a formal apology," Bianca went on, "then perhaps Horace will let you off with a slap on the wrist."

"You're mad," Stark said, staring glassily at Bianca.

"If you only knew," Bianca said, giving Stark the *squint of death.*

After gulping, R.W. Stark felt the disturbingly empty stare of Wrath. "Who is this kid?" Stark asked quakily. "And why is he looking at me like that?"

"I am the darkness," Wrath said cryptically and without unlocking his creepy corpse ogle.

"Okay, that does it," said R.W. Stark, rolling up his sleeves. "This isn't cute anymore. You oddballs need to get out of my way..."

"Nope," Jedd said, forming a human chain with the others across the shoreline.

"My bulldozers won't care about your little protest," Stark said snidely. "If you think a bunch of rural eccentrics can stop me..."

R.W. Stark nearly got whiplash when the cab door on Kraven's pickup truck slammed shut with a resounding clang. Several rubber soles were heard landing on the gravel before the very haggard *Atticus & Blart* employees ambled towards the lake. Their bloodshot eyes bulged from stress, lack of sleep and glaring screens. Likewise, their faces were gaunt and wan, and they twitched in a caffeinated manner. They resembled damned souls, once doomed to an eternity in hell, now suddenly squinting at the large, yellow ball of fire in the sky.

"What in the hell..." Stark said, disturbed.

The looming shadow of Kraven approached the now cowering R.W. Stark, whose eyes widened with a stupefied horror. He literally trembled when Kraven uttered a guttural growl from deep in his throat. Kraven narrowed his gooseberry green eyes into slits of hate, barbing Stark with his fearsome glare. After a moment of standing stiffly, paralyzed with fear, R.W. Stark suddenly ran away, flailing and screaming.

***

"Abernathy?" quavered R.W. Stark as he fumbled on his phone from the safety of his Maserati. "Call it all off... Yes, I'm serious! We cannot share a lake with that insane asylum! They've all lost their goddam minds! Especially the cute one with the flapper haircut... Forget the deposit! Move the project to Moncton for all I care! Kapuskasing! Squamish! As far away from Algonquin as you can manage!... No, Abernathy, do not do that. Do NOT go over there! I swear a group of seven damned souls and a werewolf... Don't judge me, Abernathy! *You weren't there!*"

CHAPTER FIFTY

It was plausibly the weirdest twenty-four hours of Bianca Mumford's life. Everything had happened so fast from her abrupt evacuation, surreal kidnapping to her drastic career change. Nonetheless, this was the first time in perhaps ever, Bianca felt secure. Accepted. A part of something profound and fulfilling.

She had absolutely no idea what would come next. Whether *The Whispering Beaver* survived the year was anyone's guess. But she was not swallowed by that sinking sense of doom she often had in Toronto during equally unpredictable times. Regardless of the challenges, she was part of a veritable team, saturated in emotional support, and more hugs than what would be considered necessary. And most satisfying of all, Bianca would never again have to set foot in that soul-sucking cesspool that is *Atticus & Blart*.

Although she could not find a word in the English language to describe the bizarre energy between herself and Kraven, Bianca felt safe. A trite way to describe it perhaps, but it felt a hell of a lot more stable than what she had with Glenn, regardless of how cute he looked in green sweaters. Bianca did not even mind so much that Kraven was not from Pennsylvania. She relished the notion of there always being a creepy guy in the shadows, freaking the crap out of anyone who trampled her dignity. And with a sigh of relief, lowering herself into an Adirondack chair overlooking the pristine lake, Bianca accidentally sat on Beckett.

REEEOW!

"Dammit, Cat!" Bianca shrieked, ungracefully leaping from the chair at the same moment Kraven joined Bianca on the porch and blinked.

"This is my life now, isn't it," Bianca stated, looking hopelessly at Beckett who had successfully claimed the chair.

"Pretty much," Kraven said, pulling Bianca closer to his buffalo flannelled chest.

What happened next was gloweringly predictable, so divulging any specific details will be unnecessary. Predictable, that is, until the moment Bianca heard a peculiar noise: a low, guttural, hollow, mooing grunt.

"Kraven," Bianca said with a muffled moan, her lips smushed against Kraven's, "did you just moo?"

"What?" Kraven asked.

Slowly, Bianca turned her head. At eye level, was the ginormous head of a bull moose, looking directly at her.

"FOR THE LUVVA...!"

Allison McWood is an acclaimed, multi-published Canadian author, playwright and lyricist. Specializing in comedy, farce and satire, Allison's novels, plays, musicals and children's books all feature her signature quirkiness. Her writing has not only charmed readers and audiences across Canada, but her works have also been taught at Universities around the world from Vancouver to Lucknow, India. Holding a specialized Literature/Renaissance Drama degree from Toronto's York University, Allison is also a Shakespearean dramaturge, and Marlovian scholar.

When she is not writing, you can either find Allison in her red canoe, reading way too many books, playing air guitar, petting all the dogs or sipping cappuccino in a cute cafe.

www.instagram.com/annelidpress/

www.ingramcontent.com/pod-product-compliance
Lightning Source LLC
Chambersburg PA
CBHW021129260626
47169CB00005B/1522